Frost Hollow Hall

EMMA CARROLL

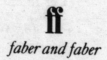

faber and faber

First published in 2013
by Faber and Faber Limited
Bloomsbury House,
74–77 Great Russell Street,
London WC1B 3DA

Typeset by Faber and Faber Ltd

Printed and bound by CPI Group (UK) Ltd, Croydon CR0 4YY

A CIP record for this book
is available from the British Library

ISBN 978-0-571-29544-9

FSC
www.fsc.org
MIX
Paper from
responsible sources
FSC® C101712

2 4 6 8 10 9 7 5 3 1

To Owen, always

A TERRIBLE TRAGEDY

A most terrible incident has occurred at Frost Hollow Hall, the country estate of Viscount Barrington near the village of Frostcombe.

Lord Barrington's only child, Christopher, died tragically yesterday afternoon whilst skating alone on a frozen lake in the grounds. It appears that he fell through ice too weak to bear his weight, and came to grief in the cold water.

The alarm was raised some hours later when he failed to return for dinner. His body was then discovered close to the edge of the lake.

Lord Barrington is said to be devastated; Lady Barrington lies in a perilous state under the care of doctors. The Honourable Christopher Barrington, known as 'Kit', was heir to Frost Hollow Hall, and a popular fellow in the Frostcombe area. The village is in deep shock at his sudden and untimely death.

WINTER 1881

1
THE DARE

I was proper fed up with waiting. I'd been on look-out now for two whole hours and there was still no sign of Pa. At every noise my spirits rose, only to be dashed as I glanced at the clock.

He was late. *Two hours late and getting later.*

Outside, the frost hadn't lifted all day. It coated the inside of our windowpane too, so it was a job to get a good view of anything. Just to look decent, I'd kept on my best Sunday frock, though the fabric was thin and I was shivering cold. I'd even had a go at tidying my hair, and now that was escaping from its plaits. Nothing was going to plan.

'For flip's sake, Tilly, *do* something useful,' said Ma irritably, as I flopped down into my seat for the thousandth time. 'Shame you're so useless at sewing, or you could help me.'

'And take that smart frock off. It's only Pa coming home, not the Queen!' said my sister Eliza, who couldn't sew either, though no one seemed to mind about *that*.

I shot her a look but didn't bite back. In truth, I was too distracted to care. Pa was due home today from a stint on the railways. There'd be money at last, which would put food on the table and pay the rent that we owed. More importantly, he'd have kisses and kind words for me.

A sudden noise and I jolted in my seat.

Someone was at our front door. It wasn't a proper knock. It was a low, secret sound like an animal scratching to get in. And it seemed I was the only one who'd heard it.

My heart sank. It was too quiet to be Pa. The noise came again. It was louder now.

Eliza looked up from the fire. 'That someone outside, Tilly?'

'Seems so,' I said.

'Find out who it is, then,' she said, and shooed me like I was some sort of servant.

I turned to Ma. 'Do I have to?'

She didn't answer. She was staring at the door, her lips set tight. I knew that look, and it made my heart sink more. It wasn't Pa she was thinking of, but the overdue rent and the landlord who came knocking for it. Chances were it was him again.

'Tell 'em I'm not in,' said Ma, when clearly she was. I went to say so, but Ma raised her hand.

'Just do it, will you!'

I didn't much fancy a clout round the ear, so I made for the door. I opened it just a sliver. The air coming in was bitter cold. It wasn't the landlord stood there. What I got was the back view of a person jiggling something under his coat like he was just about to drop it. When he turned round to face me, I shut the door quick and leaned against it hard.

Will Potter. Will *blasted* Potter. What the heck was he doing here?

'Tilly!' he hissed at the keyhole. 'Come outside, won't you?'

My heart started going like the clappers in my chest.

'Tilly! You there?'

I prayed he'd go away.

He'd been clowning about in church today, singing stupid words to the hymns and pulling faces all through the sermon. Annie Woods and Hannah Brown had giggled under their bonnets, daft things; I swear I'd looked the other way. God help me if I'd actually smiled at him without thinking.

Eliza was watching me. 'Who's out there, then?' she said.

'No one much. They've gone now.'

'Good,' said Ma, clearly relieved.

Eliza waited 'til I'd moved back to the fire, then fixed me with a wicked stare. 'So why've you gone all red?'

'I in't!' I cried, feeling my face go redder still.

And then Will Potter knocked again, a proper *rat-tat-tat* this time so the whole world might hear it. Eliza was the first on her feet.

I grabbed her arm. 'Don't answer it!'

'Why the heck not?' she said, laughing. 'It can't hurt, can it?'

'Just wait a bit, and he'll definitely go away.'

'*He?*'

Quick as a flash, she lunged for the door.

'Eliza, no!' I cried. 'Leave it!'

God's teeth! I didn't even like Will Potter. He was far too sure of himself, though it seemed I was the only girl in Frostcombe who'd noticed.

Now Eliza threw the door open wide, making Ma cry 'Keep the heat in!'

And so Will Potter was asked inside.

Immediately, our one downstairs room looked

smaller. I saw Will taking in the low, dark beams, the threadbare rug before the hearth and the turnips in a basket on the dresser. The only tidy thing was our table, covered in neat piles of mending work that Ma took in from the village. It paid little and hurt her eyes. But even on a Sunday, she sewed.

I felt hot and angry all at once. What did Will Potter know about being poor? *His* pa owned the butcher's shop. *And* he'd built a smart brick house on the edge of the village where the Potter family lived. In our house, we didn't even own enough chairs for us all to sit down at the same time.

'Will in't staying,' I said, as Eliza beckoned him into my seat.

Yet he'd already taken his cap off so his dark hair stood on end, and his face was one big smarmy smile. He was still shifting something about under his jacket too. I wanted to die on the spot.

'You come for our Tilly, then?' said Eliza, smirking. 'She's looking smart today, in't she? Maybe she was expecting you all along.'

'No! I weren't!' I cried.

But she winked at Ma, who was starting to see the funny side of things. I wondered how their mood could lift so fast, when just the sight of Will Potter made me feel ten times worse.

Not that he'd even noticed.

'I have come for Tilly, yes,' he said, mighty sure of himself.

'I in't going nowhere.'

And I meant it, for boys never looked twice at me. I was a small, skinny creature with a face full of freckles and wild dark hair that wouldn't stay put. Eliza was the handsome one. Ma always said it, and Eliza certainly *thought* it. Pa was the only person who'd ever called me pretty, though I reckoned he was just being nice. Besides, Will Potter could have his pick of the girls. What the heck could he want with me?

I decided he was only here to make mischief. I didn't trust him an inch.

'That in't very friendly, Tilly,' said Eliza. 'You be nice to Will.'

'But I can't go,' I said, and not just because it was Will Potter asking. Pa would be home any moment. I couldn't possibly go out now.

''Course you can,' said Ma. 'It'll stop you moping round here all afternoon. Only don't get into no trouble.'

'But Pa'll be here soon,' I said.

Ma snorted. 'I wouldn't hold your breath!'

I didn't like her saying this, not in front of Will, and that sinking feeling came back, all cold and hard in my chest.

Will turned to go. 'Well, if I can't tempt you . . .' he said.

Slow and stealthy so only I could see it, he opened up his jacket an inch or two. I couldn't resist a quick peep inside. There was leather, a buckle, something pale, the colour of wood. I'd not the faintest idea what it was. He must've read my frown, shifting the thing so I saw it better. Silver blades glinted back at me from the dark inside of his coat. I knew at once and my heart leapt.

Ice skates!

I looked right at him.

'Dare you,' he mouthed.

My mind began to race. I'd heard plenty about Will Potter's stupid dares – jumping off bridges and riding horses bareback in their fields, the sorts of things a great big show-off would do. But I couldn't imagine for one second those daft girls in church being up for such a lark.

I was.

It'd been a long afternoon, sat in waiting for Pa. A bit of fresh air might not be such a bad idea.

I glanced at Eliza, who'd got bored of us now and was toying with her hair, and Ma, who was sorting through the turnips. And I saw the glint in Will's eye, the challenge laid down.

'All right. I'll come. But just for a bit,' I said, and grabbed my shawl off the peg.

*

Outside, it was icy underfoot and the sky was already turning pale. Halfway down the lane, Will stopped and faced me.

'You ready for this?' he said.

''Course. Are we going to the river? It's frozen over down by the bridge.'

'The river's for babies. We're going somewhere else.' And he nodded towards Combe Hill, where the lane rose sharply out of Frostcombe village.

'Where, exactly?'

Beyond the village was the turnpike and the main road to Bristol. And beyond that was the biggest house for miles around: Frost Hollow Hall.

My stomach dropped. He wouldn't be *that* stupid, would he?

'Oh no, Will,' I said. 'We can't!'

It would get Ma's dander up if she knew. No one went near Frost Hollow Hall, not since that boy died there in the lake. There was talk of dogs and traps and men with sticks for anyone who went there uninvited. The tragedy had turned the Barringtons quite strange. And there were stories of queer happenings in the house too. But it didn't help to dwell on these matters; I felt edgy enough already.

'Thought you was game,' said Will. 'Perhaps I should've asked your sister instead.'

I was right about him. He really did only want to make mischief. Not that I was about to go home again, whatever Will Potter thought. Because more than anything else, I was dying for a go on those skates.

2

ON THIN ICE

We followed the road for a mile or so and then, quite suddenly, the gates to Frost Hollow Hall loomed before us. They were great tall things, the ironwork all twisted leaves and queer-looking flowers. And they were very definitely shut.

'It in't very welcoming,' I said.

Will looked at me like I was a complete hare-brain. '*Exactly*. That's why it's a dare.' And he led me to a hole in the hedge, the sort made by badgers on their travels. 'This is our way in. Now stay close.'

But I didn't fancy tucking right in behind him, so I waited 'til he'd elbowed his way through.

'Thought you'd done a runner,' he said, as I eventually emerged from the hedge.

'Just keeping me distance, so you don't get no ideas,' I said.

And though he laughed, I was glad I'd put him straight. Girls had this habit of swooning over Will

Potter and if he thought I would too, only to mock me for it, then he could blinking well think again.

We now stood in a gloomy thicket. It was quiet as death; even the birds weren't singing. I didn't care for the place, and felt the shivers go through me, though I did my best to hide it. When Will set off again, I stayed close this time. We followed a narrow path that twisted and turned between the trees. Soon enough, the woods thinned and we slithered down a hill and out onto open ground. No sign of those men with dogs, though I kept my eyes peeled just in case. We went through a gate and over a field to the crest of another hill. Here we came to a halt.

'Look at that,' said Will, gazing at the view below.

Spread out before us was the thickest, most marvellous frost I'd ever seen. The grass was so pale it might've been snow, the trees all white like bones.

'It's a frost hollow,' said Will, smugly. 'Catches the cold air and hangs onto it. That's how the house got its name.'

'Oh? Is that right?'

I had to admit it was a sight to behold.

'Where's the house, then?' I said.

Will pointed to a stand of yew trees. 'Behind there. You can't see it from this side.'

My spirits sank. I'd been hoping for a peek at the creepy old place. Then I saw the lake itself, spread out like a great metal platter, just visible through a copse of bare trees. Of a sudden, I couldn't keep still. I hitched up my skirts and set off down the hill.

'Hang about!' Will called, which only made me go faster.

I didn't stop 'til I'd reached the lake edge. Down here, the air felt heavy and chill; it hurt my chest just to breathe. All along the banks were old stone urns and statues with their arms missing. Frost covered everything in a thick white fur.

One look at the lake and my heart beat faster. It was frozen right across. I had this sudden urge to be out in the middle of it. All by myself, where no one could get on my nerves.

'Can I have a go?' I said to Will when he'd caught me up.

He shook his head. 'I'm first.'

'Oh go on, please.'

He ignored me. Crouching on the grass, he pulled the skates from his jacket. They were odd-looking things, part wood, part leather, part blade. The wooden bit was shaped to fit snug against a boot sole; on Will's great feet, they did fit perfectly. He then fastened the two leather straps over his toes and at his ankle to keep them firmly in place.

'If the ice holds me, it'll hold you,' he said, flexing his feet. 'It's safer to let me try it out first.'

'Bit late to worry about that now.'

This was a dare, wasn't it? Will had made that perfectly clear. We were sneaking about on private land. If we got caught a thrashing would be the least of our worries. Since when did *safe* come into it?

Straightening up, Will wobbled and grabbed my arm. I stood still while he got his balance.

'You don't mind me really, do you?' he said, a smile flitting over his face.

Actually, I minded him very much. He was an irksome wretch. And I'd seen that look before; he used it on all the girls. Very firmly, I prised his hand off my arm.

'I'm only here for a go on them skates,' I said, though in truth they looked way too big. Not that it'd stop me. Heck, I'd get out there in my bare feet if I had to.

The very second he was on the ice, Will started acting the clown. He skated first on one foot, then the other, flapping his arms like he was about to fall, only to right himself in the nick of time. What a daft lummox he was. I wished he'd get on with it so I could have my turn. And then, as if just to vex me, he darted off across the ice.

I was by myself.

It had got colder. By now the sun was low and red in the sky, and the air so still not even the trees stirred. High above my head, rooks circled and cawed to each other. At my back, the copse grew darker.

I began to feel uneasy again. *A boy died out here*. I pulled my shawl tight against me and shivered.

Somewhere behind me, a twig snapped. I spun round. A blackbird flew past, squawking. Except for my heartbeat, all went still again. Then, thirty or so yards into the copse, a dark shape flitted through the trees. It was a woman. She moved fast and low, away from me. She hadn't seen me yet. I held my breath, praying she wouldn't look back over her shoulder; we were done for if she did. Thankfully, she kept moving. Then she ducked behind an old stone wall and disappeared.

Bit by bit, my breathing slowed to normal. But I didn't fancy being here much longer. It was giving me the creeps. I waved to Will, though it was an age before he saw me. He was right over the other side of the lake; I wondered if he'd forgotten me completely.

Then little by little the black dot that was him got closer, 'til he slid to a halt in front of me.

'That was grand!' Will said, his face all lit up.

I pointed to the trees. 'Someone was there just now.'

His smile vanished.

'Don't fret, they didn't see us,' I said, a little bit pleased to see him rattled.

'Who was it?'

'How the flip should I know?'

'Well, it's getting late. Perhaps we should . . .'

'Oh no.'

I knew Will Potter's game, all right. If we went home now, he'd think he'd won the dare. I wasn't going anywhere 'til I'd been on the ice too.

'I didn't come all this way for nothing. Now give me them skates.'

'Tilly . . .'

I held out my hand. 'Skates!'

He pointed at the ice and said something about the middle, but I wasn't really listening.

'Sit down,' he said, coming back onto the bank. 'I'll put them on for you.'

'I'll do it myself, ta,' I said.

'No, you won't. They have to be on properly.'

So I bit my lip and sat down on the frozen grass.

Will took his time, tutting because my own boots were smaller than the skates themselves, and then fussing over the buckles. I reckoned he was doing it on purpose.

'Oh come on!' I said, as the frost soaked through my skirts. 'It'll be summer at this rate.'

He offered me his hand for a pull up but I waved him off.

'Suit yourself,' he said, and stood back as I got to my knees, then to my feet. Blimey, it was hard enough just to stay upright on the grass! As I stepped onto the ice, my feet shot out in front of me, my arms whirling like mad.

'Steady there!' laughed Will.

I wished he'd just clear off. His blasted skates didn't help much either; they were easily three sizes too big. With my heart in my mouth, I tried to go forward but tipped back, arms flapping like a goose. This was no fun at all. I gritted my teeth. I'd show Will Potter. And I'd wipe that stupid grin right off his face.

I focused on my feet. Though it pained me to admit it, Will had a knack to how he moved his – *down and out*, *down and out*. Somehow, I managed it too. And I stayed upright. I leaned forward, wobbled a bit, went faster. The skates began to glide like they had a life of their own. My hair lifted off my shoulders. Ice-cold air stung my cheeks.

This was it! I was skating!

A great rush of joy came over me. I kept going. Faster and faster. Everything around me was a blur. I grinned like a mad thing 'til the cold made my teeth hurt. And when I saw how far I'd gone, I finally turned back for the bank. There was Will. He waving both arms over his head, calling something; I didn't hear what. The sight of him soured my mood.

'What you on about?' I yelled.

'Stay away from the middle! You're too far out!'

What an old woman he was!

With a whoosh, my feet went from under me. I fell flat on my backside. I couldn't get up again. My hands and feet slithered like a drunk's. I didn't dare look at Will, though I heard him all right, laughing his ruddy head off.

'Nice linens!' he shouted. 'Show us some more!'

My face went hot. I'd had enough of his smart jibes. 'I'll throttle you, Will Potter! Just you see if I don't!'

All around me, the ice looked rough. There were lines criss-crossing it and I began to feel uneasy, for these weren't skate marks; these were cracks. As I scrambled to my knees, the ice gave an almighty groan. I froze to the spot.

Oh no! This in't right!

The ice seemed to shift beneath me. I fell forward onto my hands. Right in front of me, the ice turned dark. My heart began to pound. I staggered upright, fell down again.

'For God's sake!' cried Will. 'Get over here! Quick!'

He stood at the edge with his arms outstretched. I was too far out to reach him.

3

THE OTHER SIDE

Black, stinking water spewed over the ice. It sucked at my skirts. And it was cold. So cold it knocked the breath clean out of me. Another great cracking sound and the ice gave way. I clawed like a mad cat, but there was nothing to get hold of. The water kept tugging. My clothes grew heavy. Slowly, gently, the lake closed over my head and all went quiet but for the blood pounding in my ears. I went down and down into blackness. My chest was too tight. I couldn't breathe. Then my feet touched something soft. I stopped sinking.

Panic kicked in. I thrashed and flailed. Mud got in my mouth, my eyes. Then, somehow, I was swimming up towards daylight. I saw sky and trees, all blurred through the ice. My lungs felt fit to burst.

Help me! Help me!

I lashed out madly. But there were no cracks or holes here. The ice stayed solid as marble above me.

Dark spots danced before my eyes. Arms, legs, head, everything went heavy. All I wanted was to sleep. I pictured Pa, come home at last and wondering where I was. And Eliza and Ma looking at the clock and starting supper without me.

The queerest feeling came over me.

Something warm like a person's breath tickled my cheek and I was no longer fighting for air. The water now seemed full of the strangest pearly light. A boy in a billowing white shirt floated towards me. I wondered if I was dead, if I'd crossed over to the other side and this was an angel coming to meet me.

He was the most perfect creature I'd ever seen. His golden hair moved gently with the currents, and his eyes were strange, beautiful things coloured like lavender. As he came closer, the light followed, as if it was coming from right inside him.

I stared. I couldn't move. He stared back, his eyes all wide at the sight of me. He reached for my hand. His skin felt icy cold, but his hold was steady. If I was dead now, it didn't matter. Here was my very own angel, beautiful and full of light.

He took my other hand and pulled me away from the deeper water. I let him take me. I knew I'd go anywhere with him. Then as grey daylight came through the ice again, I saw we were heading towards the bank. I pulled back.

I didn't want to face Will Potter, or Ma or Eliza. Right now, I didn't even care about Pa. I wanted to stay right here with this beautiful boy. Yet before my very eyes, he began to fade 'til he was no more than a speck of brightness in the water. I tried to swim after him, but my skirts got caught in the weeds, and I couldn't break free.

He was gone.

Next I knew, I was up on the bank. I saw a pair of feet, then heard Will saying, 'Tilly? Can you hear me?'

Blackness.

I sensed I was a bird high up in a tree, looking down on the lake. Somewhere near the middle was a person-sized hole, all dark like a stain. And over on the bank was a girl – me – sprawled lifeless across the grass. Will Potter was crouched beside me, calling and calling my name. Steam rose off my skirts, and my hair, worked loose, lay wet against my face. Suddenly, my whole body jerked into life. I retched water and weeds and goodness knows what all over Will's boots, and he didn't so much as flinch. He thumped my back and kept talking, though his face was stricken and pale.

I came back to myself.

Head, legs, arms, everything hurt. I swore I'd been jabbed in the ribs a thousand times. It was agony even to draw breath. My eyelids were stone-heavy. All I wanted was to stay still and sleep. But I grew aware of a tugging at my feet. Rough fabric pressed up against my cheek. I was jolted this way and that. I sensed darkness, then daylight, then dark again. I came to on a strange doorstep, with Will's arms wrapped tight around me.

A buzzing noise filled my head. Everything started to spin. The darkness came back.

I woke to the sound of voices. I was lying down on a hard surface. My chest was on fire. As I rolled over to cough, a pan was thrust in my face, ready to catch the foul-tasting water as it streamed from my mouth and nose. The room tipped sideways. I reckoned I was about to throw up. I shut my eyes until the tipping stopped. Everything went quiet.

Next thing I heard was a woman's voice. 'We'll be for it if *she* comes in.'

'But look at the state of the child. We can't just fling her back out in the cold,' said another.

'Can you get us a ride to the village?' It was Will, sounding far away.

I tried to focus my eyes but it made my head hurt, and I drifted off again.

'Quick! Mrs Jessop's coming!'

The voices were back. This time they sounded sharp and loud. I wondered if I should be scared. But it was too much effort. I slipped back into sleep.

I awoke to hear footsteps. A new voice said harshly, 'Fell through the ice, did she?' A hand gripped my shoulder and shook me hard. 'Is she dead?'

My eyes flew open. A stranger in a dark frock loomed over me. She didn't look altogether friendly. Then her face turned suddenly pale. Her hand hovered close to my cheek; to slap me or stroke me, I didn't know which.

'Take her away at once!' she said, and was gone.

*

They bundled me out of the door and into the back of a cart. Someone had draped a blanket round my shoulders and I was mighty glad of it since by now I couldn't stop shaking. Wide awake at last, I felt sick as a dog. And a thought nudged away at me, but I couldn't for anything work out what it was.

Will sat beside me all the way home. I didn't have

the strength to protest when he put his arms round me. He was warm and quiet, and after a while I got used to it.

When Ma opened our front door, her face was like thunder.

'Where've you been?' she cried. 'You've been gone hours!'

Then she saw the state of me and her hand flew to her mouth. Will tried to explain what had happened. It didn't sound good. We were very clearly in the wrong, and I knew I'd be in for a right earful.

'I'm sorry, Mrs Higgins,' Will said, and finally let go of me.

My legs gave way before I could get inside.

DREAMING: 1

I'm in the middle of the lake. The ice groans. I tilt forward. The water pulls me under. Everything is hushed. Down and down I go, in a stream of tiny bubbles.

'Help me!' I cry.

No one hears me. The water deadens everything. Darkness closes in. I'm a goner this time, I'm sure of it.

Out of nowhere, a light darts towards me like a will o' the wisp. My heart leaps. The light becomes a shape. It's him again, the boy in the white shirt.

He stops a few steps away. I see how his hair curls over his collar, and how his eyes seek out mine. I've never seen anyone so lovely. I go all fluttery inside. Trouble is, I know what happens next. Any second and he'll lead me to the bank. But I don't want to be saved just yet. I want to stay here like this.

He comes closer. I can barely meet his eye. It's then I see how sad he looks. Something is clearly very wrong.

'Tilly,' he says.

How do I hear him? And how on earth does he know my name?

4

FOLLOWING A DREAM

Early next morning, I woke with a start. Thin, grey light filled the room. It took me a moment to gather my wits and realise I was safe at home in bed. Behind the old curtain that split the room in half, Ma and Pa would still be asleep. Eliza lay next to me snoring, and I was glad of her, all familiar and warm, even though she had more than her share of the blankets.

The dream left me feeling strange. My shift was damp with sweat and my heart thudded uncomfortably. What's more, a thought had lodged inside my brain, going round and round like a moth bumping at a lamp. It was such a mad idea. No one would ever believe it. They'd laugh right in my face.

I shut my eyes. I tried to go back to sleep. But the thought wouldn't go away.

Something, *someone* had been out there in the lake. What's more, he'd saved my life. Just when I'd been breathing my last, he'd appeared out of nowhere, all lit up like a star.

Yet if he'd really been an angel, he'd have taken me up to heaven. I've have gone with him, too. Instead, he took me back to the lake edge so that I might live.

Now he was here in my dreams, only it shocked me to see him so changed. There was real pain and sorrow in his face. What's more, he knew my name. How the heck was *that* possible? It didn't make sense. Not one bit.

From behind the curtain came sounds that Ma was stirring: her little cough and the wince as her feet touched the ice-cold floor. No sound yet from Pa. But knowing he was here lifted my spirits, and I couldn't lie still any longer. The cold made me dress fast, tugging on my everyday frock, which was too short and too tight under the arms. Just the effort of it made me dizzy, and I grabbed hold of the bedstead until the feeling passed.

Ma called out, 'Tilly? That you?'

'Yes, it's me.'

'You well enough for work?'

My eyes smarted with tears. *A kind word wouldn't go amiss.* But she was cross with me. And I supposed I deserved it.

'I reckon so,' I said, because this was the answer she wanted. It wasn't much of a job I had, just a pupil-helper at the village school, cleaning slates and carrying coal and showing the young ones how to read. But it brought in some pennies and it meant I'd got quite clever at my letters.

I heard rustling as Ma reached for her clothes.

'You were a little fool yesterday,' she said sharply.

I braced myself, hoping she'd be quick with her telling-off.

'Fancy going to Frost Hollow Hall!' she said, yanking on her frock. 'Of all the places! Don't you know nothing?'

I wondered if Pa might wake up soon and take my side. But Ma wasn't finished yet. 'It could've cost you dear, going up there on that ice. You're lucky to be here at all.'

Right now, I didn't feel it.

Ma appeared from behind the curtain. She looked like she'd hardly slept a wink. 'You and that Will Potter's both to blame, you silly beggars. Honestly Tilly, I'd have thought you'd know better.'

Wait a minute! Hadn't she urged me to go with him? I certainly hadn't *wanted* to go, not 'til I'd seen his skates. And I was just about to say so when I caught sight of the empty bed behind her. Pa must be already up. Perhaps he'd made us a surprise breakfast, with fresh bread and bacon and hot sweet tea. He'd done such a thing once before.

*

Yet there was no special meal on the table. There was no Pa neither. He still hadn't come home. Breakfast was stale bread and cheese with the blue bits cut off.

'Blame your father,' said Ma, slamming plates down on the table. 'Due home yesterday with six weeks' earnings, and no word from him. What the heck's he playing at?'

She only ever mentioned the money. All this time he'd been away and not once had she said she missed him.

'Perhaps he's only . . .'

Eliza interrupted me. 'Don't stick up for him. He'll be sleeping it off under a hedge somewhere. Or following one of his big dreams.'

I'd have got a thick ear for saying such things. Not Eliza. As far as Ma was concerned, she could say what she flipping well liked. At least Pa *had* dreams. He didn't want to be poor for ever. Why would he? I didn't see it making us very happy.

'Well, eat up,' Ma said. 'And don't count on nothing for supper.'

I wasn't hungry. It was enough that Pa wasn't here. My dream was still troubling me too. It hung over me like a fog, making it hard to think about anything else.

'You seeing Will Potter today, Tilly?' Eliza asked.

'No. Why should I?'

'Oh, I thought you two was courting now.'

'It was a dare, nothing else.' I knew she was ragging me for a reaction. But really Will Potter was the least of my worries.

She narrowed her eyes at me, chewing slowly. 'Well, you look like you've seen a ghost. And you was twitching and turning in your sleep last night too.'

'What d'you mean?' I said, uneasy.

'And stop shredding that bread,' said Ma. 'Eat it or leave it so someone else can have it.'

It was a measly slice to start with, although Eliza seemed to have landed herself a decent-sized chunk. Even her cheese looked passable. I pushed my plate away. Here we were then, just like always; Eliza and Ma on one side, me on the other.

Except I didn't feel right and I needed to tell someone, though I'd no idea how to put it into words.

'I've just had the queerest dream,' I said.

'Oh aye,' said Ma, only half listening.

'I was in the lake again and couldn't get out. There was a boy under the water, and he seemed so . . . well . . . sad. I mean proper, heartbroken sad.'

Ma tutted. 'Perhaps that'll learn you, then. You shouldn't have gone poking about up there in the first place.'

She moved to the window where the light was best and picked up her sewing work. I waited for her to start chiding me again; she didn't.

But Eliza had stopped eating. Her eyes were fixed on me.

'*Christopher Barrington*.' She said his name dead slow, savouring it like it was something tasty.

'What about him?' I said.

'He drowned in that lake, didn't he, Ma?'

'Don't start filling her head with nonsense. She's in her own little world as it is.'

'I am *not*!' I said, surprised Ma had even noticed.

Eliza carried on. 'Kit, they called him, short for Christopher. Sad that he died so young. He was quite a looker, I've heard.'

'Oh Eliza!' Ma said.

'Well, it's true! Got his looks from his mother, apparently. She's meant to be a right beauty, though no one's seen her for years.'

'Why are you telling me this?' I said, because I'd heard it all before.

Everyone in Frostcombe knew the story. Kit Barrington was the rich, handsome heir to Frost Hollow Hall. An only child, he'd drowned in the lake, and his mother was quite broken by his death. She shut herself away from the world in her big old house and was still up there now, to this day.

To me, it seemed a sad sort of tale. To Eliza it was pure 'sensation', right out of a penny dreadful story. She loved a gruesome yarn, where beautiful people met with grisly ends and ghosts came back from the grave to spread secrets. And by the way she'd sat forward in her seat, she was certainly warming to her theme.

Ma had stopped sewing too.

'It was a terrible business for Lady Barrington, losing her only child,' she said quietly. 'Folk say the house is a queer place. No one wants to work there nowadays. Word is they've hardly got enough staff to keep the place going.'

A little shiver passed over me. I didn't know this part of things. And it wasn't like Ma to gossip.

'What sort of strange?' said Eliza, eagerly.

Ma started sewing again. 'Oh, I don't know.'

'He's buried up there, in't he? Got their own fancy graveyard, so I heard.'

'Enough now!' said Ma, quite sternly so that even Eliza took heed. 'This is tittle-tattle and I've got work to do. And so have you two. If your father don't turn up soon, we'll be fending for ourselves. We owe four weeks' rent as it is.'

I hardly needed reminding. A cold sweat pricked my brow. I stood up too fast, sending knives and spoons crashing to the floor.

'Careful girl! Watch what you're about!' cried Ma.

'I need some air,' I said. 'I'm all right, really.'

Eliza gave me a long look. 'You're jumpy as anything.'

'No I in't.'

'Oh yes you are,' she laughed. 'Fancy dreaming about a dead boy. That's right queer, that is.'

I'd heard enough.

'It weren't your Kit Barrington in my dream! If you must know, it was ...' I stopped short, not knowing what to say.

Eliza sat back in her seat, smirking. 'Go on then. Who was it? Will Potter?'

'Shut up! I in't telling you no more about it!'

'Suit yourself.'

God, how I wanted to throttle her.

'I'm going to work,' I said, feeling sicker than ever.

I didn't even make it to the door. My eyes went all fuzzy and the ground swung up to meet me. When I came to, Ma was gazing down at me.

'You in't going nowhere,' she said.

She didn't look too happy about it, neither.

5

GHOSTS AND ANGELS

I spent the morning dozing in a chair by the fire. There wasn't much left to burn on it, but it was the warmest spot in the house. With Eliza gone to her job at the mill, and Ma down in the village pleading for credit at the shop, time passed quietly enough.

Then near midday, someone knocked at our door. Thinking it might be the landlord, my stomach dropped. I opened the door just a crack. Will Potter was on the doorstep.

'You've got some neck coming round here,' I said.

He grinned. 'And you look peaky. Not working today then?'

It struck me as a daft thing to say. 'Does it look like it?' I said.

'Bit cold out here,' said Will, pointedly.

I'd no plans to let him in, but he'd already got one foot past the door, so it was hard to protest when he grasped my arms and steered me back inside. I shrugged him off and sat down again. As he settled into the chair opposite, all easy and relaxed, I wondered how I'd ever get rid of him. He started nattering on about his pa's butcher's shop, and wasn't it funny how a dog had run off with a string of sausages.

'Lucky dog,' I muttered, thinking of my own sorry breakfast.

Then with a flourish, he pulled something from his pocket and held it towards me on the palm of his hand. It was a snowdrop, looking rather the worse for wear. The petals were crumpled and the flower's head was almost flat.

'Is this a joke?'

'No.' His face fell. 'It's the first one I've seen. I thought you might like it.'

I stared at him. 'Why are you here?'

'To see how you are,' he said, and for once he seemed almost serious.

I raised my arms weakly. 'Well here I am, still alive.'

Will gazed at me for so long I felt myself grow hot. Then he said, 'You nearly drowned in that lake. I couldn't reach you though I tried and tried.'

My stomach turned. I preferred it when he larked about.

'You're very lucky to be alive, Tilly,' he said, his eyes

still on me. 'You know that, don't you?'

A beautiful angel had saved my life. I *was* lucky. My palms were sweating now and my heart began to thud. Perhaps Will knew more than he was letting on; maybe he'd seen the angel too. I was desperate to share it with someone.

'Will, at the lake yesterday, did you notice . . . ?' I trailed off.

'Did I notice what?'

What would I tell him? That an angel took my hand and guided me to safety? Heck, I'd tried to explain it to my own family and hadn't got very far. I couldn't tell *Will Potter*. As if he'd believe me, when I hardly believed it myself.

'Doesn't matter,' I said.

We stared into the fire.

'I went back to Frost Hollow Hall this morning to thank them,' said Will.

'Thank who? For what?'

'The kitchen staff, for taking you in.'

I was having trouble keeping up. But in a dark corner of my brain something stirred, and a hazy sort of memory came back to me.

'We went there yesterday, did we?' I said, with a shiver.

"Course we did. Don't you remember?'

'What I mean is . . . did we go inside the house?'

'I've just said so, haven't I?'

I doubted even a cad like Will Potter could charm his way into Frost Hollow Hall. Not if there were men with dogs and sticks. But he seemed a bit too familiar with the place for my liking. Something didn't add up.

'You know the Hall quite well,' I said.

'My pa delivers meat up there and sometimes I help him. Why?'

'So you know the family, then?'

'No, I never see the Barringtons.'

'So how come we ended up there? In the kitchens, weren't it?'

'Look, I know Cook and she's a good sort, and the maids are all right too.'

'They weren't that friendly,' I said, remembering that face looming over me.

'The housekeeper, Mrs Jessop, you mean? Come to think of it, she did take a strange turn when she saw you.'

I stared at him in disbelief. 'So you *do* know them, don't you?'

He shrugged. 'I know some of the staff a bit, yes.'

I couldn't hold back any more. I let rip.

'Some flipping dare *that* was, then!'

'What d'you mean?'

'Ooooh, Frost Hollow Hall!' I cried. 'The big spooky place what no one goes near?'

Will moved uneasily in his seat. 'So?'

'But in fact you *do* go there, *and* you know the staff! How the heck does that make it any sort of dare at all?'

'Easy, Tilly! Calm down!'

'Calm down?! Why didn't you just get us an invite to tea? It would've been a flip's sight easier!'

'But no one goes near that lake. Not since Master Barrington died,' said Will. 'And there's other things too, dark, queer stuff. And now there's even talk of a ghost. I heard all about it today.'

'Huh! And I bet no one's never seen it.'

'One of the maids says she has. Some plates got broke last night, and she swears they just flew off the shelf at her. But I don't think the others believed her.'

I shut my eyes and took a deep breath. Suddenly I felt very tired.

'Will,' I said. '*I* nearly died up there.'

'I know,' he said, looking very shifty indeed. 'And I feel awful about it, I really do.'

For a long moment, neither of us spoke.

Then he got to his feet. 'I'll see myself out.'

'You do that.'

He'd almost got to the door when he stopped and said, 'But you didn't die, did you? Someone's watching over you, Tilly Higgins.'

DREAMING: 2

I'm under the ice in the blink of an eye. A hand touches mine, the fingers so cold I shiver. When I realise it's him, my angel, I light up inside. Only he looks too tense, too pale. I see his mouth is moving but I can't hear the words.

'What is it?' I ask. 'What's wrong?'

Yet the more I talk, the less I hear. I stop. Wait. And it's as if the answer is right inside my own head.

'I can't rest in peace until the truth is known.'

'What truth?' I say, confused.

He doesn't answer.

It's cold down here, too cold. His hand rests on mine like ice. I'm scared. He senses it almost before I do. I can't bear him to look at me, and I try to turn away. But the lake bed is sticky. It sucks at my boots, grabs at my skirts. I'm held fast. I can't move. The fear turns to panic. Inside my head I hear his voice again, clear as glass.

'Now it's your turn to save me,' he says.

What on earth does he mean?

I see my own panic in his face. I almost feel his too-fast heartbeat. He moves back and begins to fade.

'Who are you?' I say, because no angel would be this unhappy.

I want to go to him but I'm still held fast. My skirts are tangled in a mass of weeds. The more I tug, the tighter they hold me. The boy stops. He doesn't answer, but he comes back to me, and with one deft move frees my skirts.

I owe my life to this boy. It's my turn to help him. And I would, if only I knew how.

Now he tries to tell me something. It's something to do with my frock. I twist this way and that to see what he means, but it stirs up mud and the water turns so cloudy I can hardly make out a thing.

'Who are you?' I say again.

But my words are lost in the water.

6

SOME SORT OF TRUTH

The first thing I clapped eyes on was my best Sunday frock, hung like a shadow on the back of the door. Ma had put it there to dry out. Just the sight of it now made me go shaky and shivery like I'd a fever coming on. And that question still echoed around my head: *Who was the boy in the lake?*

A strange notion gripped me that the answer was here in the room. That it was, in fact, *inside* my frock.

I was out of bed in a flash.

Up close, the fabric had that outdoors smell. Quickly, I ran my fingers along each sleeve and around the neckline. The cotton was damp and chill like pastry, and thin in the places where it was almost worn through. More slowly now, I traced each pleat, each fold, moving down until I'd reached the hem. Nothing seemed amiss, though I noticed how loud my heartbeat seemed. Perhaps I was poorly still. Or maybe this was all part of the dream.

Then, at a spot where the hem had come loose, I touched something small and hard. I pinched at it, rolled it in my fingers, feeling its shape through the cloth.

What was it?

I eased the thing out. It fell cool and heavy into my palm. I closed my fist tight round it, scared I'd drop it, though by now I knew from the feel of it what it was.

How the heck had it got into my frock?

My head reeled. In my dream, the boy had barely touched me. I'd no memory of him giving me anything. Then I remembered. In freeing my skirts, he'd touched the hem. He'd saved me, and this was my reminder. Now I had to do the same for him.

I tiptoed over to the window and lifted the curtain for what little light there was. By now it was just before dawn. The pane was covered with ice. When I breathed on it, the ice melted away and I saw that it was snowing outside.

Ever so slowly, I opened my fist. In my hand was a small gold ring. I stared in wonder. Tiny heart-shaped leaves were carved into its surface. It was right lovely, the gold all warm-coloured like honey. So the boy had saved my life and given me a ring. Yet I still didn't know his name.

I began to feel uneasy. This ring was clearly worth a bob or two, but poor folk like me didn't have fancy jewellery, not unless we'd nicked it. Everyone knew that.

I turned the ring over. Something was written on the inside of it, words almost too small to see. I held it closer to the light.

Christopher Edward Barrington

My insides turned cold.

It couldn't be ... *could it?*

I pressed my forehead against the window. Any minute now, I'd wake up. But the ring felt real in my grasp. In the dream the boy hadn't answered my question. Now he had. This *was* the answer, wasn't it? The boy under the ice wasn't an angel. He was Kit Barrington.

Only Kit Barrington was dead.

My breath seemed trapped in my throat. I must be delirious. It couldn't be real. I even considered waking Eliza up, because of a sudden I was fearful. It all felt too much, too strange. I hadn't the wits for *this*. I didn't ask to be part of some dark business, where dead people were haunting my dreams.

It was very nearly light now. Behind me, the bedsprings creaked as Eliza turned over. I realised how chilled I was, how my teeth were chattering and my hands shaking with cold. I crept back into bed, all the time keeping hold of the ring, which seemed to grow warm in my grasp.

Sure enough, the fear began to lift. Did it matter if Kit *was* a ghost? I had no reason to fear him. He'd saved my life, after all. And he really was the finest-looking boy I'd ever seen. What's more, he was counting on me to help him. It felt like an honour, really it did. My own ma wouldn't trust me to darn a flipping sock.

As I lay listening to the hush of falling snow, and the church clock as it chimed the hour, I grew calmer. I pushed the ring onto my finger. It slid over my knuckle, cool and tight, as if it had been made for me.

*

When I woke again it was proper morning. The room was full of cold white light. Snow light.

'Still snowing,' said Eliza. 'Ma's up already, clearing the front path. Don't know why she's bothering.'

She'd propped herself up on the pillows, and even though I was only half awake, I sensed something was troubling her.

'Tilly?' She sounded serious. It didn't bode well. 'Can you keep a secret?'

My heart sank. I was rubbish at keeping secrets. But she'd got my attention, so I pushed my hair out of my eyes and sat up. I must have nodded because she said, 'Good,' and started rummaging under the bed. She pulled out a book. Between the pages was what looked like a piece of paper.

'Now, this is the secret part what you're not to tell,' she said, taking the paper out and smoothing it over her knee. 'Ma would go hopping mad, and we don't know for certain.'

I'd not the faintest notion what she was on about.

Three words jumped off the page:

'WHITE STAR SHIPPING'.

This didn't make matters much clearer.

'When Pa went off to the railways, he left his best jacket behind. I found this in the pocket,' said Eliza, meaning the piece of paper.

'You went through his *pockets*?!'

She shrugged, unfazed. 'Someone needs to ask questions. People don't just not come home. I've asked folk in the village too.'

'And?'

'No one's seen him. Not even at the alehouse.'

'So where d'you think he is?'

She turned to face me. Her eyes were bright. 'You know he had those dreams?'

I did, all too well.

One day, Tilly, he'd say, *we'll find a house with some land and keep our own pigs for market, and we won't owe nobody nothing. Won't that be grand?* Then Ma would tell him not to be daft because you couldn't do it all on thin air, and she'd share looks with Eliza, who'd start yawning. Neither of them had ever listened. Not like I did.

'Looks like this was one of them,' she said to me now. 'And what a dream to have!'

The piece of paper was a flyer, the sort that people handed out in the street when they wanted to sell you something. I started to feel sick as I focused on the words.

'STEAM SHIP' and 'STEERAGE CLASS'.

'£7 A TICKET.'

'LIVERPOOL TO NEW YORK IN UNDER TEN DAYS!'

'He wouldn't!' I cried, staring at Eliza in horror.

'But *America*! Just imagine it!'

'Well, if he did go he'd take us with him.'

'Huh! Would he?'

I wasn't sure either. How many hours had I sat at his

feet, listening to him paint a merry picture of the life we'd one day have? And now I struggled to even re-member what his voice sounded like. I hid my face in my hands and began to cry.

'Blimey Tilly!' Eliza gasped. 'Where d'you get *that*?'

I parted my fingers to see my sister kneeling over me, her hair tucked behind her ears. Her eyes were nearly popping out of her head.

Oh flip!

I was still wearing Kit's ring. I whipped my hand back under the covers. Too late. She grabbed my wrist hard.

'Let me see!' she hissed.

I snatched my arm back. 'Keep your beak out of it!'

'I'll just have to tell Ma, then.'

'Try it,' I said, 'and I'll be telling your secret too.'

7
DOUBLE DARE

Eliza didn't speak to me at breakfast. She left for work without saying goodbye. Quite honestly, I was glad to see the back of her. Now I could hide Kit's ring away without her seeing. I couldn't risk carrying it with me; I might lose it or get done as a thief. In the end, I chose our bed as the hiding place, stuffing the ring in an old stocking and sliding it under my side of our mattress. If Eliza did try to nick it, I'd be sure to wake up like a shot. Then I wound my shawl tight round my head and shoulders and set off to school.

It wasn't snowing any more, but the sky was still grey and heavy, and the air so cold it woke me up and got me thinking. Not miserable thoughts about Pa; these were good ones all about Kit. For the first time in my life, I felt I'd been trusted with something proper important. I was glad of it, and proud, but it weighed on me too since I'd no idea how to help him. All I knew about Kit came from village gossip, which didn't seem much use when I was trying to seek out a truth. What I needed was to get closer to the real Kit Barrington. That way I'd find out the facts.

The big question was *how?*

Frost Hollow Hall had locked front gates and people patrolling the grounds. Will Potter might know the place, but if my hazy memory of Sunday served me right, it wasn't the most welcoming house in the world.

Not that I'd let that put me off. Kit was counting on me now, and it was such a stirring thought my spirits truly began to lift. I marched on, a person with a purpose. Though the snow was only a few inches deep, it made the whole world look different, like a spell had been cast over Frostcombe village, turning the cow byres and cottages into things of magic.

Then I saw Will Potter.

He was hanging a side of beef outside his pa's shop. Two daft girls stood watching him, simpering and giggling as he played the idiot. When he saw me, he waved and called my name. The girls pulled faces and elbowed each other. I felt my cheeks grow hot. Putting my head down, I kept walking, all the while an idea growing in my head.

At school, I couldn't focus on anything much. Nor could the pupils. The snow made them restless, which got the class teacher Miss Fletcher so rattled she was near to blowing her top. To cap it all, the stove wouldn't stay lit, so by lunchtime it was too cold to even write properly. Poor Miss Fletcher had had enough. The class cheered when she told them they were being sent home. It was my place to stay behind and tidy the slates and put reading books back on the shelves. Though clearly today I wasn't doing a very good job of it.

'Go home, Tilly. Your mind's elsewhere too,' said Miss Fletcher, as she put on her coat. 'But I'll expect you bright and early tomorrow.'

'Yes, miss!'

I rushed for the door. With three good hours of daylight left, I'd no intention of going home. I headed straight for the butcher's shop.

*

Will was there, sweeping the floor. He looked at me coolly, taking in the snow on my skirts and the plaits coming loose at my shoulders. I fixed him with what I hoped was a meaningful stare.

'I've been thinking about that dare of yours. You know, the one what wasn't really a dare at all and I nearly . . .'

He held up his hand. 'If you've come to give me another earful, then buzz off. I'm busy.'

I was taken aback. I'd pictured him still all sorry for himself, dying for a chance to be friends again. It irked me that he wasn't.

'That's not why I'm here,' I said, trying to hold my temper.

'Oh? Well, you're not here to be civil, clearly. You didn't even say hello this morning.'

It wouldn't do to fly at him now. 'I want to go back to Frost Hollow Hall.'

'You're mad.'

Will turned his back and started sweeping again. I stayed put in the doorway. Eventually, he seemed to realise I wasn't going away. 'So what's it got to do with me?'

'You said there were places at the Hall even more daring to go to than the lake.'

'So?'

My heart beat quick. 'Now *I've* got a dare for *you*.'

'Really?'

'We have to go to Kit Barrington's grave.'

He looked horrified.

'Well? Will you come?'

He shook his head. 'Not a chance!'

'Why not?'

'You know why. The Barringtons are important customers. We can't afford to lose them. My pa'd kill me if he knew what we'd been up to. I reckon we got off lightly last time.'

'You call what happened *getting off lightly*?'

'I didn't mean it like that.'

'Of course,' I said, flicking a plait over my shoulder, 'you might just be scared.'

'No, I'm not!'

'Prove it.'

Will leaned on his broom and sighed. 'Kit's grave, Tilly? *Really*?'

The way he said it made my heart go even faster. 'It's one of them places you was talking about, in't it?'

'You wouldn't want to get caught there,' he said.

'And d'you know how to get to it?'

'I've an idea, yes.'

'So will you show me?'

He puffed out his cheeks. 'Heck, you really know

how to pick a dare!'

'You started it, remember,' I said.

'Does this mean we're friends, then?'

It didn't sound quite so bad now he'd said it. I nodded. 'All right.'

He put down his broom and disappeared off to speak with his pa. He returned with his hat and coat.

'I told him we was going for a nice cosy stroll,' he said, grinning.

'Is that so?'

He could think what he liked, just so long as he got us to Kit's grave.

'I've only got an hour, so let's get cracking,' Will said. 'But I still think you're mad.'

8

FLIGHTS OF ANGELS

At the gates of Frost Hollow Hall, I took a long breath. 'Straight there and straight back. Got it?'

Will turned up the collar of his coat. I could tell he was nervous too, and making a bad job of hiding it. He looked over his shoulder once or twice and then peered through the gates.

'We're going that way, are we?' I nodded at the wide drive leading away from us into a thicket of trees.

'Yep. But we'll need to be quick.'

'What we waiting for then? We in't here to admire the view.'

'All right, all right,' he tutted, and pulled down his cap.

The gates were shut. I reckoned I was small enough to squeeze through the bars, but Will had found another badger hole in the hedge, so we clambered through there, and went quickly round the first bend of the drive. I was hoping for a view of the house, but all I could see was snow. I kept walking straight ahead. Will yanked me back by my shawl.

'Not that way! You'll leave footprints! Now stick close,' he said, crossly.

We turned a sharp left off the drive and slowed our pace, though my heartbeat seemed to quicken. The way was too narrow to walk side by side, so Will took the lead and I fell in behind. Wild gorse and bracken grew over the path and branches bent low across us. It looked like no one had walked this way in years. The snow was deeper here. It came up to the tops of my boots and soaked my skirts. I hitched them up, best I could.

Will stopped suddenly. I ploughed right into the back of him.

'Can you climb that?' He pointed to a waist-high stone wall.

''Course.'

He vaulted over it with a quick flick of his heels. I pulled my skirts between my knees and tucked the hem in my waistband at the front. I ignored his offer of a hand up and scrambled over. On landing, I looked around me. What I saw made me shudder. We stood in a dismal, dank little graveyard. I didn't fancy going much further in.

It struck me just how quiet it was here, the eerie kind where even a breath sounds deafening. Before us, the ground swarmed with little metal headstones, poking up through the snow like teeth. Each one was red with rust, and between them were great tussocks of dead grass. The place looked uncared for, forgotten about. They might've been pets' graves, though I'd not have buried a dog in such a spot if you'd paid me.

What a poxy place!

Kit Barrington wasn't buried here. Any fool could see that straight away. We'd come all this way for a big fat nothing. And now my plan looked stupid too: I'd wanted to see Kit's grave, to know how his family remembered him. Stupid me for thinking Will might help. And even stupider him for reckoning he knew all the flipping answers. It was about time Will Potter got a piece of my mind.

One little grave stood out from the rest. It had been tended, and recently too. The brambles had been cleared, the ice scraped off and a fresh snowdrop lay beneath the headstone. I crouched down to read the name on it:

Ada
Taken Too Soon

No date. No surname. Just four simple words. But it stirred me strangely and my eyes filled with tears. She was dead in the ground, this Ada. Yet someone still cared enough to come out here in the cold and tend her sorry little grave. It seemed so very sad. But then if I was dead I supposed my pa might do such a thing for me, and the thought made me well up even more.

It was colder than ever now and it had started snowing again. I wiped my face and stood up, looking for a way out of this godforsaken place. I realised then that I'd lost Will.

I called out. 'Where are you?'

The noise sent rooks bursting from the tree tops, their hateful racket setting me right on edge.

'Will? Where the flip are you?'

'Over here, slow coach!' He was standing by the far wall. I hurried over to him.

'What are we doing *here*?' I snapped.

He rolled his eyes like I was a total lummox. 'This is where they bury the servants.'

'But I want to see Kit Barrington's grave! And you said you knew where it was!'

'This place is a shortcut, that's all. Not scared, are you?'

This was mighty rich, coming from him.

'Fat chance!' I said. 'But you better know where we're going, I'm warning you!'

Will led me through a gap in a holly hedge and this time onto a clearer path, wide enough for us to walk together. A blackbird hopped from bush to bush up ahead, singing sweetly in the chill air.

'The Hall's half a mile behind us. You won't see it from here,' he said as I turned to look. 'Come on, we're nearly there.'

The path curved to the right and into a clearing flanked by yew trees. Leading off from the centre were more little walkways, each one ending with a stone urn or a pillar or marble cross, all covered in snow. People lay buried here too, it seemed. Only this place was grand, with its clipped hedges and fancy carvings. The quiet was different too; not bleak and queer, but painfully sad in a way that made my throat ache.

Will nodded up ahead. 'Here it is.'

Standing pale against the leaves was a most magnificent sight. An angel stood before us, taller than a man, with wings spread wide and head bowed, clutching flowers to its breast.

I stood still, completely overawed.

'Go on then. Have a look,' said Will, nudging me forward.

Hardly knowing where to put my feet, I stumbled forwards. I reached out to touch the angel's hand; I wondered for a moment if it was real. The stone was smooth and cold against my fingers. Looking down, I saw the name carved into the base at the angel's feet:

Christopher Edward Barrington
Fell asleep February 6th 1871
Our Beloved Kit
'Goodnight sweet prince
And flights of angels
sing thee to thy rest'

Before this moment, I might just have convinced myself that I'd had a fright and imagined everything: the boy under the ice, the dreams, the ring. Not now. Kit was dead. The gravestone made it real. And what a fine grave it was.

I knelt down and stared at the stone angel towering above me, tears streaming down my face. Someone had laid a wreath of fresh winter roses at the foot of the statue; Lord and Lady Barrington, most probably. They'd have knelt here too, just as I was doing now. This was Kit's final resting place.

Only I knew he wasn't truly at rest.

9

THE DAY HE DIED

I didn't know how long I knelt there; minutes, maybe more. Will's voice brought me back to myself.

'This isn't a dare at all, is it?' he said, his gaze fixed on me.

'Don't,' I said, getting to my feet.

It felt too much. I squeezed my eyes shut 'til all I saw was swirling patterns. Bit by bit, my mind slowed down. When I opened my eyes again, the snow was still falling. The quiet had changed too; now it was all muffled and thick, like in a room when the drapes are closed.

'You'd better tell me why we're here,' he said. 'And I want the real reason.'

I fiddled with a thread end of my shawl, unable to think of a single thing to say.

'Please don't,' I said again.

'You seem so heartbroken, that's all,' he said, more gently this time.

I looked at him unsteadily, and felt myself flush. 'I am, I suppose, though it hardly makes sense to be.'

Will looked past me at the gravestone and breathed in sharp.

'What is it?' I said.

'Look at the date Christopher Barrington died,' he said. 'Just look. It's right strange.'

I turned to peer at the inscription.

February 6th 1871

Kit died ten years ago. I knew this already. I wasn't sure what Will was getting at.

'What's strange about that?' I said.

'Today's the eighth of February.'

'So two days ago on Sunday it was . . .'

'The same date. The sixth.'

A chill spread through me. 'That's . . . some coincidence, in't it?' I said, hearing my voice tremble.

'Kit Barrington died in that lake,' Will said. 'You didn't. But you *was* drowning, Tilly. I tried crawling across the ice to reach you but you'd just . . . well . . . vanished. You was under for ages. I was certain you'd come a cropper. And then, somehow, you just floated up again, right near the edge so I could drag you out.'

I shifted uncomfortably.

'How the heck *did* you stay alive?' he said.

'I . . . um . . .'

'And you're right, that date *is* a coincidence, don't you think?'

His eyes seemed to peer inside me. And before I could stop myself, the words fell from my mouth.

'I've something to tell you,' I said. 'It sounds barmy, but promise me you'll listen.'

'Go on then. I'm all ears.'

'I didn't die in the lake because somebody saved me. And that somebody was Kit Barrington.'

Will gave a little laugh. 'You're right. It *is* barmy.'

Now I'd started, I wasn't going to stop, though thank God he couldn't see how my legs shook. 'I swear it was him,' I said. 'He took my hand and . . .'

'How the heck could Kit Barrington save you? He's been dead ten years!'

'But he was under the water. I saw him.'

'*Really?*'

'It was him! I can prove it!'

'How?'

'Last night I found this gold ring with Kit's name engraved on it.'

'Where?'

'In the hem of my dress, the one I was wearing on Sunday.'

Will held out his hand. 'Let's see it then.'

'It's at home.'

Will pulled a face.

'It is!' I said. 'I in't daft enough to carry it round with me! People'd reckon I'd nicked it!'

'Fair enough,' he said, still looking unsure. 'But what does this ring prove?'

'At first I thought he was an angel come to take me to heaven. But then I didn't die. And now I've found the ring, and, well, I reckon it's a sign.'

'Of what?'

I felt uncertain myself, saying it out loud. 'Kit saved me for a reason. And now he wants me to help him.'

'How can you help him? He's dead!'

I shook my head. 'Not quite, not properly. He's not at peace, anyway.'

'You been reading those penny dreadfuls again?' said Will. 'Messages from beyond the grave and all that?'

He did have a point.

'I can hardly believe it myself,' I said. 'He says there's a truth to be revealed and until that's done, then his spirit won't rest.'

Will went silent and looked at the sky. Eventually he said, 'Come on, we'd better get going. I said I'd only be an hour, and this snow's getting heavier.'

'Don't you dare walk away!' I cried, grabbing his arm. 'You promised you'd listen!'

He shook me off. 'But it doesn't add up.'

'Why not? Yesterday, you said there'd been talk of a ghost up here.'

'*Inside* the house, yes. But it could just be servants' gossip. I've heard nothing about ghosts being *outside*. And certainly no one mentioned the lake.'

We glared at each other.

Then Will said, 'This is all too strange, Tilly. We need to leave it be.'

'You're scared, in't you?'

'Don't be daft,' he snapped.

'Then listen to me. It's a queer story, how Kit Barrington came to die in that lake. No one knows what *really* happened. But he's unhappy and he needs my help. And the date on the grave might just be the start of it.'

'How do you know all this?'

My insides went fluttery. I hoped it didn't show in my face. 'He comes to me in my dreams. He's desperate.'

And he's the most beautiful thing I've ever seen.

Only I didn't think it'd help to say this.

Will scratched his head and took a great deep breath like he was suddenly weary of it all. I wished I'd brought the blasted ring to show him. It might have proved I was telling the truth.

'You're the only person I've told this to,' I said. 'No one else will listen.'

Will met my eye. Then he turned to look at the stone angel. 'You know my uncle Bert, the stone cutter?'

I did. And I wondered where this was heading.

'Well, he told me about graves. See that there?' He pointed to the flowers in the angel's hands. One of the heads was broken at the stem and hung down limply. 'It's s'posed to be like that. It means he died too young, too suddenly – cut down in his youth, and all.'

'So do you believe me?' I said. 'That Kit Barrington needs my help?'

Will put his cap back on. 'I don't know what to think.'

But he'd stopped smirking, at least, and I felt so overcome that my eyes filled with tears.

'You think I'm mad,' I sniffed.

'I always have done,' he said. 'And you'll have your

work cut out trying to solve this business. But I reckon you're right to start here at the Hall. There's something about this place . . .'

I knew what he meant.

'I bet someone here knows more than they're letting on,' he said.

'But Kit's family loved him. You only got to look at this gravestone.'

The snow was falling thickly now. It was a job to see beyond the hedges, or to the path beyond.

Suddenly, close by, a dog barked.

'Someone's coming!' hissed Will. 'Quick! Follow me!'

We didn't get far.

As we stepped back out onto the path, our way was blocked by a rough-looking man with a big stick in his hand. An enormous black dog growled at his side. I sensed Will freeze up beside me.

'Well, well, well,' said the man, and spat something solid into the snow. 'Two tykes from the village paying their respects. In't that touching? We'll have to see if it softens his Lordship's heart.'

Grabbing us both by the scruff of our necks, he marched us in the direction of the Hall.

10

HOT WATER

Despite Will's cussing, the man kept a firm grip on us all the way down the path. I stayed quiet. The dog nosed around our ankles and would've sunk its teeth in at a moment's bidding, but it didn't scare me. Because as we walked, this queer, calm feeling came over me, like I'd been tied with an invisible thread and someone at the Hall was on the other end of it, reeling me in. There was no going back.

We went downhill until a high wall rose up before us. There we stopped in front of a doorway. The man pushed it open with his elbow.

'Get in there,' he grunted.

We stumbled into a dim courtyard, lit only by a few lamps at the windows. I guessed dusk wasn't that far off, but the great buildings themselves seemed to block out what daylight was left. As my eyes got used to the gloom, I saw railings and steps leading down below ground.

'Down 'ere. Both of you. And don't move!'

The man flung us forward. We tumbled down the flight of steps. I landed on my knees at the bottom, and found myself facing yet another doorway. Will was stood a few feet away, rubbing his hands and muttering under his breath. The man and his dog had gone.

'You all right, Tilly?'

My knees stung as I stood up. 'Think so. Where's *he* gone to then?'

'To fetch Lord Barrington, I reckon,' said Will. 'We're for it; you know that, don't you?'

I could handle a thrashing, if that's what he meant. I bet my ma hit harder than most men, anyway. I squared my shoulders and smoothed down my frock. If this was my chance to meet Lord Barrington then I wanted to look neat, at least.

The door flew open. But it wasn't Lord Barrington, not in the slightest. It was a woman. She was tall with hair piled high on her head, wearing full skirts and a wide-shouldered blouse. A great bunch of keys hung at her hip.

'Will Potter,' said a voice I knew from somewhere. 'Delivering meat is one thing, but roaming the estate is quite another. And twice in two days! This is trespassing of the highest order . . .'

Her words trailed off as she saw me.

'*You* again,' she said.

Staring back at me was the same pinched face I'd seen here on Sunday. She was the housekeeper, Mrs Jessop. And she didn't seem any friendlier today.

I spoke before Will got the chance. 'We took the wrong path, that's all.'

'You'd do well to lose that tone, young lady,' she said, eyeing me coldly.

'Please excuse Tilly, Mrs Jessop,' said Will. 'She don't always know her manners.'

I jabbed him in the ribs.

'Ouch!'

Mrs Jessop raised her hand for silence. 'Both of you listen carefully. You won't be whipped because his Lordship is leaving shortly on business. Though if it were down to me, I'd have you flogged right away.'

'So we in't seeing him, then?' I said, spirits sinking. I'd been hoping for a quick peek, at least.

She glared at me. 'No, you are not! You'll be working your punishment instead. I'm one maid down since Gracie Waite is sick in bed.'

'Gracie's sick?' said Will. 'Is she badly?'

So he knew this *Gracie* person too. I bet she was another simpering half-wit. They seemed drawn to

Will Potter like flies.

'It's nothing to concern yourself with,' said Mrs Jessop.

'Right. Well then. I've got to get back to the village. Reckon I'm already late,' said Will, looking worried of a sudden.

But the idea of working here thrilled me. What a chance this was! I'd get to see inside Kit's home, to meet people who'd known him. Heck, my plan to get closer to the real Kit Barrington was turning out better than I'd hoped.

I fixed Will with such a look he apologised at once. 'Beg pardon, Mrs Jessop,' he muttered. 'Didn't mean to sound off.'

'And you'd do well to stay quiet,' she said. 'First trespassing, and now trying to shirk punishment. What on earth would your father say?'

He looked up sharply. 'You won't tell him, will you?'

'Won't I? This sort of behaviour hardly looks good for his business. Maybe we'll have to go elsewhere for our meat.'

'Please. Don't say that.' His voice was tight. 'You're our best, most finest customer. Her Ladyship's ordered from us for years.'

'Will . . .' I tried to stop him but he shrugged me off.

'We need the custom! I'll do anything! Please!'

Mrs Jessop raised her hand. This time Will was having none of it.

'It weren't me! *She* made me come here with her stupid ideas!'

I realised then that he was pointing right at me.

'Why you filthy low-down worm!' I said and went to wallop him. He stepped back just in time, so my fist whizzed past his ear.

'Enough! The pair of you!' Mrs Jessop cried.

Shooting each other the darkest of looks, we shifted apart, and right then I was glad of Mrs Jessop, since I'd have throttled him otherwise.

Damn Will Potter! Why the heck did I tell him anything?

'All right,' she said to Will. 'You can clean out the hens.'

He nodded eagerly.

'They'll peck at you, and they haven't been cleaned out in days,' she added, wryly.

His face fell just a little. The sight of him being handed a pail and sent back up the steps made me feel much better. Chicken muck was just what he deserved.

'And you can wipe that smirk off your face,' Mrs Jessop said to me. 'You're going to the kitchens.'

She pulled me into the light and shut the door behind us.

As I stepped inside the Hall, all thoughts of Will vanished. My heart began to pound. Here I was in Kit's house. Any minute I'd see the people who had cooked his meals, made up his fires. Any one of them might know something, even Mrs Jessop. But I had to be careful and not speak out of turn. Any questions could wait; I was in enough trouble already.

'Keep up, I haven't got all day,' Mrs Jessop called over her shoulder.

I quickened my pace and looked about me. We were walking down a flagstone passageway, where gas jets flared on the walls and little high windows showed the falling snow outside. Many doors went off the passage: a laundry room full of drying clothes, a still room where someone was pouring ale into jugs, and a larger room full of gleaming glass and silver, with a fire burning in the grate. We stopped at this doorway. A man in a smart black suit was dusting glasses and placing them on a tray with great care. From the way Mrs Jessop addressed him, I guessed he was someone important. It was certainly different from how she spoke to me.

'Mr Phelps, this young lady will be scrubbing the pots from luncheon, and there's a boy outside doing the chickens.' Mrs Jessop pushed me forward. 'Tilly, this is Mr Phelps, the butler. He's in charge here.'

Mr Phelps looked me over. 'Extra hands, eh? Goodness, what luck! And where did you find them, Mrs Jessop?'

'Up to no good, that's where I found them. Wandering about like this was some sort of pleasure gardens, not a private estate.'

'There's nothing an honest day's work can't put straight,' said Mr Phelps, frowning. 'And we've plenty to do here.'

Mrs Jessop gave a curt nod. 'Any bother and the strap's where we always keep it.' I must've looked like a startled rabbit because Mr Phelps gave me a tiny wink, then went back to his polishing.

'Right you are, Mrs J., right you are,' he said.

Back out in the passageway, we carried on through a set of glass doors and the heat of the kitchen hit me. A maid passed us carrying armfuls of plates. Up ahead, voices were shouting, 'More ice, over here,' and 'Watch your back,' and then 'Clean that fat up, won't you, before we break our necks.' The clattering of pans and slamming of doors deafened me. Mrs Jessop stood aside as the same maid came back past, this time with a basket of vegetables. She had sleek brown hair, most of which was hidden by her cap. I was struck by how pretty she was.

'Thank you, Mrs Jessop,' she said politely.

'I'm sorry you're having to work down here today, Dorcas,' said Mrs Jessop. 'It's not fitting for a head housemaid, but there we are.'

Then we followed her into the big kitchen itself.

The heat was stifling. Pans and kettles steamed away on a massive black range, and the opening and shutting of oven doors wafted even more hot air about the room. The space was huge and brightly lit, with a high ceiling and more little windows. A vast dresser stacked with basins and jugs covered an entire wall. The maid had joined another girl in a white pinafore. Together, they were sorting through the vegetables. The giant table and great tall ceiling seemed to dwarf them both. This space looked made for twenty kitchen hands, not just two.

We went up to a small woman in a waist apron who appeared to be the cook. She moved about like a whirlwind, though she stopped mid-clatter when she saw us.

'This is Tilly,' said Mrs Jessop. 'She's standing in for

Gracie. Let her go when it's our suppertime.'

Cook looked me up and down.

'Scullery,' she said and pointed to a door off the back of the kitchen. 'Get your hands washed and I'll be in to show you what's what.'

I looked to Mrs Jessop but she was already making for the door. *What an odd way of walking*, I thought, watching her straight back and swaying skirts. *Her feet could be on castors. Her keys don't jangle at all.*

After the kitchen, the scullery felt cool and quiet. Cook folded her arms and looked at me.

'Now then missy, I've seen you before. You're the girl Will brought in on Sunday, in't you?'

I kept my eyes down.

'Well, you look recovered, thankfully. But honestly, can't you get enough of this place?'

I wasn't sure quite what to say.

'What was you up to this time, then?'

'Nothing much,' I said.

'Oh come on, out with it. I in't got all day!' she said, but in a kindly way.

'We was trespassing.'

Cook sighed. 'Oh aye, Jake and his dog catch you then?'

I nodded. So the brute of a man had a name.

'Stealing rabbits from his snares, was you?'

'No!' I said, sharply. 'I never stole nothing!'

Cook laughed. 'You must've been up to something.'

I wasn't sure how much to tell her. So I said, 'I'm to scrub pots as punishment.'

'Why you want to fool around up here is anyone's guess. And in this weather too!' she said. 'But do your work well and there might be a place for you. We're always short of hands. Not many folk want to work here, these days.' She saw the look on my face. 'Don't get too excited though. It in't your job yet.'

But already my mind was racing. Who wouldn't want to work in such a grand house as this? I'd bite their hand off for the chance. Nosing around here all day, I'd find out plenty about Kit. Such a job was sure to pay better than helping at school. And I might even make Ma proud, for once.

Cook told me to roll up my sleeves and gave me a cap and pinny to wear. Then she filled two pails, one with soapy water, one with clean. A shout came from the kitchen that something was burning and she made for the door.

'The soft soap's for the china, soda's for the pans,' she said, pointing to some jars on the windowsill. 'And there's sand and salt for the copper pans. Brings 'em up a treat. Now get your hands washed!'

The door swung to and I was on my own. The sink had hot running water. *Hot running water!* I turned the tap on-off-on-off just for the fun of it and washed my hands until the skin went pink. Then the pots started coming from the kitchen. I got to work as best I could. All the soaking and scrubbing quickly turned my hands raw and wrinkly like newborn mice. The hot water made me sweat and my hair kept escaping from under the cap. Bending over the sink made my back ache too. After an hour or more of it, I'd really had enough.

I was mighty glad to see Cook again, especially since she'd brought me a cup of tea and a pastry.

'Get this down you,' she said, noticing the scrubbed draining board and racks full of drying pots. 'Haven't you done well here?'

I gulped the tea and stuffed the pastry into my mouth. I was famished, and tired too. How could anyone scrub pots all day and not fall down dead in a heap?

I handed back the cap and apron.

'If you're lucky, you might need these again,' said Cook.

I didn't want to seem ungrateful, but I began to

wonder what I'd discover about Kit stuck in here all day with my nose in a pot.

'This position what's going,' I said. 'Is it only working in the kitchens?'

'Not as such. It's for a proper housemaid. It'd be a smashing job for a girl like you.'

'Good,' I said, relieved.

'But things is topsy-turvy here. We're so short-staffed, you'll have to try your hand at all sorts.'

It was better than nothing, so I put on my best smile. 'I'd do anything to work here, really I would.'

'I can see that. Now get yourself off home.'

I was half out the back door when she called, 'So where was it Jake caught you then? Go on, tell us.'

She'd been kind enough to me. It couldn't hurt to say.

'The Barringtons' graveyard. Looking at the stone angel,' I said.

Her face went pale. 'Oh no! Not Master Kit's grave? What on earth was you doing up *there*?'

The way she said it made me go cold. I'd have done better keeping my mouth shut.

11

GONE

I'd no intention of waiting for that rat Will Potter. It was almost dark by now, and though the snow had stopped falling, the sky was clear, making the cold seem sharper than before. I went up the drive with a heavy heart, sure I'd blown my chances of a job at the Hall. Who in their right minds would hire a sneak like me? I was absolutely useless.

Nearing home, I saw a huddle of people on our front step. The door was open, casting a pale light over them. They were too many all at once to be ordinary visitors paying a call. One by one, they turned to watch me coming up the lane, their faces so grim that a sense of dread came over me, and I began to feel sick and ill.

Something was very wrong.

I walked slowly towards them, fearing what they might tell me. One of them was our neighbour Ruby, jiggling her squawking baby on her hip, and talking quickly in a low voice. She hadn't yet seen me.

I stopped at our gate. 'Ruby? What is it?'

'Tilly! You're here!' she cried and rushed towards me, seizing my arm. 'Thank goodness!'

'What is it? What's happened?'

People stepped aside to let me through and I felt a hand on my back, pushing me into the house. Ruby closed the door behind us.

'Be gentle with your ma. She's had an awful shock,' Ruby said.

My stomach lurched.

Someone's died. Pa. Is it Pa?

I reached out to steady myself.

He's dead. That's why he hasn't come home.

I stumbled into the room like a blind thing.

'Ma?' My voice shook.

A little grey shape sat huddled on the chair.

'Ma?'

She turned her head just a bit, like she wasn't sure who was speaking. Her face was whiter than the wall behind her.

'What's going on?' I rushed to her side. 'Ma? Please! Speak to me!'

She looked right through me, then turned away.

'We thought you'd both gone after him,' said Ruby. 'You and Eliza.'

Every part of me turned cold.

'What do you mean?'

'Your father. He was seen boarding the Bristol coach this afternoon. Eliza was with him. Word was you were there too.'

The room swam in front of me. I pushed past her for the door and threw up all over the front steps.

*

I sat in a daze until Ruby finally got up to leave. Her baby was crying again and she had five more still to feed at home.

'I'll have to go now, Tilly,' said Ruby, kindly. 'You've not a scrap to eat here, poor things. I'll send something by if I can.'

'Ta, but we'll manage,' I said.

In truth, I didn't see how. But I didn't cry. I felt drained and empty, like I'd run out of ways to feel.

Once Ruby had left us, the room seemed too quiet. Ma hadn't moved in her seat. And I wondered if I'd ever get up again either, since I hardly trusted my legs to hold me. Yet I couldn't bear the silence between us.

'Shall I get the tea on?' I said.

Ma stared at me, blank-eyed. 'Tea?'

'I reckon we might need it.'

She sighed deeply. Her nose was red and her mouth drooped down at the corners.

So this was it, then. Just the two of us.

It did little to comfort me. In fact, it felt awkward, like being with someone I hardly knew. Any moment she'd tell me she'd been right all along, that Pa was no good, and I was a fool to have thought otherwise.

But she didn't speak another word.

The room had grown so cold my breath came out like smoke, and the frost had set hard on the windows. I put a blanket over Ma's knees and got to work, managing to coax the stove alight and putting a pan of water on to heat. There really wasn't anything left to eat, but at least we'd have hot tea. I wetted the dregs from the morning's pot and busied myself getting the cups out. It felt better to be doing something.

Outside, it was proper dark. As I went to close the curtain, I saw the stars were out, and before I could help it, I was thinking of Pa and Eliza. They were out there somewhere, under this very same sky. And I wondered if Pa was looking at the stars like I was, and thinking the same about me? I shut my eyes to make a wish.

Keep him safe. Bring him back home. And Eliza too.

Like a blow to the chest it hit me.

He'd gone, hadn't he? He really *had* gone. He wasn't coming back. And he'd live out his dream with Eliza, not me.

I shut the curtain quick, unable to bear it. I swore I'd never wish on a star again.

*

Once the water had heated, I made tea, stirring the scrapings of an old twist of sugar into Ma's drink.

'Here,' I said, placing her hands round her cup. 'Don't spill it.'

As she sipped, she shut her eyes.

'That better?'

She nodded slowly and opened her eyes, looking at me in a way I wasn't used to. Then she pulled something from her pocket. It was a piece of paper, folded up very small.

'Eliza left this on the table,' she said, handing it to me. 'I found it when I came back from the village. And then Ruby came by with the news that she'd been spotted.'

'What does it say?'

'I in't looked. Read it to me, will you? And don't

leave nothing out.'

Ma wasn't so good at reading. Right then, I wished I wasn't either, bracing myself as I unfolded it. It was the White Star flyer, the very same one Eliza had shown me just this morning. Written on the back of it was a note. The writing was most definitely my sister's.

Dear Ma

By the time you read this I'll be gone. Don't try to find me because I shan't come back. See, I've found out where Pa is and what he's up to, and I'm going after him but not to bring him home. He's at the Buckland Inn, and is leaving today to catch a boat from Liverpool to America . . .

My heart caught in my throat. Buckland was the next village, just a few miles over the hill. It was ten times worse knowing this. He'd been so close and still hadn't come home. What the heck had stopped him?

Ma looked paler than ever.

'Shall I keep going?'

She shut her eyes and nodded.

. . . and I'm going after him. He doesn't know I'm coming. It'll be a terrific surprise! I used to think Pa's

big talk was just stuff and nonsense. Then I found this advert. That's when I knew he meant it, that dreams can come true. All I do is read stories where adventures happen to other people. I'm sick and tired of it. You see, I fancy a bit of fun myself . . .

It was agony to hear. This wasn't how things were in our family. It was me who sided with Pa. *Me*. Whenever he'd talked about the house or the land or the pigs we'd have one day, Eliza'd seemed bored to tears.

Now I could hardly bear to look at Ma, who'd fallen back into a shocked sort of daze. I read the final lines.

. . . So please don't be too sad. I shall tell Tilly myself that I'm leaving and if she wants to tag along, I don't suppose I can stop her. Goodbye Ma.
    Your Eliza

My heart jolted. We'd had cross words this morning. Of course Eliza hadn't come to find me.
Or had she?
We'd been sent home from school early. And all afternoon I'd been up at Frost Hollow Hall.

I was suddenly deeply glad. For who knows what I might've said to her? I wasn't even sure myself.

the room was now Eliza wasn't here.

look at the empty chair, which just this

been heaped with her clothes. Now the

o big, the covers too neat. Our room had

his tidy before. I put the candle down and

ankets.

ttress was bare.

the heck was the bed sheet?

ed to God she hadn't nicked that and all, since

't have another one.

foot caught on something soft. The sheet was

hidden under the bed like someone had stuffed

re in a hurry. In amongst it was a dark shape. I

bed the candle and thrust it before me. The shape

a stocking, the very one I'd hidden Kit's ring in.

y heart began to race.

Oh no. Please. No.

I bent to pick it up. It felt horribly light and empty in my hand. As I sank to my knees and started to sob, I already knew what Eliza had done. Anyone bold enough to take the rent money from her mother's pot was never going to leave a gold ring behind.

I was crying so hard, I could barely breathe. I didn't care that Ma might hear me. I screwed the stocking up

'Well, I didn't see her,' I said.

A hopeful thought came to me then.

'Pa might not want her with him. He'd have to pay her passage, wouldn't he? And she never showed much interest in his plans before.'

Ma shook her head, sadly. 'Someone saw them, remember? The coach left at two o'clock this afternoon. They looked happy enough, so I was told.'

Anger welled up in me. This wasn't a pleasant picture at all.

'I've lost her, haven't I?' Ma said.

I'd never seen her cry before. Now she did it quietly, the tears streaming down her cheeks and onto her frock. I felt truly terrible. Here I was, her very own daughter and I didn't know how to comfort her.

After a bit, she wiped her face.

'I blame your father for all of this,' she said, bitterly. 'Good riddance to him. But why did he have to take my Eliza?'

'He didn't exactly *take* her. She chose to go.'

She didn't seem to hear me. 'He always did fill your heads with stupid notions. I told him not to, but he'd never listen. And now this has happened. I hope he's mighty pleased with himself!'

I bit my lip. I loved it that Pa hoped for better

things. They weren't *stupid notions* to me. But it was no good explaining this to Ma. Her dander was well and truly up.

'And d'you know the worst thing?' she said.

Oh heck, there was more?

'Yesterday, I got paid. I was putting a bit by for the rent.' She reached for the little brass money pot on the mantel and took the lid off to show me how empty it was. 'Look! Cleaned out! All gone! See what he's done to us, that father of yours?'

'Pa didn't take it! How could he?'

'Oh grow up, Tilly! I realise Eliza *took* it. But only to go after your pa, just to get her to Buckland or Bristol or wherever she was hoping to find him. Which really makes it his fault.'

Even now she couldn't blame Eliza.

'Well, she didn't have to take it,' I said, crossly.

Ma shook her head. She was trembling with anger.

'Your pa is a waste of blinking space and it's about time you realised it!'

She might as well have twisted the knife already in my chest.

'And it's about time *you* realised that the sun don't shine out of Eliza's backside!' I said, before I could stop myself.

All went
I hadn
ready for
didn't hit m
feet, like it wa

I couldn't be
pany was better th

'Please, stay a bit
said.

She'd already reache
for one day.'

So I gave her what was le
she'd have forgotten my outb

'You have it,' she said, handi
a good girl, Tilly. I knew you
leave.'

My eyes prickled with tears.
shoulder lightly, just once, and moved

*

Soon after, I went to my own bed, tired t
bones. I wasn't even planning to get undresse
wanted to fall down and sleep. But glancing abo
my heart sank. I cursed the candlelight, since it

me see how bar
I could hardly
morning had
bed looked to
never been t
lifted the bl
How odd
The ma
Where
I hop
we did
My
half
it th
gral
wa
M

in a tight ball and hurled it at the wall.

No father. No sister. No ring.

What did anything matter now?

I crawled into bed and willed sleep to come.

DREAMING: 3

My fingers are white like bones picked clean by fishes. I can't feel them at all. Above my head, the ice holds fast. Every step, every breath is exhausting. My chest is tight, I can't breathe deep enough. I'm tired of this place. It's too cold, too dark. If only I could just lie down. The dark gets darker. My eyes begin to close.

Out of nowhere a pale shape comes towards me. It's him, the boy; Kit Barrington.

Goodness, the look of him! All I can do is stare. His beauty works on me like magic. But his eyes are pleading, desperate. I should be doing something, I know I should, but my head is all dizzy and I can't think straight.

I see his mouth form the words: 'Help me!'

As he moves closer, panic flares up in my chest.

Why me? Can't he see that I'm useless?

The tiredness is overwhelming. My arms and legs go heavy. I want to sleep, to give up on this and never open my eyes again.

He's crying now. I shake my head. He's got me all wrong. I'm no help to anyone. He grips my hands tight, the chill of his fingers biting into mine. He's holding onto me for dear life. He needs me. I'm his only hope.

Even his tears are beautiful.

12

GOING INTO SERVICE

When I opened my eyes it hit me all over again. I swore I'd been punched in the heart. I pulled the covers over my head and curled up tight in a ball. It didn't make the hurting go away. The early-morning sun shone in through the window just like this was any other Wednesday.

Except it wasn't.

Slowly it dawned on me. There was little to be done about Pa and Eliza. But there was plenty I could do for Kit, especially as a maid in his family's house. Lying here feeling sorry for myself wasn't helping no one.

Ma got up soon after I did. She looked a mess. Her frock was stained and her hair unpinned, and she moved about the place like a sleepwalker. I'd expected more ranting, more fury. Not this. It made her seem sadder than ever.

I'd just got the stove lit, when a sharp knock at the door made us both jump out of our skins. Ma's look turned suddenly wild.

'Don't answer it!' she hissed. 'He'll be wanting the rent again.'

'I know you're in there, Clara Higgins,' said a voice from the doorstep. 'And I'm warning you, if you don't open this door, I'll break it down myself.'

'We can't put him off for ever, Ma.'

Wiping my hands on my skirts, I opened the door. The landlord stepped back, surprised.

'Oh aye, doing your mammy's dirty work then, are you?' he said.

Up close, he looked like a prize rodent. He had small eyes set in a very red face, and when he spoke, his front teeth seemed too large for his mouth.

'My, you've grown into a pretty young thing, haven't you?' His gaze ran over me in a way I didn't much like.

Shame I can't say the same, I thought, and folded my arms. 'Exactly how much do we owe you?'

'More than you can afford by the looks of it,' he said, leering. 'I'm warning you, I've got another family I could move in here tomorrow.'

'We need a bit more time.'

He came closer. 'You've had time, missy.'

Though my heart was racing, I stood my ground.

'You'll get your money, I promise.'

'I want it now.'

'Well we in't got it now.'

He moved closer still. I smelled the gin on his breath. ' You ain't too growed up for a clip round the ear . . .'

Ma pushed past me in the doorway. 'Take this, you vulture!' she cried.

Something gold spun through the air. It hit the landlord square in the chest. For one confusing second, I was sure it was Kit's ring, and a sob broke from my mouth as I went to grab it. The landlord got there first, scrabbling through the snow like a terrier at a foxhole. He held up Ma's own wedding ring between his thumb and forefinger. I looked at her in total dismay.

So this was what it had come to. We'd finally sunk this low.

But she wouldn't meet my eye. She was breathing hard and glaring at the landlord.

'Cheap gold,' he said, getting to his feet. 'It'll buy you a couple of weeks, then you're out.'

Without another word, Ma pulled me back inside and slammed the door. She collapsed into her seat, exhausted.

'What we going to do, Tilly? We can't find that money in two weeks.'

I was still in a state of shock. 'You gave him your wedding ring.'

'I had no choice.'

'But your *wedding ring*?'

'Leave it be,' she said.

My eyes stung. I felt my throat go thick. A gold ring stood for love, didn't it? Pure, proper love. Here was Ma throwing hers out the door like it counted for nothing. Maybe it didn't any more for her or Pa. And as a thought, *that* hurt quite enough. Then there was Kit's ring. I'd left it in a stocking, for flip's sake, where anyone with half a brain might find it.

And someone had.

If I clapped eyes on my sister now, I'd rip her beating heart out. Though in truth I doubted she even had one. She was no better than that foul-faced landlord. In fact, she was worse, thieving from her own flesh and blood. I blamed *her*, fair and square. Yet I felt sore too since some of the blame lay with me. Kit had given me a precious thing and I'd not taken proper care of it. If a gold ring stood for love, then what the heck did that say about *me*?

'Go to the mill and ask about Eliza's old job,' said

Ma. 'They might give it you if you're quick.'

I stared at her. 'The *mill*?'

'We need money, Tilly. And it's time you got a serious job, a girl of your age.'

'But there's a housemaid's job going. It's what I want to do, really it is,' I said all in a rush. 'Though it'll mean living in.'

She looked at me blankly.

'And it'll pay more than I get at the school.'

'Are you set on it?'

'I am.'

'So where's this job to?'

'Frost Hollow Hall.'

She did a heavy sigh. 'I thought you'd seen enough of that place.'

But that's just it, I wanted to say, *I haven't seen enough of it by far*.

'It's a good position,' I said. 'I'd be lucky to get it.'

Ma's face darkened. 'It's a fine household, yes, but there's been ill luck and broken hearts a-plenty in that family. No one stays working there for long.'

'You said that was just idle gossip.'

'Some of it, maybe,' she said. 'But if you want to go into service, you'd do better trying somewhere else.'

I shook my head. I didn't fancy clearing up after just

anyone. My heart was set on this job. It was my chance to be a fly on the wall, a part of the furniture. And all the talk of queer happenings made me want to work there even more. Only I couldn't explain this to Ma.

Yet she must've seen that my mind was set, because she got to her feet and put a pan of water on the stove.

'So when you going to ask about this job?'

'Soon as you can spare me, I suppose,' I said, thinking how pale she looked.

She nodded. 'Right. We'll have you ready in an hour. Can't send you to Frost Hollow Hall looking like a ragamuffin, can we?'

With that, Ma seemed to spring into life. While I shined my boots and found a clean shift, she busied herself brushing out my best Sunday frock and sponging down the bits where mud still clung to the skirts. She'd spread it across the table, which got me picturing the kitchens again up at Frost Hollow Hall and me laid out, half dead from drowning. A shiver ran right down my back. *Poor Kit.* No one had pulled him free. His spirit was still in that dreadful lake, even now.

Then Ma said, 'How did this hem come loose?'

She was frowning at the place in my skirt where Kit had hidden his ring. My heart gave a painful thud.

'Oh . . . um . . . Must've caught it somehow.'

'Hmmm,' she said, biting the black thread with her teeth. 'They wear uniform up at the Hall, I s'pect. Tear that, and you'll be mending it yourself.'

'Promise I'll be careful.' I would too. And not just because of the sewing. I'd be wearing something neat, for once. Something that might actually fit.

Ma went upstairs and came back with her best red flannel petticoat.

'For you,' she said. 'To make you feel smart, even if your frock has seen better days.'

I jumped to my feet. 'Blimey! Really? For me?'

'Not 'til you've had a proper wash.'

The pan of water was warm by now, so I poured it into our tin bath and stripped off, teeth chattering. The water was grey when I'd finished. Then I wrapped myself in an old sheet and sat by the hearth to dry out my hair.

As I watched the flames, I began to feel very sorry that I had to leave Ma at all. We only had each other now. By this time tomorrow, who knew where I'd be and what I'd be up to? So much was changing. And so very fast. My head ached with it all.

'Buck up, then!' said Ma, bringing me back to myself. And she might've meant herself too, for she'd turned all thoughtful again too.

I dressed quickly, glad to be in clean clothes for once.

'Last touch,' Ma said. She twisted my hair into a knot on the top of my head and pinned it in place. 'You look . . .' Her lip began to tremble. 'Very respectable indeed.'

She steered me towards the gloomy old mirror above the mantel. When I saw my reflection, I gasped. I'd never worn my hair like this before, all swept off my shoulders and held up with pins. My eyes were huge dark things and my neck seemed so slender and pale, I barely recognised myself. I turned this way and that, unable to stop smiling.

What would Kit think of me now?

'You're blushing at yourself!' Ma said, smiling a little too. 'But goodness me, how fine you look! Why, you're pretty as a rose!'

And she sounded surprised, like she'd never really noticed before.

13
FROST HOLLOW HALL

'Not at work again?' said Will, as I passed his pa's shop half an hour later. The village clock had just chimed ten. Miss Fletcher would be wondering where I was, but I didn't have time to stop at the school and explain. I didn't have time for Will Potter neither. He was sweeping snow from the front steps, and though I tried to ignore him, he put down his broom and fell in beside me.

'You look different too.'

'Keep your beak out,' I said.

Though the sun was shining, the cold made the tips of my ears sting. What's more, I was sick with nerves. And the last person on earth I wanted to see was Will.

'No need to be unfriendly.'

I glared at him. 'You snitched on me.'

'So I did.'

'It was a lousy thing to do.'

'I'm sorry.'

'Lost your bottle, did you?

'Maybe. But the Barringtons are our finest customers, see. If we lost that account, then ...' He trailed off, looking uneasy.

'So Mrs Jessop didn't tell your pa, then?'

'No, luckily. But only after I'd cleaned those chickens out within an inch of my life.' And he smiled at me then in that slow, lazy way of his that was meant to win me over but actually got right up my nose.

'Glad it worked out so well for you,' I said, hitching up my skirts. 'Now I'm in a hurry so leave me be.'

As I walked on, my anger grew. I bet *he'd* had breakfast this morning, I bet he'd seen his pa today. And he'd have supper waiting for him when he'd done his day's work, with his whole family all sat round the table. It didn't seem fair. Not one bit.

I quickened my pace to get shot of him, but he stuck to me like a limpet all the way up Combe Hill.

'Go away, Will,' I said, through gritted teeth.

'Not 'til you tell me where you're going.'

I did my best to walk even faster. But it was tricky underfoot where hooves and cart wheels had turned the snow to slush that had then frozen hard. Will offered me his arm.

'I don't need your help,' I said, though in truth it was a job to stay upright.

'Suit yourself.'

Out on the main road, the ground got easier. We walked on in silence, until finally Will said, 'You're going to get work at the Hall, aren't you?'

'You don't know everything,' I snapped, feeling myself going red.

'I knew it! You're such a rubbish liar!'

'Am not.'

'I'd heard they was after a housemaid,' said Will. 'You'd be just the ticket. You'd find out all sorts about Kit Barrington, working there.'

'P'raps.'

I looked at him sideways. It wasn't worth telling Will anything, not after the stunt he pulled yesterday, bleating to Mrs Jessop about my *stupid ideas*. But I felt so sick, I wasn't thinking right and besides, Will knew how much this job meant to me.

'I just hope they'll have me,' I said.

'You've swept a floor before, haven't you?'

''Course!'

'Well then.'

'Trouble is, things is changed.'

'So I heard,' said Will.

My heart sank. 'What've you heard?'

'That your pa and sister are gone away, and times is hard.'

News travelled fast in Frostcombe. But at least he'd spared me the gory details. It hurt enough already; I couldn't bear for someone as smug as Will Potter to point out all that was wrong with my family.

'If I mess it up, we'll be in the workhouse,' I said. 'Ma's counting on me.'

'So's Kit Barrington,' he said, sharp as you like. 'Or so you say.'

'I don't need *you* telling *me*, ta very much!'

'Get amongst them Barringtons, then,' said Will. 'Find out what makes them tick.'

'It in't that easy. If they catch me snooping, I'll be done for!'

'Then make sure they don't. Keep your gob shut and your eyes open.'

It was all very well for Will to dish out advice, when he didn't have to lift a finger himself.

'Just be careful, that's all,' he said, suddenly serious.

'Since when did you care?'

We fell silent for a moment, then his face lit up with a grin.

'You've changed your hair, haven't you?' he said.

'Yes,' I said, patting it gently. 'Is it all right still?'

'It looked better before, if you ask me.'

Oaf.

I thumped him.

*

The gates to the Hall were actually open for once. A man in a greatcoat was in the process of leading his pony and trap through them. He stopped to peer at us as we approached.

'You bound for the Hall, too?' he said.

'Ta, but we'll walk,' said Will.

I stopped dead in my tracks. 'You in't coming with me!'

'Oh yes I am,' Will said, tucking his arm through mine. 'I know them down there, remember?'

I yanked my arm free. 'And a fat lot of help it was last time.' I turned to the driver. 'Thank you. A ride would be grand.'

Will frowned. 'Now just a . . .'

'I'm going by myself,' I said, firmly.

Will gave me a long look. Then, without so much as a goodbye, he turned smartly on his heel. I felt a strange pang as I watched him go, like he was my last link with home and I'd not been quite fair with him. Moments later he was out of sight completely.

There wasn't time to fret. The driver had already pulled the gates almost shut and was waiting for me to join him. I grabbed my skirts and squeezed through the gap. He heaved the gates shut behind us. My heart began to thud.

'All aboard then,' said the driver.

I climbed into the trap and had barely sat down when the cart shot forward, flinging me backwards. We set off at a right pace. The cart spun over the packed snow, hurling me one way, then the other. I gripped the seat hard; it was all I could do to stay on board. Icy air stung my eyes, hair whipped my face. On and on we raced through a blur of trees. I gritted my teeth and hung on tight as I could.

And then the driver heaved on his reins. The cart slowed to walking pace and stopped. Before us the road went downhill sharply and the woods gave way to grand lines of trees on either side of the drive.

'There 'tis,' said the driver, nodding into the valley. 'The grandest house in the county.'

I followed his gaze and gasped out loud. *What an eyeful it was!*

On a day like today, the frost hollow business was as

clear as anything. Already at the top of the valley the snow had started to thaw, and yet deep at the bottom everything was still thick white. Sat right in the coldest frostiest spot of all was the house itself. For the first time I got a real sense of its vastness.

Frost Hollow Hall? Frost Hollow *palace* more like!

It was shaped like a capital E with the middle bit missing. The house was made of grey stone, and was finer than any I'd ever clapped eyes on. The roof was a jumble of chimney pots and little slanty windows, all white with snow like a fairytale castle. I bet the place was full of narrow stairways and secret passages, waiting to be explored.

Off beyond the gardens was a familiar-looking path, leading through yew trees to what had to be the family graveyard. There was no sign of Kit's stone angel from up here, though. Everything was hidden by the dark trees.

And where was the lake?

I leaned forward on my seat, shivering with cold and excitement.

There it was, set back beyond the graveyard, half screened by those great trees. It still had that dull grey look to it, like something solid and steady. Only I knew now not to be fooled.

'That's the lake, in't it?' I said, trying to sound casual.

'Aye.' The driver flicked the reins. We started moving again.

'It won't thaw out 'til spring,' he said. ''Specially not this winter.'

'And the family? What do they use it for?'

'You'll know the story. You're a Frostcombe girl. Now leave it be.'

I felt him staring at me. I kept my eyes on the road.

Soon we arrived at the side of the Hall. Up close it was just as handsome. The drive had been cleared at the front of the house, so that snow was heaped up either side. There were three floors to the house, four if you counted the attics, which meant a heck of a lot of windows. Each was made of old, watery glass, split into little panes. On the ground floor the shutters were already open, though the rooms were in shadow so I couldn't quite see inside.

A lump formed in my throat. One day this would've all been Kit's. *Should've* been.

'I'm headed for the stable block,' said the driver, cutting through my sad thoughts. 'You want the servants' entrance.' He pointed over his shoulder at the cobbled yard I recognised from yesterday. 'Grey door.

By the railings. Can't miss it.'

'Ta very much,' I said, and jumped down.

The cart pulled away, leaving me alone in the drive-way. I glanced up at the house again and began to feel uneasy. This whole place felt sad. *Bleak*. I scanned the windows. Each one stared back at me, blank and cold.

Then I saw a movement. The drapes twitched at a large window on the first floor. A dark shape stepped back from the glass, disappearing from sight. The shivers ran through me.

Someone had been up there, watching.

14

INTERVIEW WITH THE HOUSEKEEPER

I made my way to the servants' entrance. By now I felt sicker than ever. Five icy steps down and the door was in front of me. I did a quick tidy of my hair and knocked on the door. Breathed deep. And waited.

No one came.

I tried again, louder this time, and stepped back, smoothing my skirts.

Where were they all? A big house like this and no one to answer a blasted door?

I stamped my feet and blew on my hands. Maybe they'd just not heard me.

Either way, it was too cold to stand there dithering. I pushed the door open and stepped inside. The flagstone passageway and high windows were just as I remembered. Though it was daylight now, gas jets still burned on the walls. My nerve wavered, but I made myself keep going, past the laundry room and the butler's pantry. This time the glass door was shut and the lamps turned down low.

Where *was* everyone?

I kept going, heart thudding. I turned the corner.

'Oh!' I stopped dead.

Up ahead was Mrs Jessop. Her tall, dark shape filled the passageway. She saw me and froze.

'Do my eyes deceive me, or is this Tilly Higgins again?'

'Please ma'am, I've come about the job.'

She came towards me like a vapour. My knees shook hard.

'The housemaid's job? *You?*' She laughed in disbelief. 'You're persistent, I'll grant you that.'

She peered at me closely and seemed to mull something over. I waited, head bowed, praying Cook had been right, that they *were* short-staffed and needed extra hands. I didn't fancy my chances otherwise.

Mrs Jessop sighed deeply. 'Come with me.'

I followed her down another corridor, so narrow that her skirts brushed against the walls as she walked. The keys at her hip caught my eye. There had to be twenty there at least, all shapes and sizes, some tarnished, some gleaming. One for every room in the house, I reckoned.

We went up some stone steps, then she reached for her keys and unlocked the door in front of us. We entered a smallish room with painted walls and a patterned carpet on the floor. An oil lamp hung from the ceiling, which made the air smell thick and close and filled the room with yellow light. As Mrs Jessop turned to stoke the fire, a set of shelves on the wall caught my eye. They were stacked high with notebooks. Each had a date on its spine, like 'October '78' or 'June '79', and seemed to be arranged in date order. And beneath the shelves was a wide, uncluttered desk, where more notebooks sat in tidy piles.

Mrs Jessop then selected one – a small, brown cardboard-covered thing – and took a seat in the corner near the fire. She told me to stand by the desk where she could see me properly. I folded my hands and bowed my head again. I hoped she wouldn't notice how I trembled.

Mrs Jessop opened her notebook. 'So, tell me. Why should I hire you as my new housemaid?'

I looked up. She stared at me, unblinking. Her eyes were black.

'Um, well,' I swallowed. 'I am a good worker.'

'And where do you work currently?'

'Um . . . with Miss Fletcher at the school.'

Though I hoped she wouldn't bother checking this fact. Miss Fletcher had wanted me in bright and early today. Instead, I'd gone after another job. It didn't exactly look good.

'That may be so,' said Mrs Jessop. 'I shall be contacting her for your character.'

Drat, I thought, as she scribbled something down.

'There are other matters to be considered, Tilly.'

I lowered my gaze.

'Twice you've been caught trespassing in the last week alone. And now you're asking for a job?'

I felt myself go red. I didn't have a cat in hell's chance, did I? I was stupid to even be here.

'I'm sorry,' I said. 'I've wasted your time.'

I went to go. Thoughts of Ma, the landlord and Kit all rushed into my head at once, and I felt so ill and low I hardly knew what I'd do next.

'Stop right there, young lady,' said Mrs Jessop. 'I haven't dismissed you yet.'

I groaned silently and turned to face her again. *Go on then, put me out of my misery, once and for all.*

'I want a sensible girl who pulls her weight, not some troublemaker. Do I make myself clear?'

'Yes, Mrs Jessop.'

A rustling of skirts and she was stood beside me.

She smelled clean and sharp like beeswax.

'Now,' she said, stepping even closer. 'Open wide.'

'Sorry?'

Her hand shot out and gripped my jaw. I pulled back but her fingers dug harder into my flesh so I couldn't move an inch.

'Your teeth,' she said. 'I need to see them.'

It hurt to struggle, and I couldn't breathe right with her hand clamped tight round my face. I stood still. She loomed over me, all bony and pale, just like before. Only this time, I kept my eyes wide open and saw how she looked at me, tipping her head this way and that, like I was an insect trapped in a jar.

Finally, she let go. 'Good. Now hold your hands out.'

She peered at my nails and fingers, then turned my hands over to examine the palms.

'Hmm,' she said. 'Nothing a good scrub won't put right.'

'But I had a wash this morning!'

She tutted, which made me go red again. Then she returned to her seat and wrote something down in her book.

'You don't have any followers?' she said, peering at me under her brows.

'Followers?'

'Young men of your acquaintance, village boys who'll come calling for you and making a nuisance of themselves. Only we don't allow that sort of thing.'

'No, Mrs Jessop.'

'Not even that butcher's boy?'

'Most definitely not!' I said, a little too hotly.

She pulled a face like she didn't quite believe me, then pressed her fingers to her lips and frowned.

'Very well, it's a week's trial. You'll be paid five shillings next Wednesday. Any nonsense and you're out.'

I could hardly believe my own ears.

'Oh thank you, thank you! You won't regret it, I promise!'

I rushed forwards her like a daft thing, catching my foot on the corner of the carpet so I stumbled against her desk. Notebooks, pens, cards all slid to the floor.

'Heck, I'm sorry!'

I fell to my knees to gather up the mess. In a flash, Mrs Jessop was beside me, her skirt hem inches from my face. *Spotless black merino. Not a speck, not a hair upon it.* As I glanced up, she looked at me almost kindly. Then her face darkened.

'Give me that notebook.'

I looked down at the book in my hand. It didn't

seem much, just an old tatty thing. Its pages were open and covered in tiny handwriting. I passed it to her without a second glance.

'Now get up, for goodness' sake!'

Tutting loudly, she turned to tidy the desk. My heart was in my mouth. She was bound to change her mind now and send me packing. But instead she said, 'Did you bring any things with you?'

I shook my head.

'Does your mother know you're here?'

'Yes. But she don't know I'm staying,' I said.

That soft look crossed her face again. Then she squared her shoulders and headed for the door

'We'll get a message to your mother,' Mrs Jessop said, briskly. 'And now you can join the others. They're having their break in the servants' hall.'

15

BELOW STAIRS

I followed Mrs Jessop down yet another passageway. We went through a door into a well-lit room, where eight, maybe ten people were gathered round one end of a long table. Tea was being poured, plates of buttered bread passed round. At first glance, it looked proper cosy, and my poor stomach rumbled at the sight of such a lovely meal. Yet despite a good fire, the room was chill. It felt big and bare, and not altogether welcoming. The people sat with their backs to us, speaking in low voices.

Mrs Jessop cleared her throat. The talking stopped abruptly and faces turned our way. I wiped my hands on my skirts, swallowing hard. Mrs Jessop went over to a man in a dark jacket who was sat at the head of the table. I'd seen him before. He was Mr Phelps, the butler. Mrs Jessop spoke rapidly in his ear. He nodded a few times and looked at me before dabbing his mouth with a napkin and getting to his feet. Everyone else got up too.

'Sit! Sit!' he cried, waving them back into their seats.

They sat down again.

'Now then,' he said. 'This is our new housemaid, Matilda Higgins from the village.'

I felt myself shrink inside my clothes.

'Welcome to you, Matilda.'

Mrs Jessop said, 'Mr Phelps, it's Tilly, not Matilda. Just so we're clear.'

'Thank you, Mrs J.' Mr Phelps shot her a look before addressing two maids sat across the table from him. 'Now Dorcas, you'll need to get *Matilda* kitted out. Gracie can assist you.'

The older maid nodded. I'd seen her here yesterday, hadn't I? She was the pretty head housemaid who'd had to chop vegetables. Everything about her was neat and clean, including her white frilled cap which sat perfectly in place.

Next to her was a younger plump-faced girl with dark, dancing eyes. She looked nearer my age. I tried to smile. The dark-eyed girl grinned back, showing a gap between her two front teeth. Dorcas, though, looked at me coolly, and I felt myself colour up again.

'Ah, Mr Phelps,' Mrs Jessop butted in. '*I* should like to take charge of Tilly directly, for today at least.

Dorcas has plenty to do already.'

Mr Phelps twitched like a fly was bothering him. The other people watched.

'In this house it is not a housekeeper's duty to train up new staff,' he said. 'It is the responsibility of the head housemaid, and Dorcas is more than capable of performing such a task.'

'But on this occasion . . .'

'Thank you, Mrs Jessop.' Mr Phelps held up his hand. 'We must try to keep to our proper roles where possible. Now, let us finish our meal.'

Mr Phelps took his seat again and beckoned me over. 'Matilda, sit with Gracie and have something to eat.'

As I slid into a seat next to the dark-eyed girl, I noticed Mrs Jessop had gone.

'Hullo, I'm Gracie Waite.' The girl held out a buttery hand, then snatched it back again. 'Oops, sorry! Should've wiped it first.'

So this was the famous Gracie who'd taken to her bed yesterday. She certainly didn't look sick today. And she seemed so friendly that I liked her at once.

'Hullo,' I said.

'What's with you and Mrs Jessop then?' Gracie said, her eyes darting over my face.

'She's keeping a watch on me, I s'pect. Thinks I'm a lost cause already.' And I told her about knocking the notebooks on the floor.

Gracie's face fell. 'Oh lordy! Not them notebooks!'

'What d'you mean?'

But she started to giggle, and I saw she was just having a bit of fun.

'I shouldn't laugh,' she said. 'Mrs Jessop keeps a record of everything. But don't look so worried – all housekeepers write a journal. Only she's very particular about hers.'

She passed me some bread, but my guts were too knotted; I found I couldn't manage anything after all. I took a small slice and went to stuff it in my pocket, thinking I'd be starved come midday. Gracie grinned as she watched me.

'We have our dinner at one o'clock. It's a big hot meal with pudding and everything. Believe me, you won't go hungry working here.'

I felt a right idiot, so I put the food back on my plate and hoped no one else had noticed.

The others started to leave the table now. I recognised the carter who'd brought me here, joking with his lad from the stables. Another maid cleared the plates away, whistling a tune as she did so. I noticed

Cook talking to Mr Phelps. And along from us, next to Dorcas, two very tall men in breeches and brass-buttoned coats laughed as they downed the last of their tea. They all seemed happy enough. I thought of how cosy they'd looked when I'd first clapped eyes on them. Maybe I'd just imagined the rest.

'That's Samuel Ketteridge, the footman,' said Gracie, who'd noticed me staring. 'And the lanky one's Peter Watson, the second footman.' She went pink as she said his name.

Dorcas then got to her feet. 'Right Tilly, let's get you sorted.' As I stood up, she turned to Gracie. 'You're to make up a bed for Tilly in your room.'

Gracie pouted. 'Do I have to go up there?'

'It's daylight, you silly fool! Nothing's going to harm you.'

'That's what you said on Sunday, and then look what happened . . .'

Dorcas cut in. 'And now you've got someone to share with. Isn't that nice? Just what you wanted.'

So Gracie went one way and we went the other. Right at the end of the passage we came to a small room with cupboards all along one wall. It was icy cold in here. No fire burned in the grate.

Dorcas shut the door behind us.

'I know who you are,' she said. 'Half dead you were when Will Potter brought you in. We laid you out on the kitchen table to get the water out of your lungs. Lord knows, you were lucky not to perish.'

I kept my eyes down.

'But I trust there'll be no more dramatics.'

'Mrs Jessop's already warned me,' I said, then thinking this sounded pert, quickly added, 'I promise to do my best, honest I do.'

'Good girl.'

I caught Dorcas's eye and she smiled, two dimples appearing in her cheeks so she was prettier than ever. I bet Will Potter thought her handsome when he came here on his deliveries, though I couldn't imagine her looking twice at a louse like him.

Dorcas went to a drawer and got out a tape, then started to measure me up. 'You're quite small, aren't you?' she said, looking me up and down like I was a pig and she was the blinking farmer. 'Hope we've got something that'll fit.'

She climbed up on a chair and started rooting around in a cupboard full of linens.

'Your uniform,' she said, handing me a pile of clothes. 'Try them on for size.'

Shivering, I stripped down to my slip, grateful for

Ma's gift of a decent undergarment. First, I tried on a striped grey cotton dress like the ones Dorcas and Gracie were wearing. The fabric was stiff and smelled of soap.

'You wear this in the mornings when you're cleaning and laying the fires,' Dorcas said as I wriggled into it. 'Turn around. Raise your arms. Hmmm . . . fits you well.'

Next she gave me a plain pinny and a white cap.

'These go on top. You'll need to keep your hair tucked right under. Here, like this.' She smoothed my hair back tight to my head.

Then she handed me a finer dress in black wool. I rubbed it between my fingers. So soft and warm; I'd never worn such a thing in my life.

'Nice, isn't it? You'll wear it in the afternoons and evenings for when you're called upstairs.'

'Upstairs? To the Barringtons?'

She frowned. 'That isn't going to be a problem, is it?'

''Course not. I'll be fine,' I said, when really my insides were fluttering.

'Good.' She locked up the cupboards and pocketed the key. 'You'll need to be in this house.'

16

THE BACK STAIRS

By the end of the day, I'd run right out of floors to scrub. My hands were red raw and my back was killing me. All I wanted was my bed. I'd not got within sniffing distance of the Barringtons, neither. Each time they rang down, it was Dorcas who took up their trays. She seemed to double up as housemaid and lady's maid, and Mrs Jessop did the rest, though the way they rolled their eyes at the ceiling showed they didn't much care for this arrangement.

If only they'd asked me! *I'd* have carried a tray upstairs gladly. I was dying to see more of the house, and not just its flipping floors. But Dorcas didn't ask me. Nor did Mrs Jessop. My smart black dress stayed hanging on its peg all day.

At suppertime, we ate ham and cheese in the servants' hall. Gracie saved me a place next to her and chattered on about this and that, but I was so tired, it was a job to stay awake. I began to feel low, thinking of Ma at home by herself. As for Pa and Eliza, well, I didn't dare think too long about *them*.

It was almost a relief when the meal was over.

'Good night to you all,' said Mr Phelps, getting to his feet. Gracie said he had his own quarters where he retired every evening, and that they were almost as grand as above stairs.

Once he'd gone, Mrs Jessop ordered us to clear the table. As Gracie did one side, I did the other. She worked fast and soon caught me up.

'Give me those.' She took an armful of plates off me, whispering, 'You do Mrs Jessop's. She don't like to be kept waiting, and she's got her beady eye on you for some reason.'

As I reached for Mrs Jessop's plate her arm shot out to stop me. 'Show me your hands.'

I glanced down at my poor fingers. Six solid hours of soap and carbolic, and they were chapped almost to bleeding. It was obvious I wasn't used to such hard work, and I felt rather ashamed.

'For goodness' sake, child! Show me!' she snapped, and pushed back my sleeves before I could object. She took hold of my hands quite firmly and turned them over. 'Hmm,' she said. 'I see.'

Across the table, Dorcas watched us. She frowned

in a way I couldn't quite read. Then a service bell rang. Everyone stopped what they were doing. Mrs Jessop dropped my hands with a sigh. A voice called out, 'Drawing room! Her Ladyship!' and another of those looks passed between Mrs Jessop and Dorcas. The bell tinkled again. Mrs Jessop got to her feet.

'I'll do it,' she said, irritably.

Soon as she'd gone, the mood seemed to lift. Cook brought round a platter of cakes, and the footmen poured mugs of ale. Voices got louder and laughter broke out as the table was pushed against the wall and chairs pulled up to the fire. Trouble was, it made the room seem emptier, somehow. Away from the fire, it was bitterly cold. Shadows seemed to thicken in the corners, and the noise echoed off the walls in a way that made even the laughter sound hollow.

A sad sort of feeling came over me. Then Gracie re-appeared at my side.

'You all right?'

I just about managed a smile.

'Get yourself some cake, why don't you? I'll finish up here,' said Gracie and took the last plates out to the kitchen.

So I grabbed myself a little fruit cake, and took one

for Gracie too, then pulled up two chairs near to the fire.

'Give us a tune!' the carter said, as Samuel Ketteridge sat down at the piano in the corner.

The footman took off his fine jacket and rolled up his sleeves. Then he flexed his fingers and grinned in a way that reminded me of Will and I felt a pang, though it was probably just because I was tired. The piano wasn't much in tune, and he kept missing keys, but soon he found his way with a jaunty tune that got our feet tapping. Then came a soppy song about a long-lost sweetheart, which had everyone dabbing at their eyes. Despite the jarring echo and the draught at my back, I hoped he'd play all night and never stop. With everyone else sobbing along with me, it gave me good reason to be sad.

After few more songs, people stretched in their seats and began making their way to bed. I realised then that Gracie hadn't joined me. I guessed she was still out in the kitchens.

A hand touched my shoulder. 'Here, take this.'

I turned to see Cook offering me a cup of hot milk. I took it gladly.

'First night's always tough. But you'll get used to it,' she said. 'Gracie's been here a year now, and she's . . .'

A scream from the kitchen cut her short. Then came an almighty crash. It was the sound of china smashing to the floor.

Dorcas leapt to her feet. 'Is that Gracie? *Again?*'

'I'll deal with her this time,' said Cook. 'Though we can't keep covering up for her.'

I glanced sideways at Dorcas, who'd taken her seat again and was chewing her lip fretfully.

'Don't ask,' she said, reading the question in my look. 'Gracie's got this silly notion into her head, when really she's just mightily clumsy.'

Poor Gracie. She'd cleared the table faster than I had, and carried armfuls of plates like she'd done it thousands of times. She didn't look clumsy to me. And she'd been kind, offering to clear up when she saw I was dead on my feet. It didn't seem right she should get an earful. Downing my drink in one quick gulp, I took the cup back out to Cook.

I stopped in the kitchen doorway. Gracie was sobbing and twisting her apron in her hands. She looked in a terrible state.

'But I didn't drop it, I swear!' Gracie cried. 'It lifted itself off the table. I was nowhere near it.'

'You have to stop this nonsense!' said Cook.

'It's true! On me mother's life!'

Cook folded her arms. 'So this china all over the floor here, *and* the stuff what's been smashed these last few days . . . all this is down to a *ghost*?'

'I've said so, in't I?'

'It's you not drying your hands proper, that's what it is! I've told you time and time again how it makes the china slippy, and you just don't listen.'

'So how come I never dropped things before?'

'Perhaps you was more careful then.'

'Oh, why won't you believe me?' said Gracie, blubbing more than ever.

'Fact is, china's getting broke every day now, and you're in such a lather about it, you're making yourself ill. You got away with it on Tuesday. We said you had a headache. But sooner or later Mrs Jessop'll find out. And what do you suppose we'll tell *her*?'

Gracie grabbed Cook's arm. 'The truth. That there's something queer down here, below stairs I mean. Something's really *wrong* . . .'

Seeing me, they stepped smartly apart. Gracie picked up a broom and started sweeping. Cook put on a smile.

'Tilly! Feeling better? Don't mind Gracie. She's had an upset, that's all.'

Some upset! The girl was as white as paper. I'd

heard enough to not be fooled, and my head suddenly filled with all that Will had told me. This looked like more than just gossip. It seemed that Frost Hollow Hall *was* haunted inside as well as out. I shivered with excitement. For the ghost here had to be Kit's, didn't it?

'You all right, Gracie?' I said, trying to sound steady.

'She'll live,' said Cook, grabbing the broom from Gracie and pushing her towards me. 'But take her up to bed before Mrs Jessop hears all this wailing.'

I said a silent thank you. Cook mightn't want to talk about ghosts, but I blinking well did. Once I'd got Gracie on her own, I'd ask her what had really been going on.

'C'mon then.' I tucked my arm through hers. 'You'll have to show me the way, though.'

But Gracie wasn't shifting. 'I in't going up them back stairs without a candle.'

'For goodness' sake. You've been up and down 'em hundreds of times,' said Cook, though she took a candle from a drawer and lit it. 'And don't you go filling Tilly's head with your daft ideas.'

Far too late for that.

Cook put the candle in a tin holder and handed it to me. 'Turn right out of the kitchen and keep walking 'til you reach the back stairs. Then it's all the way to the top.'

We set off down the passage. Gracie's hand trembled on my arm and she was breathing quick and shallow.

'Bet you think I'm a right baby to be so scared,' she said.

''Course not.'

Though I wondered how anyone could be this fearful of Kit Barrington.

'I in't normally like this,' said Gracie. 'But something's started up these last few nights. And it in't just the china. I've sensed someone following me up to bed.'

A little thrill ran through me. We stopped at the foot of the stairs.

'You go first,' she said, pushing me forward.

The stone steps went up steeply. To me, it was just another dark passageway, and this house was full of them.

'Come on, then,' I said.

I held the candle out in front and, gathering my skirts, took the steps two at a time. I didn't see the point in lingering. As we made our way upwards, the darkness grew thicker, blacker. It seemed to smother what little light our candle gave off. Out the corner of my eye, I saw strange, creeping shadows on the walls. Any excitement I'd felt began to ebb away. A shiver ran down my back, though I hardly knew why. There was no reason to be scared.

'Slow down, can't you?' Gracie called, as I reached the first landing. She'd fallen quite a way behind. As she caught up, she seized my arm.

'Don't you go leaving me,' she said.

'Keep up, then,' I said, peevishly. 'We in't on a Sunday stroll.'

Another flight up and of a sudden, the air turned icy cold. It set me off shivering so hard it was a job to hold the candle straight. Gracie was right behind me now. I heard her breathing and the scuffing of her boot soles on the steps. The shadows stretched long and monstrous on the wall beside us. I told myself they were only ours. Nothing to be frightened of.

Two shadows. One for me. One for Gracie.

My breath caught in my throat. For there weren't two shadows, were there?

There were three.

I stopped dead. Gracie stumbled right into me.

'Oh!' she cried, grabbing at my arm.

'Careful! Or we'll fall and break our necks!'

But she clung on so tight I lost my balance and, in panic, threw out my hands to save myself. I fell against the wall and dropped the flipping candle. It went clattering down the steps, tin holder and all. It stayed lit for a moment, a little speck of light in all that darkness. Then it flickered and went out.

I hardly dared move. It made no difference if I shut or opened my eyes. The darkness was total.

'How much further is it?' I said to Gracie, trying very hard not to think about that third shadow. I must've imagined it. There was no way of knowing now.

'We're halfway,' she said. 'Reckon we should go back for a light?'

'No. Let's keep going.'

I laid my hand flat against the wall and felt my way slowly, one step at a time. Gracie whimpered behind me.

'It's all right if you go slow.' I tried to sound calm, though I certainly didn't feel it. 'Just don't grab me again.'

A few steps up, I sensed someone close behind me. Very close.

It wasn't Gracie.

The person started whispering. Their voice was low

lly, that weren't me,' she said. 'What you felt
been the ghost.'
ed to believe her. Or part of me did. But how
thing on the stairs be Kit Barrington? He'd
life. And now he was desperate for me to
. So why the heck would he want to scare me?
n't know what I felt,' I said, eventually. 'I just
bed, that's all.'
don't believe me neither, do you?' said Gracie,
y. 'And there was me thinking you might be my

e I could answer, she marched off. I followed
vn a passage and into a large, cold room. I
ist make out two narrow beds either side of the
breast. In the corner was a chest for storing
And there were my things from home, folded
ile next to it. It churned me over to see them
d I felt very low indeed.
e,' I said.
peaking to you.'
dressed and got into
it. I took from
vas mine. Strip
he icy sheets an
to warm, thoug

felt it,
'I felt y

and quick. It was impossible to make out the words. With growing horror, I smelled something too, a sickly-sweet scent like honey. I turned round.

'Who's there?'

The whispering stopped. Darkness pressed in on me. Then, right close to my ear, someone sighed. I felt their breath, cold and queer against my neck. I shuddered. Jumped back. My foot slipped, and suddenly I was falling backwards, grabbing madly at thin air. I fell hard on my tailbone onto what felt like a rough wood floor. It must be the landing we'd just passed. Gingerly I got to my feet, trying to ignore the pain. All was quiet as the grave.

'Gracie?' I called out. 'Where are you?'

The only noise was my own echo. Gracie had vanished.

17

TALK OF A GHOST

Someone was coming towards me. I prayed it was Gracie. That she'd had seen sense and gone back for a candle after all. Any second now we'd have light again. But as the footsteps drew closer, there was no light. The dark stayed thick as anything.

'Gracie?' I said, then went cold all over.

It *was* Gracie. *Wasn't* it?

The footsteps sounded different. Lighter. Quicker. All I could see was darkness. I smelled it again, that sweet honey scent, and got ready to run; upstairs, downstairs, I didn't care where.

Someone was close.

The whispering started just inches from my ear, a hissing, lisping sound that made my scalp prickle. A hand gripped my upper arm. I shrank back in horror. Tried to pull free. But the grip was fierce. Fingernails bit through the sleeve of my frock. The more I struggled, the tighter it held me, 'til I was sure my

arm would be twisted
Thrashing and kicking
seemed to slacken. I yar
the last flight of stairs.

At the top was anoth
shone in through a sm
stopped to recover myse
Gracie caught up with r
shaken.

'What happened?' she sa
you was right in front of me, th

'I didn't go nowhere. You
peared.'

'Did not,' she said. 'I wa

I was having trouble m
hurt like hell, and tired as

'Try a trick like that ag
Gracie Waite!'

She blinked. 'A trick li

'You grabbed my arr
lowed me right close 'til
heck are you trying to p
Her mouth fell ope
didn't you?'
u, playing p

'No, Ti
must hav

I want
could th
saved m
help hir

'I do
want m

'You
al huff
friend.

Befo
her do
could ju
chimne
clothes.
up in a j
again, ar

'Graci
'I in't
She un
good nig
window
between
bed bega

A few feet away, Gracie tossed and turned in her bed. She'd been all kindness and smiles an hour ago; now she wouldn't even talk. When I shut my eyes, I felt those pinching fingers again, and started weeping silently into my pillow. I felt truly wretched. What a dreadful house this was! I was beginning to wish I'd never set foot in the place, and had stayed at home with Ma.

I stopped mid-sob.

Gracie was right. Something *was* wrong with Frost Hollow Hall. Never mind that there were too few servants, or that Lady Barrington kept herself hidden away. I'd known all that before. But this ghost business seemed to have started only in the last few days.

Weren't spirits meant to haunt the place where they'd been done a terrible wrong? That's how it worked in a penny dreadful story. Not that I believed all that, but I didn't have much else to go on, and right now it made a sort of sense. Maybe something had happened here in the house, *and* out on that lake. Trouble was, this wasn't some daft story that Eliza might read. This was happening in front of my very eyes.

What's more, the ghost on the stairs had seemed spiteful. Yet the Kit I knew was as gentle as an angel. It didn't add up that he'd turn all angry and mean, unless something had happened here to make him that way.

My head was reeling. I'd never sleep now. Eventually, I sat up.

'Gracie?'

She didn't answer.

'Not asleep, are you?'

'No.' She still sounded cross.

'I'm sorry I was angry with you.'

'Huh!'

Silence.

I tried again. 'Please, Gracie. I so want us to be friends.'

Her bedclothes rustled as she turned towards me. 'There is some sort of spirit here. I'm not making it up. And I'm not pulling pranks.'

'You'd better tell me what's been happening, then.'

For ages she didn't speak. Then she said, 'You won't laugh?'

'Promise.'

'But it scares me even to think of it.' And she started to cry.

'Get in with me if it'll help,' I said. I had to keep her talking.

Gracie padded across to my bed and climbed in.

Her hair spread over the pillow, tickling against my cheek. I propped myself up on an elbow so I could just about see her outline in the dark. She lay still, her gaze fixed on the windowpane above our heads.

'It's been happening these last few nights.' Her voice was shaky. 'At first, I thought it was just me being daft. The footmen often tell spooky stories of a night in the servants' hall, and I do get scared easy.'

I reached for her hand. 'What's been happening?'

'A feeling I get. Like someone's right behind me.'

'On the back stairs?'

''Specially on them back stairs. Sometimes it's so close I feel it breathing on me,' she said.

My heart thudded. 'And does it pinch you?'

She hesitated. 'No. It don't touch me.'

So it was just me, then. The thought did little to steady my nerves.

'And the broken china?' I asked. 'Does it scare you so much that you drop stuff?'

I felt her tense up. 'They think it's just me being clumsy. But I don't drop nothing. Honest I don't!'

'So what happens?'

Gracie turned to face me. 'It's so strange, I can hardly explain it. What happens is things move by themselves.'

I shuddered. It sounded horrifying.

'What's doing all this, Tilly?' she said.

Don't ask me that. I turned away so she couldn't see my lying eyes. Because I couldn't tell her. I couldn't tell anyone. Not if I wanted to keep my job.

'I don't know,' I said. 'Only I felt it too and didn't like it much.'

Gracie went quiet again. After a bit she said, 'P'raps we should keep this to ourselves.'

'I wasn't planning on telling Mrs Jessop.'

'No, don't you see? It's just ...' Gracie shivered. 'Well . . . it's all about the dead in this house. Everything is. And it in't right.'

'Oh?' I thought of Samuel Ketteridge and his love songs, and the chatter in the servants' hall. True enough, this house was a cold, shadowy place, with too few servants to run things right. But tonight at supper it had seemed happy enough.

Gracie turned away. 'You'll be laying fires tomorrow. You'll meet the Barringtons. Then you'll see what I mean.'

DREAMING: 4

The water's clearer than before. I see every detail of Kit's fine face. It takes my breath away. His hand takes mine. The cold of it numbs my fingers and sends an ache all the way up my arm. Slowly, gently we float towards the daylight. At the surface the ice stops us so we're trapped like butterflies at a window. Kit lets go of me. He reaches up and pushes with all his strength. The ice doesn't budge an inch.

His head drops, his shoulders shake. I can't bear to see him like this.

Yet something strange is happening. There's a handprint in the ice, at the place where Kit touched it. And now it's gone dark like it's starting to melt. My heart leaps. I point wildly.

'Look!' I cry, though he can't hear me. 'Look!'

He reads my face and when he turns and sees it too, the ghost of a smile appears.

18

LAYING FIRES

'Get your backsides out of bed!'

I tugged the covers over my head.

'I'm counting to three . . .'

The voice came closer. It didn't sound like Ma.

'All right Dorcas, we heard you.'

The warm shape next to me wasn't Eliza either. My guts went tight as I remembered where I was.

Gracie swung her legs round and got out of bed, letting icy air in under the blankets. She fumbled in the dark for her clothes then lit the stub-end of a candle. I sat up and rubbed my eyes.

'Time for work,' she said, holding the little flame towards me. 'Gawd, you look done in already!'

'Feels like the middle of the night. What time is it?'

'Just after five. Come on now, hurry!'

Getting out of the warm bed was agony. As I reached for my clothes, I saw two bruises on my upper arm, and with a jolt remembered last night on the stairs. Something, *someone* had grabbed me hard.

'Blimey Tilly!' Gracie had seen them too. She came closer with her candle. 'Who did that to you?'

'Don't know,' I said, because I couldn't quite believe Kit would do such a thing.

'Well, it's bruised up a right treat,' said Gracie. 'Looks like someone pinched you. Let me see again.'

'Not now,' I said, pulling my frock on quick. It was much too early for more ghost talk.

The water at the washstand was frozen. But I didn't want to appear before Dorcas looking like a dog's breakfast, and the ice broke easy enough. A quick smooth of the hair, a fix of the cap and I was ready. Gracie led the way with the candle. She didn't seem flustered this morning, and was back to her usual, chirpy self. There was nothing remarkable about the staircase either. If it hadn't been for the marks on my arm, I might have thought I'd imagined the whole thing.

At the bottom of the stairs, the warmth from the kitchens hit me. The gas jets burned so bright it made me blink. We went straight to the servants' hall where Dorcas was waiting, looking neat as a pin in her striped frock. First she straightened my cap so it sat properly on the back of my head. Then she showed me how to tuck up my skirts to keep them from the dirt.

'Now, we work quick as lightning,' she said, fixing me with her pretty grey eyes. 'We're back below stairs by seven thirty at the latest. That's when the family rise, and it's not proper to be caught at your work. The Barringtons don't want to see you covered in coal dust.'

But hadn't Gracie said I'd see them? *Today?* I tried to keep the disappointment from my face.

'The fires'll need a lot of coal this morning,' Dorcas said. 'It's perishing cold.'

'The usual rooms?' said Gracie.

'Yes.'

'What, *all* of them? Even the bedroom? Can't we skip it today, just this once?'

Dorcas rolled her eyes. 'You know the rules.'

'But it's such a pain, lugging coal all the way up there.'

I glanced at Gracie, and noticed shadows under her eyes. She was also twisting her apron again.

But Dorcas was having none of it. 'There'll be fires where fires is needed. That's what you're paid to do.'

She turned to me. 'You take this.' And she handed me a wooden pail topped with a tray of brushes and rags. 'Gracie, bring the coal up to the library.'

Gracie sloped off, muttering to herself. Dorcas led me back out into the passageway. Doors slammed. Cook shouted orders. The kitchen maid scurried to and fro with armfuls of plates and baskets of vegetables. Round a corner and up some steps, we came to a door covered in green felt. Yesterday, I'd seen Dorcas go through it with countless trays. On the other side of the door was *above stairs*. And that meant the Barringtons. My heart beat faster as Dorcas reached for the door handle.

'Stop a moment,' said a stern voice behind us.

We both turned. Mrs Jessop stood in the passage. 'Where are you taking her?' she said, meaning me.

'To do the fires, Mrs Jessop,' said Dorcas. 'We need to get on.'

As Mrs Jessop's gaze rested on me, my insides went all of a flutter like I'd done something wrong again.

'Very well,' she said. 'There's a jar of ointment in the kitchen for Tilly's hands. See that she uses it. We can't have our staff looking ill-treated. This is a fine house with standards. We need to remember it.'

Dorcas shot me a sideways look.

'One more thing,' Mrs Jessop said. 'Gracie must do the front bedroom. Tilly will be needed down here once Cook starts the luncheon.'

And with a whisk of her skirts, she was gone.

Dorcas narrowed her eyes at me. 'Can't keep her oar out where you're concerned, can she?'

'It's 'cos I'm new, I s'pose.'

'No.' She shook her head. 'It's more than that. Anyway, we've got work to do. Come on.'

She opened the door and we stepped out into a vast hallway. The door closed behind us. Everything went quiet and still as a church.

'This way,' she said.

I stared about me. Honest to God, you'd have fitted our whole house inside this very hallway and still had room for a garden. The ceiling was high and arched, the floor all dark red marble and so polished it seemed a shame to walk on it. Rows of paintings in thick gold frames hung on the walls. And up ahead, to my right, a staircase curved up and up, the handrail done in fancy wood. No back staircase this: lamps shone from the walls, right up to the first landing and beyond.

'Tilly!'

I stopped gawping and hurried over to where Dorcas waited. We went through a door into a dimly lit room. Bookshelves reached from floor to ceiling, so I reckoned this must be the library though it was as cold as the attic in here, and the place was quite a shambles. Books covered every surface – floors, desks, tabletops. Chairs were strewn about, rugs kicked up at the corners, and dirty glasses littered the mantelpiece. The fire was a heap of cold ashes in the grate.

Dorcas looked about her, hands on hips. 'He was up late again last night, by the looks of it.'

'Lord Barrington?'

'Mind you, he's usually in London. And when he's here, he don't sleep well. Not now.'

My ears pricked up at this; I was dying to hear more, but Dorcas had started clearing the glasses and tidying the chairs. She beckoned me over to help. As we knelt down to straighten the rugs, she dropped her voice to a whisper.

'I've worked here over ten years now, and I've seen how things have changed.'

'Really?'

'Ever since Master Kit died. Nothing's been right here since then.'

'What d'you mean?'

'Well,' she sighed. 'They say people never get over the death of a child. It's certainly true in this house.'

An ache filled my chest. How sad this all was.

'You've gone pale. Not sick, are you?' said Dorcas. She looked uneasy, like she'd said too much and it wasn't her place to gossip. Getting to her feet, she rubbed her hands briskly.

'I'm all right,' I said.

But I got up too fast and leaned on a nearby chair to steady myself. Glancing down, I jumped clean out of my skin.

A sleeping man was sprawled in the chair. At least, he was only just asleep, since he twitched and stretched like he was about to wake up. I backed away in shock.

'What *is* the matter?' said Dorcas. As I pointed to the chair, her face softened and she lowered her voice. 'Oh! Is it his Lordship?'

How the flip was I supposed to know who it was?

'Right, Tilly, stop dreaming!' she hissed. 'I'll open the shutters, you do the lamps, then we'll see to the fire. If we're quick and quiet, he won't even know we've been.'

Once Dorcas turned her back, I took a good long look at him. Lord Barrington's legs were crossed neatly at the ankle and his head rested back against the cushion. He looked familiar too. Achingly so.

I took a shaky step backwards.

This was Kit's pa; one peep at him told me that. He was fair, like Kit, and though his eyes were shut, the same long lashes curled out from under his lids. How odd to be stood here, staring at Kit's own flesh and blood!

Then I sensed Dorcas beside me. 'Handsome, isn't he?' she whispered. 'You should've seen the son.'

I gasped out loud.

She'd known Kit; living, breathing Kit!

It was a struggle to contain myself. But if I opened my mouth now, it'd come out all jumbled up and sounding crazy. She didn't believe Gracie's ghost talk, so why the heck would she believe mine?

'Now come over here,' said Dorcas. She pulled back the hearth rug and put a cloth down on the floor. She bid me kneel beside her.

'Watch,' she said. 'There's a knack to lighting these open fires.'

It was a job to tear my gaze from Lord Barrington. But I paid attention best I could; I'd never lit a fire in a fancy fireplace like this before. And it was an art, the way Dorcas did it. She cleaned the grate then blacked it 'til her hands were filthy and the hearth shone. Next, she took kindling sticks and paper and had it aflame in an instant. She added what coal was left, then sat back looking pleased.

'Never use more than seven kindling sticks, that's

the rule,' she said. Then she turned to me. 'Look lively! There's still the dining-room and sitting-room fires to do.'

'And that *bedroom*,' said Gracie, who'd appeared in the doorway with two full coal buckets.

Dorcas put a finger to her lips. 'Ssssh! His Lordship's asleep in here. Get yourself upstairs.'

'Can't I do the dining room instead?' said Gracie.

'Now then . . . I'm warning you!'

A groan came from the chair. Dorcas froze. I held my breath. Lord Barrington's legs twitched and he turned over.

'I'll go with her,' I said.

Dorcas glanced at the mantel clock, then back at us.

'All right, give me that coal and get gone. Be quick, mind, or Mrs Jessop'll have my guts for garters.'

Out in the hallway, Gracie grabbed my hand. 'Bless you. It's not about lugging stuff up and down stairs. I'm used to that.'

'What is it, then?'

'It's that bedroom. I hate it. It gives me the creeps. Always has done, ever since I started work here. They keep a fire burning up there every day and we in't allowed to let it go out, not even at night-time.'

'Sounds a bit odd,' I said.

'Well, it was his room, see. The boy, their son what drowned.'

A thrill went though me.

'Tell you what,' I said, thinking fast. 'Why don't I go on up and do the fire? You could just bring the coal.'

It'd only give me minutes. And I'd no idea what I'd find up there, apart from this fire business. Even so, it was a pretty exciting start.

'Would you do that? *Really?*' Gracie's face lit up like I'd given her a gold sovereign.

'I left you on the stairs last night, remember? I owe you.'

'But there's other stuff to do in there too. It's all very particular.'

'Well, I'll make a start. The rest we can do together,' I said, which seemed to please her. 'Now tell me, which room is it?'

'Up the stairs, turn right. Last door on your right. It's at the front of the house.'

I waited 'til she was out of sight. Then I grabbed my skirts and legged it up the stairs.

19

WAITING ON THE DEAD

At the top of the stairs, I turned right. Up ahead was a passage full of doors. My brain went blank.

Which room was Kit's? Left? Right?

Then Gracie's words came back to me, and I headed for the furthest door. I counted each one as I passed it, stopping at the last to wipe my hands on my skirt. The handle felt cool as I gripped it. I checked over my shoulder. Gracie worked fast, so I didn't have long. Five minutes maybe, ten at the most and she'd be back with her buckets of coal. I pushed the door open. Legs shaking, I stepped inside.

The lamps were lit and the room was unusually warm because a good fire glowed in the grate. I stared about me. Books lay open on a table, fresh clothes were draped over the chair. There was a half-empty glass of water, a pen with its lid off, bed covers all crumpled and slept in.

My stomach dropped. It was the wrong room.

Someone had spent the night in here. Any minute they might be back, and I'd get caught where I shouldn't be.

Too late.

The door handle turned. Someone was coming in.

I froze. There was nowhere to hide. My heart started pounding and my mouth turned dry. Here I was, snooping again. It didn't look good at all.

A pair of grubby hands and a bucket of coal appeared. Gracie stuck her head through the half-open door. I gasped with relief.

'I got this from the library. Dorcas didn't need it all. Here, take it,' she said.

She handed me the bucket. I took it, bewildered. So I was in the right place. This *was* Kit's room.

Over by the hearth, a pair of filthy riding boots caught my eye. They stood upright like someone had just stepped out of them. A chill came over me. What queer business was going on here?

'Gracie, why . . . ?'

'I'll be back in a minute. I'm just going to get the water.'

'What water?' Suddenly I didn't want to be left here on my own.

'Every morning I bring up a jug of hot for the

washstand. It sits there and goes cold.'

She must have seen the shock in my face.

'I know. Mad, in't it? It's her Ladyship's special request, though God knows we've got enough to do without waiting on someone who's dead.'

My head began to spin. 'So ... wait ... this ...' I waved an arm at the books, the used pen. 'Is it all Kit's? Are these things *his*?'

Gracie shuddered in the doorway. 'Yes. As it was on the day he died, exactly. No one's been allowed to move nothing since. We just dust, that's all.'

It was too strange for words. All right, so people wore black when their loved ones died. The Queen had pined for poor Prince Albert for years on end. Yet this room, so full of Kit, was like a blinking museum. My heart was beating very fast. The room felt too warm, too close.

But before I knew it, I'd crossed to the bed. The head-shaped dip in the pillow was still there, and the covers had been thrown back carelessly. It was like he'd just got up and left the room, like he'd be back any minute to get dressed in the clothes laid out on his chair. Heck, I even reckoned the sheets might still be warm. If I just slid my fingers in ...

'Don't touch nothing!' cried Gracie.

I snatched my hands back quick. She looked at me oddly.

'Do the fire like you promised and keep your hands off the rest,' she said. 'And I'll be back in a jiffy.'

She shut the door behind her.

Everything was quiet and hushed, but for the murmur of flames in the grate. This had to be the saddest, strangest place I'd ever been. I didn't know quite what to do with myself, feeling a great ache grow inside of me. I went over to the window, pulled back the drapes and eased open the shutters. My breath misted up the cold glass. I rubbed it clear and saw it was almost daylight now. The sky was pale, the lawns deep white and the driveway flanked by banks of snow curved round to the main steps beneath me.

Wait.

This was the window, the very spot, where yesterday that figure had watched me arrive. It had slipped my mind completely, but now I shrank back from the glass, shivering.

So someone *did* use this room. Or maybe it wasn't a person at all, but that *thing* that'd followed us up the stairs last night. The *thing* I struggled to believe was Kit.

I looked nervously over my shoulder, wishing that

Gracie would hurry up so we could get back downstairs again.

But I still had the fire to do. I went to the hearth and got down on my knees, just like Dorcas had done. There was still plenty of heat in the coals, so I added more and swept out the ashes. The sight of a good fire cheered me a little. Once I'd gathered up the brushes though, the flames had died down and the grate suddenly filled with smoke. I cussed loudly, blew on the fire, took off the extra coals, added a few sticks. Nothing worked. Soon it was dead as a doornail. And I was up to my elbows in soot.

The one task I'd been left to do, I'd messed up. I started to panic. I had to get this flipping fire going. As I crouched down, I sensed the door opening behind me. It closed again softly. Something told me it wasn't Gracie. I turned round dead slow, almost too scared to look.

20

A KIND OF SPELL

A stranger stood before me. She was slender as a reed, with pale cheeks and dark curled hair. Her eyes were tight shut like a person in a trance. What a beauty she was! I hardly dared take a breath for staring. She was dressed from head to toe in black. Her frock, a high-necked thing with narrow skirts, was well cut but plain, set off only by the gold brooch at her throat.

Something stirred me.

These were full mourning clothes. What a person wore for a loved one newly dead. Yet set against the woman's white skin and lovely face, the effect was not just sad, but *tragic*.

She opened her eyes, and turning towards the hearth saw me.

'Goodness!' she cried, clutching her chest. 'You gave me quite a fright!'

Same here, I thought.

Her eyes were dark and huge, and gazed at me closely.

It dawned on me then who she was. I felt sick to my very boots.

'Lady Barrington ...' I scrambled to my feet. 'I won't be a minute, your Ladyship, if you'll excuse me.'

'My, you *have* been busy, haven't you?' she said, smoothly.

I glanced at my black hands and even blacker cuffs, and quickly hid them from view, hoping to God she couldn't see the cold grate behind me.

'You must be Matilda, the new housemaid.'

I nodded.

'Mrs Jessop tells me we're lucky to have you.'

I was taken aback. Wasn't *I* the lucky one, getting work here after being caught trespassing?

'It's such a job to find decent staff these days,' she said.

Which made sense to me now, stood here in this creepy room. Maybe they *were* lucky, in a way, for Gracie was right; this place really was all about the dead.

Lady Barrington seemed to lose interest then. She went over to the window and turned her slender back on me to look out over the lawns. I wondered what she was staring at. From the tilt of her head, she seemed fixed on a certain point, way beyond the trees.

The lake. Of course.

Did she do this every day, like some sort of vigil? My heart turned at the thought.

'So Matilda,' she said, gazing on out of the window. 'Tell me about yourself. I do so like to *know* my staff.'

I was unsure how much to say, and uncertain how to address a grand person's back.

'Um . . . well . . .'

She stepped away from the window then, easing herself into a chair and beckoning me to stand before her. I was glad, since it meant she still faced away from that shameful fire, though I couldn't hide it for ever.

'Tell me about your family,' she said, as I stood in front of her.

I'd have been happier telling her how fast I could scrub a pot.

'I live in the village,' I said.

'*Lived*,' she corrected me. 'This is where you live now. And your parents? Are they well?'

'You could say that.'

'Oh?'

'Well, your Ladyship . . .'

'Come closer, so I can see you properly,' she said, smiling warmly.

I inched forward. Close up she was even more lovely. Her hair was held up at the sides with little combs, the rest fell in thick curls about her neck. Her hands, smooth white lady's hands, were folded neatly in her lap.

And those eyes.

Fine things they were, but blank, somehow. It made me think of my ma now Eliza had gone. Her eyes had that emptiness too.

I knew it wasn't proper to stare, but I couldn't help it, and found myself studying Lady Barrington's brooch. It was round, gold-edged, with a pale woven pattern of flowers in the middle. What a pretty thing it was.

She noticed my interest. Her fingers went to her throat. 'Isn't it lovely?' she said. 'It's very dear to me. The flowers are made from his hair, can you see?'

His hair? Oh Lord!

I fought the urge to back away, instead making myself lean in close to look at the brooch, knowing exactly whose hair was inside it. And it was just as pale and fine right here in the daylight as it was in the dark of my dreams. Her Ladyship studied my face. I dreaded to think what she saw there.

'Remind me of your parents' surname?' she said, suddenly.

I straightened up. 'Higgins, your Ladyship.'

This seemed to please her. 'You look familiar, that's all. So then, tell me about your family.'

And she was so sweet, so warm, I felt myself fall under a kind of spell.

'My sister and my pa are on their way to America as we speak,' I said.

'How thrilling!'

'Not really. They didn't tell us they was going. It came as a proper shock. And my sister nicked stuff from us too. Money and . . . all sorts.'

I stopped, wondering if I'd been too free with myself and spoken out of turn. But her Ladyship seemed keen to keep me talking.

'How dreadful for your mother,' said Lady Barrington. ' Is she bearing up?'

'I reckon her heart's been broke.'

Something caught her fancy in this and she sat forward in her seat. 'Oh? And has it been hard for you?'

'It in't been easy,' I said, carefully. 'See, they never said goodbye.'

Lady Barrington breathed in sharp. '*Such* a tragedy,'

she whispered, turning so grave, so drawn, I thought she might faint.

'Your Ladyship?'

'Give me a moment, please,' she said, and took a tiny bottle of salts from her skirts and sniffed delicately. The colour came back to her cheeks.

'Are you all right?' I asked.

She gave me a most beautiful smile. 'Quite well. And as I have you all to myself, there's something else I need to ask you.'

One look at her face and I reckoned I'd tell her anything.

'Are *you* recovered?' she said.

'Pardon?'

'From your ordeal on Sunday. It must have been frightening for you.'

So Mrs Jessop really *had* filled her in. When I went to speak, the words seemed to stick in my throat. 'Yes, your Ladyship. I am ... I mean ... It *was* ... Um ... thank you.'

'A young man saved you, am I right?'

The words wouldn't come. My eyes seemed fixed on her brooch. If it were mine I'd have pulled it apart, just to touch Kit's hair again. But it wasn't mine. And she was waiting for an answer.

'Yes, your Ladyship,' I said. 'He did. I ... I was lucky.'

'You were, Matilda.' Her chin trembled. 'And the name of your rescuer ...?'

I hesitated. The spell was broken. There was plenty I couldn't tell her. Heck, I couldn't even meet her eye.

'Will Potter, your Ladyship.'

'Ah yes, the butcher's son. Clearly, you owe him your life.'

'Yes, your Ladyship.' And it wasn't such a lie. Will did bring me in from the cold, after all.

I prayed this was the end of it, that she'd heard enough and wouldn't bring up the trespassing part of things.

Sure enough, she rose from her seat and moved towards the bed, where she spread her hands over the pillow, like I'd almost done myself. It felt private, somehow. I didn't like to watch.

'Please, get on with your work now,' she said over her shoulder.

I didn't need telling twice. At once, I crossed the room and knelt at the hearth, hoping to block her view. I had to get this blasted fire lit again. My hands shook as I stirred the ashes. Then the door opened behind me. It was Gracie with a steaming jug of water.

Alarmed, I glanced at her Ladyship. She was still leaning over Kit's bed in a kind of daze.

'Quick!' I hissed to Gracie. 'Help me get this fire lit before her Ladyship sees!'

Gracie's face fell. 'You in't let it go out, have you?'

'Not on purpose, no! Now get in here and help me!'

We only had seconds. In a flash, we'd emptied the grate and started again. Every brush, every scrape felt ear-splittingly loud.

'Come on, come on!' I muttered under my breath as the flames licked the paper.

Gracie laid the sticks on top then added on some lukewarm coals. A small, feeble fire began to take. Quickly, I swept up and emptied the ash into my bucket. It would be hours before the room was properly warm again.

Lady Barrington straightened up, drifting back to her place at the window without so much as a glance at us. I breathed out. We'd done it! The fire was lit.

Then I dropped the pan. I flinched as it clattered against the hearth.

'Sorry!' I whispered to Gracie.

'Are you *quite* finished?' said Lady Barrington, a new edge to her voice. She turned from the window.

Her gaze slid past me to the wretched fire I so desperately didn't want her to see.

She let out a cry. 'What on earth . . .? This isn't a proper fire! This won't do at all!'

Flying across the room, she barged past me so I stumbled sideways into a table full of books. She fell to her knees at the hearth and scrabbled around in the coal bucket like a mad thing. In no time, her fine white hands were black with dust. Her hair came unpinned, falling across her face and down her back. The sight was sickening.

'Your Ladyship, please . . .' I said, trying to stop her.

She took no notice, muttering over and over, 'Don't worry, my darling, we'll keep you warm.'

I was horrified. Gracie had begun to cry.

'Get Dorcas quick!' I said to her. I didn't know what else to do.

Gracie legged it out of the room.

I turned to Lady Barrington and crouched beside her. 'Please get up, your Ladyship. You must let me do the fire. You'll ruin your frock.'

'We'll get you warm . . .' she kept saying, her face wet with tears. 'You'll be better, once you're warm.'

It was no good trying to talk sense to her; I might as well have spoken to the wall.

I got to my feet, legs shaking. That moment, the door flew open. Dorcas's face was stern.

'Get downstairs, Tilly,' she said to me. 'I'll deal with this now.'

I couldn't seem to move.

'For goodness' sake, just do it!'

She stepped aside to let me pass. 'And don't say a word about this to Mrs Jessop,' she said in a low voice. 'We keep it to ourselves, understood?'

I gripped the banister all the way down the stairs. My legs could barely hold me. Somehow I found my way through the felt-covered door, and once I was below stairs again, all the shouting and banging brought me back to myself.

''Bout time an' all,' said Cook, when she saw me. 'Blimey, you look a funny shade. Wash your hands, then come and stir this sauce for me.'

It was the simplest task I'd had all morning. Honest to God, I was glad of it.

21

SWEETHEARTS

After luncheon, we set to cleaning the silver cutlery. I was thankful for the chance to sit quiet, away from Mrs Jessop's beady eye. If she got wind of what'd happened up in Kit's bedroom, then we'd all be for it. But I was the one who'd let that blasted fire go out; if anyone got flayed alive, it'd be me. Yet we didn't speak of it between ourselves. Instead, we worked in silence, sitting close to the hearth, and drinking hot sugary tea like people who couldn't quite get warm.

Mid-afternoon, when the light was fading, Peter the under-footman came in. There were tiny flakes of snow all over his smart woollen coat.

'Post's been,' he said, taking off his hat.

He was a great tall thing, all arms and legs and with fine blond hair which now lay flat to his forehead. In truth, he looked a bit of a lummox. And as he hovered by the fire to warm his hands, Gracie turned suddenly sulky.

'Dorcas, this came for you,' he said, handing her an envelope which she stuffed in her apron pocket without as much as a glance.

'Thank you. Can I fetch you some tea? You look in need of it.'

He shot Gracie a pleading look, but she stared hard at the fork she was cleaning, leaving him to dither like a spare part. I couldn't help but smile.

'Tell him to sit down, then,' I said.

'He can do what he likes,' she muttered. 'I in't his mother.'

Dorcas frowned. 'Now come on. That's no way to speak to Peter.'

'Go on, Gracie,' I said. 'Be a good sort.'

Huffing loudly, she jabbed her fork at Peter. 'Take it down the other end of the table, then. We've got work to do here.'

Peter's mouth opened like he was about to speak, then he thought better of it. He pulled himself up to his full height and strode out of the room.

'Well,' said Dorcas. 'I hope you're pleased with yourself.'

'Can we change the subject?' said Gracie, irritably.

No one said anything for a while. The fire hissed as snowflakes blew down the chimney and the clock on the wall ticked lazily. I began to feel almost sleepy.

Then Gracie spoke like she was halfway through a thought. 'No, I honestly can't think of one boy I'd trust with a confidence.'

Dorcas smiled. 'Sounds a bit dramatic.'

'Well, it's true. They all think we're half-wits.'

'Are we still talking about Peter, then?'

'He'll do for starters.'

'What do you think, Tilly?' said Dorcas.

I reckoned this Peter looked a fine one to be calling anyone else a half-wit.

'I know girls I'd not trust, never mind boys,' I said, thinking of Eliza.

Gracie rubbed a spoon furiously. 'I've given up on boys. I swear I have.'

Dorcas tried not to smile. 'Until Peter wins you over again. It's always like this with you two. You fall out, make up, then fall out again.'

I tried to picture how Peter might win anyone over with his baby-fine hair and great gangly legs, and gave up.

'Not this time,' said Gracie.

'Maybe you should try your luck with that butcher's boy, Will Potter, instead? He seems a nice sort,' said Dorcas.

My face went suddenly hot.

'I wouldn't count on it!' I said, a bit too quickly. 'All the girls like him . . . well . . . most of them, anyway.'

But Gracie was busy scowling at Dorcas.

'I don't need no matchmaking, ta very much. And anyway, what would *you* know about having a sweetheart?'

Dorcas's hand went to the pocket of her apron. 'You'd better mind your manners,' she said, coolly.

An uneasy silence fell over us. It was almost half past four by now, and very nearly dark outside. Shadows lurked in the corners of the room. The fire hissed and spat. Any good cheer I'd felt had gone. And despite the hot tea, I was suddenly chilled to the bone. I moved my seat closer to the hearth; it didn't stop dark thoughts returning.

Something was very wrong with this house. A spirit haunted the back stairs. Above stairs was a queer shrine to a dead boy. The place was so full of secrets. Even the servants seemed to have them, for flip's sake, so goodness only knew what Lady Barrington was keeping to herself.

A service bell rang, and someone out in the passage shouted, 'Her Ladyship! Front parlour!'

As Dorcas glanced my way, I felt the colour drain

from my cheeks.

'I'll answer it this time,' she said, reading my look. 'You two finish this cutlery off.'

I thanked her.

'Save your thanks. You'll have to face her again soon enough.' She swapped her plain pinny for a lace one and tucked the letter up her sleeve.

Once Dorcas had gone, Gracie said, 'I bet that letter's from her sweetheart.'

'Dorcas is very pretty,' I said. 'She must have men queuing up.'

Gracie shook her head. 'Only one. He writes every week, but she's cool as anything. She's got *plans*.'

'Oh?'

'To be housekeeper of a big fine house. She don't want to get married.'

It struck me as a sad thing, to choose a job over love. Maybe Dorcas didn't love her sweetheart enough, or maybe she just wanted her dream more. And a thought came to me, so quick it made me catch my breath.

Pa chose his dream over me.

Anger rose up in me, hot and strong. Never mind what Eliza had done. Pa was supposed to love me. He was on my side. He did have a heart. *Didn't he?* And yet he'd wanted his dream so badly, he couldn't take me with him. He couldn't even say goodbye.

Such thoughts would drive me mad. By now my eyes were full of tears but I wasn't about to sit here and blub. Heck no! A quick dab of my face and I turned to Gracie, hopeful she might cheer me up.

'Go on then, tell me, what did you and Peter fall out over?'

'Well,' said Gracie, smoothing her hair behind her ear. 'See, it's about that back-stairs business.'

My heart sank. This was hardly likely to cheer me.

'Tuesday breakfast I told Peter what was happening, about the funny feeling on the stairs, and the broken plates and that.'

'What did he say?'

'He said all girls have these stupid fancies, and what I needed was a cold bath and a really long walk. Reckoned it always worked on his sister.'

'Really?' I said, not exactly warming to Peter.

'But I told him it weren't no fancy. I said I'd seen plates spinning through the air clear as day.'

'Bet he didn't believe *that*.'

'No he didn't. And the stupid clot told Samuel Ketteridge. So then he started on at me, saying they'd think I wasn't right in the head and they'd send me away if I wasn't careful.'

'Oh Gracie!' No wonder she couldn't be civil to Peter. I felt guilty now that we'd teased her. Rather than asking him to stay for tea, we should've told him to sling his hook!

'And by the time breakfast was finished, I was so upset, Mrs Jessop said I was fit for nothing and made me go back to bed.'

Of course!

Tuesday was the day we'd got done trespassing and Mrs Jessop was one maid down. So it was because of Samuel Ketteridge's teasing that I'd got my foot in the door here. It was hard to be glad of it though, when I felt so sore for poor Gracie.

We fell quiet to our thoughts. The polishing was nearly done now, but for a few fiddly-looking forks. I reached for one and held it to the light.

'So you've broken off with Peter for good?' I said, squinting at the fork.

'Oh yes. It's finished. I trusted him with a confidence and he blabbed it. No true sweetheart does that.'

I looked at Gracie. 'What if Peter *had* believed you?'

'But he didn't, did he?'

'Sometimes people surprise you, and believe you when no one else does.'

She glanced at me sideways. 'You thinking about a sweetheart of your own? I can see you are!'

I shook my head. 'No, I'm not.'

And I wasn't, neither. I was thinking about Will Potter in an almost kindly way. Because compared to Gracie's Peter, Will was a flipping saint. When I'd told him about Kit, he'd listened. And for this I was mightily grateful.

22

BROKEN CHINA

Evening came and still no one collared me about letting Kit's fire go out. I'd been expecting it; Mrs Jessop had eyes like a hawk. Then, just as we were clearing away the supper things, she appeared in the kitchen doorway, notebook clutched to her chest. The look on her face turned me proper cold.

Oh God, I thought. *This is it! Lady Barrington's told her everything.*

I held my breath as her eyes slid over me. Then she opened the notebook and started flicking through the pages.

'It seems we're rather light on china. I counted out sixteen plates and sixteen side plates, and yet only twelve of each have made it back to the cupboard.'

China?

I breathed again, though Gracie started looking shifty.

'I'll check, Mrs J., and let you know,' said Cook,

quickly. 'They're probably on the drying rack still.'

'See that you do,' said Mrs Jessop, and wrote something down in her book. Looking up again, her gaze rested on me.

'You've used the ointment for your hands?' she said.

'Yes, Mrs Jessop.'

I caught Cook's eye. She had the strangest expression on her face. Cook glanced at Mrs Jessop and back at me, then whistled under her breath.

'What?' I mouthed, thinking I'd done something wrong.

Cook shook her head and went back to cleaning the range. Her hand moved slowly like she was thinking hard about something.

'I'll be in my office,' said Mrs Jessop. 'Send Tilly to tell me when the plates have been accounted for.'

Once she'd gone, I turned to Cook. 'What did I do?'

'What d'you mean?'

'Just then with Mrs Jessop. You was looking at me funny.'

'I weren't,' she said.

'Yes, you was.'

'Leave it, Tilly, and get on with clearing up.'

'But Mrs Jessop's always looking at me too and I don't know why.'

'That's enough. Don't go making trouble for your-self.'

Which made me think there *was* a reason for it. And no one ever stared at Gracie like that.

'Well, it sets me right on edge,' I said.

Cook stopped cleaning and took me to one side. 'If you must know ... well ... it's probably because you look like someone.'

'Lady Barrington reckoned so, too. Who is it?'

Cook hesitated. Looking over her shoulder, she dropped her voice. 'Someone very dear to Mrs Jessop. Someone she used to know.'

'What d'you mean, *used to*?'

'It was a long time ago, and the girl was about your age, poor soul. And I wonder if when Mrs Jessop sees you, she in't just thinking ... what if ...'

Something smashed to the floor behind us.

We both spun round. Gracie was stood by the table. Her mouth hung open in horror. At her feet, broken plates littered the flagstones.

'Not again!' cried Cook. 'This time it'll be coming out of your wages, young lady. We can't cover up for you any more, not now Mrs Jessop's noticed.'

Gracie sobbed. 'But I didn't drop them, honest I didn't.'

'Then who did? The Duke of flaming York?'

Gracie looked to me. 'Tilly, you believe me, don't you?'

'I'm sorry, I didn't see nothing,' I said.

'Please, it's not me. It's something else doing it . . . something mean . . .'

The gas lights on the wall suddenly hissed then dipped low, casting an eerie, underwater gloom about us.

'Oh heck!' said Cook. 'That's all we need, to be clearing the dishes by candlelight.'

But she made no move to find any candles. Like the rest of us, she stood stock still, looking warily about her. The room felt different, somehow. Familiar things like the table and chairs now looked queer and stark. I began to feel uneasy.

'What is it? What's going on?' cried Gracie.

Cook put a finger to her lips. But the quiet was worse. It stretched tight, like a breath held too long. Abruptly, the air changed. Now it was bitter, bitter cold. It set my teeth chattering. A sense of dread spread through me. Then I smelled it, that sweet honey smell. It was close by me. Too close.

'Oh no!' whispered Gracie. 'Look! It's happening again!'

She gazed transfixed at the pile of clean china on the table. One small white cup began to move. I couldn't quite believe what I saw. My brain wouldn't allow it. For cups didn't move by themselves. Someone must have touched it. But it wasn't any of us; we were stood too far from the table. The cup swayed from side to side, like it was about to tip over. Then it lurched forward to the table's edge.

No one moved. Our eyes stayed fixed on the cup. It seemed almost to *tremble*, like it was a living breathing thing. I watched in growing terror, quite unable to look away. Slowly, shakily, the cup lifted up off the table. For one long, awful moment, it hung in mid-air. Then it whizzed over our heads with shocking force, and smashed against the wall behind us.

'Great heavens alive!' Cook breathed.

My heart beat hard in my chest. I couldn't bring myself to turn and look at the damage, for before us on the table a whole pile of plates now moved towards the edge. They were just plates; normal everyday things. Except they weren't. They were moving *by themselves*, and had become something terrible.

Gracie rushed forwards, arms out to catch them. The plates stopped. Gracie froze. As if in spite, the plates lurched again, toppled over and clattered to the floor. Some smashed to pieces, others spun off in all directions about our feet.

The gas lights flickered, then grew bright. The last plate came to rest over in the corner. A strange stillness settled over the room.

I was shaken to the core. No one had touched those plates, I'd swear to it, at least no one *human*. This was Kit's work, wasn't it? His spirit was here making trouble, and I'd not the faintest idea why.

Gently, Cook eased my fingers off her arm.

'Get yourselves to the servants' hall,' she said. 'I'll clear up this lot.'

As she grabbed her broom and started sweeping, I went to Gracie. She hadn't yet moved. Her arms were wrapped round her waist like she was hugging herself. Her eyes were glazed with shock.

'Let's go,' I said and took hold of her hand, which felt clammy and cold. I bet mine did too.

We stopped in the doorway. Rapid footsteps came towards us down the passage. Mrs Jessop appeared, skirts flying, her face flushed. She still had her note-book in her hand.

'What an infernal racket! What on earth is going on?'

No one answered.

What was left of the teacup lay at Mrs Jessop's feet. As she stepped forwards, it crunched beneath her boot soles. Her eyebrows shot up. She bent to pick up a shard of china, and held it up so the light shone through it. I saw at once how fine and fragile it was.

'One of our best teacups, it seems.'

'Please, Mrs Jessop.' Gracie dropped my hand and started twisting her apron. Her lip quivered.

'And these plates?' Mrs Jessop pointed to the floor. She looked clearly horrified.

Cook spoke first. 'Now look, we all makes mistakes sometimes, Mrs J., and I think . . .'

Mrs Jessop turned to face Cook. 'Are you saying that this is *your* doing?'

'No,' she stuttered. 'Well, not quite . . . you see . . .' Cook wasn't often lost for words. I didn't like where this was heading.

'Only it seems to me that what's happened here to-night has happened on other nights this week,' said Mrs Jessop, coldly.

I shot a look at Gracie, who'd started sobbing quietly and was staring at the floor.

'Well . . .' said Cook.

'HASN'T IT?'

I flinched.

Cook's face was red. 'Now just a minute! I in't the one been throwing china about the place!'

'Then you'd better tell me who has.' Mrs Jessop turned to Gracie. 'Was it you, then?'

'No! Please, I never . . .'

'For pity's sake! I keep records of everything!' Mrs Jessop shook her notebook at Gracie. 'Every night since Sunday, something has been broken!'

Since Sunday?

'You mustn't . . . I can't lose this job . . . please . . . let me explain,' Gracie cried.

'No, let me explain.' Mrs Jessop licked the end of her finger and started flicking through the pages of her book. 'Yes, here we are . . .' She paused. For a split second her face paled but she quickly recovered. 'Sunday the sixth of February, two china plates missing . . . Monday the seventh of February, three cups cracked . . . Tuesday the eighth of February . . .'

I didn't hear the rest. My mind was racing ahead of itself.

Sunday February 6th. *Kit's death, my almost drowning, and now the china. Three things. Three flipping things! All on the same date!*

These things hadn't happened by chance. They all linked back to the day Kit had died, connected to each other in some queer way. I was on to something at last! It was a job not to whoop or punch the air, when everyone else still looked so grave.

But.

That wasn't quite everything, was it? Thrilled though I was, something still didn't fit. In the lake Kit had been heart-stoppingly lovely. Here in the house, his spirit was different, smashing cups and causing mischief for the sake of it.

For the sake of what?

It was like there were two sides to him, the dreamy gentle side and the spiteful, angry one. Maybe that was it. Perhaps he had good reason to show his temper, if something truly bad had happened here. Something like the truth he said had to be revealed.

A strange thought came to me then, that maybe there was more to this. Could Frost Hollow Hall have other secrets, other *ghosts*? It hardly made sense, and I pushed it at once from my mind.

The room had fallen quiet. Mrs Jessop clearly thought we were a bunch of oafs who weren't to be trusted. She hadn't listened to Gracie or Cook; I didn't suppose for a minute she'd listen to me.

Yet before I could stop myself, I said, 'What Cook and Gracie say is true. No one's been dropping china.'

'Oh?' said Mrs Jessop, turning to me. 'And who asked you?'

'I saw what happened just now.'

'Then perhaps you might tell me.'

Cook put a hand on my arm. 'You don't need to do that, Tilly.'

'Well, it in't right to blame Gracie, nor anyone else. I'm not afraid of the truth,' I said, though my palms were sweating.

'If you want to keep your position, just be careful what you say,' warned Cook.

Mrs Jessop raised her voice. 'If someone doesn't tell me THIS SECOND what is going on . . .'

'There's a spirit down here!' I said, in a rush. 'We think it's angry at something.'

Mrs Jessop went white. She pressed her fingertips to her forehead and sighed deeply. Then she looked straight at me.

'This is worse than I anticipated.'

'You can't sack her!' cried Cook. 'That in't fair!'

'It'll be Lady Barrington's decision.'

Cook looked horrified. '*Her Ladyship?* But it's you and Mr Phelps what decides on the household staff. You mustn't tell *her*!'

'It's high time Lady Barrington was told. We have

huge problems keeping hold of our staff. And is it any wonder when you're all scaring the living daylights out of each other?'

'But what good would it do, really, with her nerves such as they are? Have a heart, Mrs J.'

Mrs Jessop shook her head. 'This nonsense has got to stop. We cannot run a house like this.'

With the greatest care, she smoothed her hair and tucked her notebook under her arm. Then she came at me. Out the corner of my eye, I saw Cook try to stop her. Mrs Jessop grabbed my wrist. A hard yank and I was out into the passageway. She dragged me towards the green felt door.

'Wait!' I cried, digging my feet into the floor. 'Please! Wait!'

One look at Mrs Jessop's face and I knew there was no chance of that.

23

LADY BARRINGTON'S PLAN

We came out into the main hallway. Mrs Jessop kept a firm grip on me, rushing me along so my feet barely touched the floor.

'Please! Just listen, will you?' I cried.

It wasn't fair. None of this was fair. I twisted and turned 'til my arm burned, but her grip held fast as a vice. Before I knew it, I was raging.

'Let go! Get your stinking hands off me!'

She didn't so much as flinch, but marched me up a different set of steps towards the back of the house. It was gloomy here, all narrow passages and uneven floors. What gas lamps there were gave off a strange, greenish light. As we stopped in front of a door, Mrs Jessop tapped on it with her free hand.

'Come in,' said Lady Barrington's voice from inside. Mrs Jessop told me to wait where I was. The door clicked shut behind her.

I leaned against the wall, head spinning, heart

still beating way too fast. Here I was now in deep, deep trouble, just for speaking the truth. That was the problem with this place, nobody wanted to listen.

I stared hard at the door. Bet Mrs Jessop was in there, painting a right picture of me.

So.

I could wait here and be told to pack my bags. Or I could just go. Right now. I'd be back home by midnight.

I set off down the passage. Halfway along it, I stopped. What good would it do to run off like some snivelling baby? It wouldn't help anyone, not Ma, not Kit, not even me. I thought of my dream last night, and the smile on Kit's face. That's what I had to think of, not the pinching fingers or the broken plates.

Kit's spirit couldn't rest. If he was ever to be at peace, then I had to find the truth. And I had to make people listen. The answer lay in this house, I knew it. That's why I was here.

Behind me, I heard a door open.

Mrs Jessop called out, 'I told you to wait right here!' I turned to see her beckoning me. 'Now come quickly, her Ladyship hasn't got all night.'

We stepped into a bright parlour. There were lamps everywhere, and mirrors reflecting back each little ball of light so the room was almost dazzling. Lady Barrington was sitting on a sofa near to the hearth. She was dressed for dinner in a black frock, this time with the brooch pinned to her chest.

Next to her heart.

She seemed recovered enough from this morning, though she still had that faraway look in her eyes. I felt my own heart thudding. I hoped to God this wouldn't take long.

To the right of me, Lord Barrington got up from his chair. He looked so much like Kit it was a job to keep my eyes down. He hardly noticed me of course, speaking over my head to Mrs Jessop.

'Let Samuel know he'll need to pack for me, would you? I'll be catching the morning train.'

'Oh darling, must you go away *again*?' Lady Barrington reached out to him and he took her hand. They made such a handsome couple, what with her so dark and him so fair. I knew I was staring now, but I couldn't help myself.

'I'm needed in London. Why don't you hold a little gathering, perhaps? It would do you good. Keep you entertained.'

'Oh no.' She looked up at him from under her lashes. 'I don't feel up to that.'

'Well, Mrs Jessop is waiting to talk to you. I'll be in the library.'

Once he'd gone, Mrs Jessop nudged me forwards. I caught sight of myself in a mirror and saw what a state I looked. My apron was still wet, and my hair was escaping from under my cap. Too late to fix it now.

'Please be brief,' said Lady Barrington.

Mrs Jessop squared her shoulders. 'Matters have come to a head, your Ladyship. Our finest china has been broken on more than one occasion this week. I've got it all written down.'

And she opened that notebook of hers like some fancy detective who was about to solve a crime.

'Couldn't Mr Phelps deal with this?' said Lady Barrington, stifling a yawn.

'But the staff are full of such silly talk, your Ladyship. They're blaming . . .' Mrs Jessop hesitated. 'Well, I think it would be best if you heard about it.'

'Oh? And why is Matilda here? Is she the culprit?'

I couldn't stop myself. 'No, your Ladyship, it in't me!'

'Quiet, child! No one asked you to speak!' said Mrs Jessop.

'Well it in't silly talk!' I knew it sounded pert, but it wasn't right, all this looking for someone to blame.

'Do you know who *is* responsible, then?' said Lady Barrington.

'Not exactly.'

'Are you covering for someone?'

'I think she is, your Ladyship,' Mrs Jessop chipped in. 'She's full of foolish ideas.'

I counted to five in my head, then said, calm as I could, 'I in't covering for no one, your Ladyship. On my pa's life, I in't!'

Lady Barrington gave me a long look. I'd told her too much about my family this morning; she seemed to recall it now. 'I think you'd better leave in the morning, Matilda. That's if Mrs Jessop can manage without you.'

I felt sick. Now it had come to it, I was desperate to stay. Mrs Jessop breathed in sharply, and I saw her hand go to her throat as if her collar was too tight. We both started speaking at once.

'No, please, don't make me go . . .'

'Really, your Ladyship, a firm warning is all she needs . . .'

'Stop! Both of you!' Lady Barrington cried. 'You're giving me a headache!'

I looked at Mrs Jessop. Her expression was blank as stone again.

'Just tell me the truth,' said Lady Barrington, more gently this time. 'And then I'll decide. If someone is deliberately breaking my china, I have a right to an explanation at the very least.'

Though my mouth was dry as sand, I reckoned she *should* hear the truth. It was up to her if she refused to believe what I said.

'We think it's a spirit, some sort of ghost.'

Mrs Jessop spluttered. Lady Barrington though, looked completely stunned. She turned paler than ever and gripped the sides of her seat. I feared she was having another of her turns. Then, like the sun coming out from the clouds, her whole face lit up. For a long while she didn't speak.

'You must tell me more,' she said, eventually.

I swallowed hard. 'It comes at night and smashes cups and plates, and it gets us maids into trouble. And it follows us up the back stairs in the dark.'

Lady Barrington sat forward in her seat. Her eyes looked huge. 'And this spirit, as you call it, does it take a form? Does it ever appear as a person?'

'Your Ladyship, please . . .' interrupted Mrs Jessop. 'This is exactly my point.'

'But don't you realise? It could be him! At last!'

'No, no, not this . . .' said Mrs Jessop, shaking her head.

By now Lady Barrington was on her feet. ' It *is* him! It has to be him!'

I felt uneasy too. Did we *really* know the spirit was Kit? I was beginning to have my doubts. But Lady Barrington seemed almost beside herself, and I didn't fancy being the one to dash her hopes.

'Ten years I've waited for a sign from him!' said Lady Barrington. 'Ten whole years!'

I stared at her.

Ten years? Did she really say ten years?

Shocked and bewildered as I was, I fought to keep it from my face. Yet my head started spinning.

So Kit hadn't haunted his mother in all this time? And yet he'd saved my life *and* appeared in my dreams, all in the last flipping week. Ten years her Ladyship had been waiting. And for nothing. Yet there was a ghost here all right, here in this very house.

Lost to my thoughts, I hadn't reckoned on Mrs Jessop. I realised now she was watching me closely.

Me.

A nobody from the village, who dreamed of Kit Barrington while his own dear mother kept a fire burning in the mad hope that it might bring him back from the dead.

My mind reeled. Why me? *Why not* Lady Barrington?

Either way, I couldn't take my eyes off her Ladyship. She had a hand to her mouth. Her gaze darted this way and that, as if she was thinking like fury. Then she said, 'We shall have a séance. We *must* summon him!'

I gasped.

'If I might say so, your Ladyship, that is not a good idea,' said Mrs Jessop, grimly.

'Of course it is!' cried Lady Barrington. 'It's the very *best* idea!'

The thought of a séance turned my stomach too. But I couldn't ignore the thrill running through me. In fact, I could barely keep still.

'It'll do nothing to settle things below stairs,' Mrs Jessop was saying. 'Those girls are coiled springs. What they need is a stop put to all this.'

Lady Barrington didn't seem to be listening. She was almost feverish with excitement.

Mrs Jessop tried again. 'And do you think his Lordship would approve?'

'My husband advised me to hold a gathering in his

absence,' said Lady Barrington, her eyes glittering. 'Besides, I'll thank you to know your place.'

Mrs Jessop blinked slowly; once, twice. She looked defeated. 'Very good, your Ladyship.'

'That's settled then,' said Lady Barrington. 'We'll need a cold supper and some wine to steady our nerves. This will be our little party. No footmen. Let's do it tomorrow evening.'

It took a moment or two to sink in. Then it came back to me why I was here, the small matter of my job. I smoothed my pinny and waited, praying her Ladyship wouldn't turn me out now. I'd *die* if I got sent home before tomorrow.

Only she seemed to have forgotten all about me and sat staring into the fire.

'Will that be all, your Ladyship?' said Mrs Jessop.

Her Ladyship started. 'Oh . . . for now, yes.'

'But what about me?' I blurted out. 'What's to become of me?'

Mrs Jessop stiffened.

'Oh yes, of course,' said Lady Barrington and passed a hand over her eyes.

My legs were shaking again. She couldn't send me home, not now!

'Very well, we'll keep you. Mrs Jessop will need you

to serve tomorrow night. This is your last chance to prove yourself.'

'Thank you, oh thank you!' I cried.

But she'd already turned away and was gazing into the flames.

*

When I got back to the kitchens, Cook looked surprised to see me. Gracie leapt up from her stool and flung her arms around my neck.

'Thought you was for the chop,' said Cook. 'I in't never seen Mrs Jessop so angry!'

'This is my last chance . And I should probably keep my gob shut more often, too.'

Cook chuckled at this. She gave us each a candle for the back stairs and wished us good night. We went quickly and though nothing followed us, Gracie still held my hand all the way up and got into bed beside me, even before I'd asked her.

'So did you tell her Ladyship about the spirit?' she said.

'Yes.'

'And did she believe you?'

'I should say so.'

'You in't half brave! I in't got the guts to even talk to her.'

I didn't feel brave in the slightest. And I didn't feel like mentioning the séance neither, which I knew would stir her up; it could wait until morning. We lay side by side without speaking, and after a bit, Gracie turned over. I listened to her breathing change. Soon she was sound asleep.

I stared up at the ceiling for a good while longer. My head buzzed with all it was holding in. Her Ladyship, I reckoned, wasn't quite what she seemed. She was charming and lovely but artful with it, like someone used to getting her own way. And it unsettled me still how she grieved for Kit like he'd died only yesterday, as if she didn't quite believe he was gone.

But then I couldn't blame her. I knew what it felt like to miss someone, even when you were angry with them, even when you wanted to shout at them hard. You hoped it might be just a nasty dream, that when you woke up they'd be there again and everything would be back to normal. Except it didn't work like that. Each morning I woke to another day without my pa. And he'd only been missing five days, not ten whole years.

Though God help us if this séance went wrong. It really didn't bear thinking about.

DREAMING: 5

Above our heads, the cracks appear. Daylight seeps in, turning the water smoky grey. Kit looks up. The light is on his face. I still can't believe he's not an angel.

A sudden light startles us. Trees and blue sky loom above us. The ice has splintered, the sun pours in. I start laughing out loud. I can't help it. I'm brimming over with joy.

I start to swim upwards. But something isn't right. Kit's not beside me. I look round and see him bewildered, some feet below. He can't move. He reaches out for my hand, starts shaking his head. This is as far as he can go.

I take his outstretched fingers. They feel colder than ever. I start to shake. Ever so slowly, we sink back down to the darker water. The chill of it hits my feet, my legs, my waist. I don't understand what's happening. I thought we were nearly free of this place. But as he turns to me, his eyes are full of something I can't quite read.

24

THE EMPTINESS

I woke with a start. It was the middle of the night still, the moon shining in through the window. Gracie was asleep beside me. Nothing looked amiss. Yet dread grew in the pit of my stomach. I pulled the covers right up to my chin.

Someone else was here in the room.

'Kit?' I whispered. 'Is that you?'

No one answered.

And yet the bedroom door began to open. My heart gave a painful thud. I sat up, rubbing my eyes and wondering if this was still a dream. From the landing came the sound of footsteps. They were light and quick; I knew them at once. The spirit was back.

Hands shaking, I reached for our candle. Once it was lit, I felt braver but still hadn't the guts to get out of bed. The footsteps got louder. Gracie groaned like she was about to wake. Then, right close by, I heard whispering and with it, that dreadful smell of honey.

Terrified, I leapt straight out of bed.

The footsteps on the landing stopped.

I crept to the door and looked back to check Gracie – she slept on. My heart beat hard as I went out onto the landing. It was empty. Then, deep within the stairwell, something moved. A shuffling noise echoed off the walls.

'Who's there?' I whispered.

The spirit had come for me. I sensed it, all right. And though I was sick with fear, I needed to know what it wanted.

I took the stairs slowly. Halfway down, the shuffling stopped. I hesitated. What the flip was I doing, wandering about in the middle of the night? If Mrs Jessop caught me, I'd be for it.

Something brushed against my face. My hands flew up.

'Who's there? What do you want?'

Silence.

All around was pitch black. I almost glad, so fearful was I of what I might see. Close to my right ear, someone drew breath. I froze. Then the speaking started, quick, hissing, rambling words that meant nothing to me but turned my blood cold. In horror, I realised the spirit had hold of my wrist. I tried desperately to pull free. The fingers gripped tighter, dragging me forwards. Before I knew it, I'd reached the bottom of the stairs.

There, the fingers let go. Now the footsteps started up again, this time heading off down the passage towards the green baize door. I wanted so badly just to turn and run back to bed. Yet a queer feeling seized me that I *had* to follow, that the spirit was demanding it. And it wouldn't let me rest until I did.

The door swung open before I'd reached it. I stepped out into the empty hall. Moonlight poured in through the windows so the paintings, the furniture, the carpets all seemed touched with silver. The house was still as the grave. I knew where the spirit was taking me. It set me shivering all over. Yet my feet moved as if by themselves, taking the stairs two at a time, going up and up into the shadows.

It was dark inside Kit's bedchamber. My eyes took a moment to get used to it. Someone had pulled the drapes tight shut, though the fire still glowed in the grate.

'Kit? Are you here?'

Nothing moved.

'Answer me, will you?'

My ears strained for the slightest sound. There was

none. But something had shifted in me, too. The fear had gone and now I felt quite irked.

'You got me out of bed, so what do you want?' I whispered, hearing the rising frustration in my voice. 'If it in't you doing all this, Kit, then who is?'

Nothing replied. I was very definitely alone.

I turned for the door. This was pointless. There was nothing here. The spirit had gone. And I'd be in more trouble than ever if I got caught here now. But I couldn't leave, not yet. Not until I knew why I'd been brought here.

My candle was fading fast so I parted the curtains to let the moonlight in and looked around me. Nothing had changed since this morning.

Why would it? It hadn't changed for ten whole years.

At the sight of Kit's things, my heart jolted. I'd never get used to them, not if I had to clean this room every day for ever. And there were so many books here, all about fancy things I didn't understand like poetry and history. This was the Kit I didn't know, and it made me sad in a different way. So much of him was still a stranger to me. Once upon a time he'd been a living, breathing boy, who'd rumpled his bed sheets and muddied his boots. It was proper hard to imagine.

The Kit I knew was the boy in the lake. A boy as fine as the stars.

One book lay open. Its pages seemed to glow in the moonlight, and before I could stop myself, I'd picked it up off the table.

It was a sketchbook, filled with little pencil drawings of wings: wings in flight, wings folded, wings outstretched like an angel's. The very final page was all fancy letters in lots of different styles; curly ones, bold ones, like he was practising writing something out: 'To my . . .', then 'dear . . .' and even a 'dearest . . .' It made my heart stir. For I supposed, writing those words, he'd been thinking of his mother, and that there had been a time when the two of them had been proper close. I could so easily imagine Kit sat right here, making something so beautiful. *This* was the boy I knew.

As I put the book back in its place, a shiver passed through me. For Kit wasn't here, was he? The room was empty.

Dead.

Even the spirit hadn't followed me inside. It struck me then there was a reason for it. That I was *meant* to feel this emptiness. Meant to know that Kit's ghost wasn't here. For it certainly had settled lead-heavy inside me. The fire burned on, the books lay open and the bed was turned back ready, and yet all of it was mocking me, saying *this won't bring him back. Nothing will. He's gone for ever.*

And this was the terrible truth that Lady Barrington just couldn't see. Nothing would ever bring Kit back; I doubted even a séance could manage it. Lady Barrington would have to live with her loss. And here I was, with my own father gone and my sister too, beginning to know what that felt like.

25

HOW TO SUMMON
A SPIRIT

Once Lord Barrington had left for his London train the next morning, we got to work like mad things. Dorcas was responsible for Kit's room, since it was here that the séance would take place. She was under strict orders not to touch his things of course, but the room itself needed preparing. For this, Lady Barrington's instructions were endless– *put this chair here, drape this curtain there* –but neither me nor Gracie were trusted to help. So we did the donkey's work of bringing in coals and beating carpets, and placing huge vases of lilies in the hallway.

Gracie was glad not to set foot upstairs; part of me was too. For an uneasy feeling hung over me that Lady Barrington was hoping for too much tonight. Her absolute faith in the séance unnerved me. But I was excited too, and glad to be here to be part of it.

Later that morning, I needed linen from the cupboard and went to ask Dorcas for the key. I hovered in

Kit's doorway, taking in the scene. Though the drapes were drawn shut, the lamps all blazed, making the room unnaturally light. Dorcas was on her knees banking up the fire, even though the room felt too warm already. The mantel mirror was covered with black cloth and a space had been cleared in the middle of the room, where a circle of chairs now stood. The sight of it made me shudder.

'What is it?' said Dorcas, seeing me. She was flushed with heat from the fire.

Before I could answer, a service bell rang somewhere down the hallway. Dorcas tutted irritably and got to her feet.

'Why isn't Mrs Jessop answering it? Have you seen her?'

I hadn't. No one had seen her since breakfast.

Dorcas headed past me for the door. 'What was it you wanted, anyway?'

'The linen cupboard key,' I said.

She shot me a look like she didn't quite believe me. As we stepped out into the corridor, I saw she locked Kit's door behind her.

After I'd got my clean tablecloths, I stopped off in the kitchen for a cup of water. What with the rest of us busy upstairs, Cook was by herself and working flat out by the looks of things.

'Just the girl,' she said, passing me a bucket. 'Her Ladyship wants ice cream tonight. God knows why in this weather.'

'I'm doing the dining room. I can't stop.'

'They won't miss you if you're quick. Just follow the path out of the yard and up to the lake and then . . .'

The lake!

In a flash I said, ''Course I'll do it,' and grabbed the bucket from her.

'Hang on! I in't finished telling you yet!'

Cook said something about trees and doors that were a bit stiff but I was only half listening. I'd been so fixated with Kit's room, I'd forgotten all about the blinking lake, the one place where I knew Kit's ghost would be. My heart beat faster as I headed for the door.

'And put this on or you'll freeze to death out there,' said Cook, handing me an old greatcoat from its peg by the back porch.

*

The lake was set back behind the house, beyond the great yew hedges of the graveyard, and surrounded by copses of birch trees. I turned right out of the court-yard and headed up the path. It looked familiar enough. I'd come this way on Tuesday, when Will and me had been frogmarched to the house. But now I was heading up the path, not down it, and the snow was deeper too, making walking quite hard work. Everything was white, the hedges black and stark against it. And the air was so sharp, it made me cough when I breathed. I was mighty glad of Cook's old coat, though it was ten sizes too big and made me look like a scarecrow. Not that I cared. There wasn't a living soul out here to see me.

Up some steps and the path began to twist and turn through the bushes. Then, quite suddenly, the dark green of the yew trees loomed up ahead like a wall. I didn't think to stop and peer through for a glimpse of Kit's grave. In truth, I didn't have time.

Once I'd passed the yews, the snow thinned a little and the path took me into a copse of bare birches. Not far to the lake now; I could almost see it through the trees.

Kit would've come this way.

I turned up my collar and quickened my pace.

He'd have walked this same path, looked up at these same trees. Was he whistling to himself? Was he thrilled to be out here in the fresh air?

In my head, I could almost see him, head down, striding along with his skates slung over his shoulder. An ache built up in my throat.

He didn't know what he was hurrying towards, that moments later he'd be dead.

I shuddered. It was too awful to bear.

Someone should've stopped him, warned him that it wasn't safe. If only he'd gone riding instead, or got sick and stayed in bed. If only . . .

By now I'd reached the edge of the trees. I passed through the little gate, and caught my breath. The lake spread out before me. Everything looked flat and bleak and strangely silent. This was Kit's last view of the world.

What a place!

Putting the bucket down, I hugged the greatcoat tight against me. A fresh fall of snow covered the ice so it looked smooth and blank like paper. There were no skating tracks, no big black holes, no sign that we'd ever been out here. Five days had passed since then, just five days, and the lake had already forgotten us. Yet Kit was a boy *ten years dead*. No one had forgotten him.

I didn't know what I was hoping for; some sort of

sign, maybe, that he could hear me, that he knew I was nearby. I cupped my hands to my mouth. 'Kit! Kit!'

A startled blackbird swooped from the bushes. The silence returned. Nothing moved. I was the only living thing out here, small and dark and shivering, in the middle of all this white.

'Can you hear me, Kit?'

I hardly expected an answer. I thought of his bed-chamber back inside, with the too-bright lamps and chairs pushed close together. And I pictured her Lady-ship, all expectant, all lit up with love.

Would he come tonight? Would he *really* come? Or like last night, would his spirit choose to wait outside?

I hid my face in my hands and tried to breathe slowly. It was all too close. Too real. I felt sure I'd never get through the rest of the day, never mind the evening. Any scrap of excitement I'd had was gone. Now all I felt was dread.

26

THE ICE HOUSE

The ice house was easy enough to spot. It was on the far side of the lake, set back under another thicket of trees. It looked like a hovel, with grass growing on the roof and a little crooked entrance set below some steps. I made my way over and pulled hard on the door. It wouldn't budge an inch. Another good yank and it flew open with such force I went staggering backwards in the snow. I didn't fancy it closing again, not with me on the wrong side of it, so I set off in search of a stone to prop it open. Just behind the ice house was the remains of an old wall. From it I chose a sizeable chunk of flint and retraced my steps.

A strange feeling came over me then, that I wasn't quite alone.

I turned round. Something dashed between the trees. It was a woman, dressed in black, moving deeper into the woods. Twigs snapped underfoot. A bird shrieked. The woman stumbled and dropped to her knees. She had a shawl over her head and most of her face, and her skirts seemed to be caught in the undergrowth. She tugged hard. Even from where I was stood, I heard the cloth tear as she ripped her skirts free. Standing up again, she glanced over her shoulder like she didn't want to be seen. I ducked behind a tree, heart pounding, and kept absolutely still. Bit by bit, I peeped round the trunk. The woman had disappeared.

With a jolt it came back to me. I'd seen her here before, on Sunday, as I'd waited for my go on the ice. Even now, when I was *meant* to be here, the sight of her still unnerved me. She'd looked like a person up to something. But I fought down the urge to sneak after her, since I'd have Dorcas on my back and Cook too if I didn't get a move on.

Armed with my piece of flint, I propped the icehouse door open and peered inside. It was dank and dark, and as I stepped in it felt even colder than being out in the snow. Just above my head was a brick arched ceiling, underfoot was old wet straw. The passage was proper narrow; I had to stoop down and tuck my elbows right in. I prayed it wasn't far.

Further in, the cold got stronger. I gripped the bucket and felt with my free hand. Ten feet in now and the bricks were slick with ice. Ahead was another arch. I kept going until the floor seemed to stop. As my eyes grew used to the gloom, I saw I was standing on the edge of a wide pit. It was full to the brim with something grey, like slush at the side of a road. I nudged it with my toe. *Ice*. Not the neat white blocks I'd pictured, but a great jumble of the stuff. Someone had left a shovel lying beside it, which I was grateful for since it meant not having to use my bare hands. I scooped what I could into the bucket, pressed it down hard, then put in some more 'til it was full to the brim and mighty heavy to lift.

All done, I turned to go. Up ahead was an oblong of daylight – the doorway! I was glad as anything to see it again, hurrying towards it with the bucket swinging against me. Of a sudden the light disappeared. The darkness was total. I stopped dead, my heart beating faster. For a moment, I wondered if I'd blacked out. But then I put out my hand and felt solid bricks on either side of me.

I was trapped.

I cursed that flipping door and the stupid rock that was meant to keep it open. My heart thumped wildly. I had to get out. I rushed at the door, ready to pound it with all my might. Then, just as suddenly, the doorway appeared again. Only now a figure stood in it, blocking my escape. The person saw me. They gasped and stepped back outside.

I hesitated. The person had gone part way up the steps and stood there, waiting. I inched forwards, seeing only the torn hem of a skirt and a pair of filthy boots.

'Come out of there, for pity's sake.'

I knew that voice. My stomach sank.

I went out into the daylight, blinking nervously. Mrs Jessop looked down at me from the steps.

'I was just getting the ice for Cook,' I said. 'I've been as quick as I could.'

I wondered if she'd been snooping on me. But then I saw how rattled she looked, like I was the last person she'd expected to see.

'You'd better get back,' she said. 'Don't let me keep you.'

Mrs Jessop stepped aside so I could pass. Up close, she was short of breath. Her hair had come loose about her neck, and her frock was splattered in mud. Normally she was so stiff and proper; the sight of her now unnerved me. It was a job not to stare.

All at once I knew.

It was her I'd seen running through the woods,

today *and* last Sunday. And here she was now, holding something tightly balled up in her hand. I thought it might be a handkerchief. But as her fingers tensed, it crackled like paper.

'Tilly,' she said as I sidled past her. 'Don't tell anyone you've seen me out here, will you?'

I coughed uncomfortably, unsure what to say. But I knew my place: she was the housekeeper and I was only a maid.

'Yes, Mrs Jessop . . . I mean no, Mrs Jessop,' I said.

Her eyes looked red and her nose all sore like she'd been crying. A tiny bit of me almost felt sorry for her. It must have shown in my face because she turned right away from me.

'Go on then, go!'

'But Mrs Jessop . . .'

'Just go, will you? For once in your life, child, do as you're told!'

Her voice sounded broken and strange, and it scared me. I raced up the steps and kept going, heading straight for the gate. The bucket thumped hard against my leg. I ran and ran until I was almost through the trees and out the other side and my lungs felt like they were on fire. As the Hall came into view, I slowed to a walk, Mrs Jessop's words still ringing in my ears. She was up to something, all right, and flipping desperate about it. She'd have to be, asking *me* to keep a secret of hers, when just yesterday she'd near got me sacked!

And I remembered Eliza with her White Star advert, how she'd said it was a secret and I wasn't to tell. The memory of it turned hot and sour inside me. There were too many blasted secrets flying around, and I was sick of being asked to keep them.

27

THE BUTCHER'S BOY

Back in the courtyard, I noticed a white horse tethered up to the wall. The sight of it lifted my mood. Because it wasn't just any old nag; this one belonged to the butcher. And right now I quite fancied seeing a friendly face.

'Hullo? That you, Will?' I called out, hopefully.

The horse flicked his ears but no one appeared. The yard was deserted. And then it came back to me, how we'd parted company without even a farewell, and I felt low again.

The back door opened just as I reached it. And there was Will. He was smiling from the tail end of something funny. He actually looked quite pleased to see me.

'Here you are! Cook's been searching all over for you!'

An odd thing happened to my stomach then. It was only a few days since I'd last seen Will, but he looked different: taller, smarter and, actually, I couldn't help but admit it, rather handsome. Suddenly, it was hard to meet his eye.

'What you doing here?' I said.

'Some sort of party tonight, apparently. An extra order for us.'

'Good for you,' I said, and though I'd wanted to be nice, it came out sounding bitter.

'Now don't get tetchy again,' he said.

I put on my best smile. And it wasn't that hard, since he was being all cheery and had clearly forgotten to be cross with me.

'Anyhow, I paid a visit to your ma yesterday,' he said.

My smile vanished. '*Why?*'

'We had some chops going spare. Thought it might help. If you like, I can send something else by next week too.'

'We don't need no charity,' I said.

'Just for a bit, then, 'til you get paid or something.'

I stared at my hands as they gripped the bucket handle so tight the bones showed white through my skin. In truth, I was taken aback by such kindness. I'd not expected it, and I confess I wasn't sure I deserved it. My nose started tingling, and I feared I might cry.

'Thank you, that's good of you,' I said, eventually.

And I began to wonder if I'd got Will just a little bit wrong. He'd snitched on me, all right, made it my fault that we'd got caught at Kit's gravestone, so that Mrs Jessop's eagle eye was never off me for long, even though I worked here now. But perhaps he'd had his reasons. It wasn't a joy being poor and hungry. I'd not wish that on no one. And I knew about loyalty too. There were times when I'd put my pa first just like Will had done with his.

I took a deep breath. 'And was Ma all right?'

'She was hard at the sewing. I didn't stop long.'

'Really? Was she?' The day I'd left, she'd looked so frail and ill, I'd worried she'd never work again. This was glad news indeed!

'Yep. Said she had enough work to keep her busy for a week.'

I was thrilled to hear it. And before I could stop them, the tears sprang up in my eyes. Will didn't poke fun or say something smart: he stood quietly until I'd gathered myself, and though I still didn't trust him completely, I found myself saying, 'Can you spare me five minutes?'

He shrugged, all easy. 'If you like.'

In truth, I was *that* desperate to talk to someone,

and Will knew more of this strange business than anyone. On the far side of the yard was a row of empty stables. I put the bucket down and led him to the nearest one.

'In here.'

I shut the door behind us. The stable was dark and dusty but it hid us from view. Will leaned back against the wall, arms folded like he had all the time in the world.

I took another great breath. 'You said I'd find things out, working here. And I have. Only I can't make sense of it all, so maybe you can help.'

'Try me,' he said.

'Kit's family still in't right from him dying. His ma wears full mourning and his pa can't sleep at night.'

'So they took his death hard. That's not so strange.'

'But they keep his room like it was on the day he died. Even the pillow's still got . . .' I heard the catch in my voice and stopped.

Will touched my arm. 'It's all right. Keep talking.'

'And there's the fire too. It's meant to never go out, only it went out on me, and her Ladyship got into such a state, I swear she turned into a madwoman.'

'Over a fire?'

'Honest to God.'

'Maybe she just misses him. She didn't have any other children, did she? I'd bet they were mighty close.'

'That's probably true,' I said, thinking of the sketchbook I'd seen last night and all those 'dear's and 'dearest's written inside it. 'And this party tonight, well . . .' I hesitated.

'Well, what?'

'It's a séance. But you in't s'posed to know that.'

Will gave a low laugh. 'Oh, my word!'

Now I'd let the secret out, I couldn't stop. 'Her Ladyship's desperate to contact Kit. She's not had a sign from him, not once in ten years.'

Will chewed on his lip and stayed silent.

'Say something, then!' I said.

'Well, it's just that . . .' He looked at me. 'She's seen nothing and yet here you are, meeting his ghost in the lake, getting his ring and having these dreams about him.'

I felt myself go red. 'Yes, I know.'

'You've got to admit it's strange,' Will said. 'I mean, you never knew him nor nothing. So why's this all happening to you?'

I shrugged.

Because he trusts me? Because for once in my life someone thinks I'm brave and capable?

Not that I expected Will to understand.

He frowned. 'So. Let me get this straight – is there a ghost here or not?'

'Yes, there is,' I said, with a shudder. 'Lady Barrington might not sense it, but I sure as anything do. And it's pretty angry at something.'

'Any idea what?'

'Not really. But I'll tell you this, it don't seem to appear in Kit's room, and it in't anything like the boy I dream about.'

'So why would Kit save your life and then turn angry?'

'That's what I need to work out. But I wouldn't mind betting it's to do with her Ladyship. I mean, why hasn't he shown himself to his own mother? It just don't make sense.'

Will narrowed his eyes like he was sizing me up. I wondered if he'd believed a word I'd said. Then ever so gently, he pushed a lock of loose hair over my shoulder. I flinched like he'd slapped me.

'What the heck you doing?'

'You look tired, that's all.' He cocked his head to one side. 'And I've got to ask, why are you wearing that ridiculous coat?'

I glanced down at the tatty old greatcoat. True

enough, it looked worse than ever next to Will's smart grey coat and matching cap. I supposed he always looked that dapper on his delivery rounds, but a mean little voice in my head wondered if he was all done up just to impress Dorcas or Gracie.

'Cook gave it me. I've been to get ice,' I said. And as Will knew so much already, it wouldn't hurt to tell him. 'The housekeeper was up there, acting all strange. She told me not to say I'd seen her.'

'Well, well, well. I wondered when you'd mention her.'

'I try to keep out of her way, but she's always watching me.'

'She's a strange one, all right,' said Will. 'I bet she's got some secrets up her sleeve.'

'She in't all bad,' I said, but in truth I didn't know what to believe. 'Though this séance seems to have rattled her, good and proper. She's been right against it from the start.'

Will grinned. 'What I'd give to be listening at the keyhole tonight!'

But I didn't see much to smile about. The very thought of the séance made my stomach turn. What's more, I'd be flayed alive if I didn't get back inside.

'I'd better go,' I said.

Before we could say any more, Gracie appeared in the doorway.

'What you hiding out here for?' she cried to me. 'We need you back inside. Dorcas is having kittens!'

Then she saw Will.

'Oh!' she flushed. 'Beg pardon.'

I realised how it must've looked – Will and me stood so close that our heads were almost touching. Trust Gracie to get the wrong end of the stick.

I hurried out into the yard to collect my bucket. As I turned to say goodbye to Will, I saw he was talking to Gracie. He'd got back on his horse and she was smiling up at him, twisting a strand of hair around her finger like a simpleton. And I knew the look on Will's face, all right – all dancing eyes and flashing grin. He often looked at me like that.

'Gracie!' I snapped. 'You coming?'

'Sorry!'

She scurried over. I slammed the door behind us.

'He's smashing, that Will Potter is,' sighed Gracie, as we made for the kitchens. 'He in't your sweetheart, is he?'

I stopped in my tracks. 'No he flippin' well is not!'

'All right, just askin',' she said. 'No need to bite my head off.'

I took a deep breath. 'Sorry, Gracie. I'm just a bit on edge today.'

What I didn't say was that seeing her with Will had made me feel a whole lot worse.

28

THE SÉANCE

The first tray of sandwiches went up at seven. Dorcas came back down looking tense and pale.

'The medium's arrived.'

'What's she like?' said Gracie, who was sat by the stove and under strict orders to stay there.

Dorcas pulled a face. 'Vulgar. Calls herself *Madame Martineau* to sound foreign, when everyone knows she's just Mrs Martin from the next village.' She turned to me. 'Take your tray up quick, they're about to start.'

I went upstairs with cake and little silver dishes of ice cream. My hands shook so hard the spoons rattled. It was a wonder I didn't spill the lot.

Jiggling the tray onto my hip, I knocked at Kit's door.

'Enter.' Her Ladyship sounded nervous, high-pitched.

I went in. The room was hot and dark, and as I felt

my way to the nearest side table, I heard the chinking of teacups, and a voice I didn't know.

'Are we all ready?' it said.

'Yes,' said her Ladyship. 'Please leave us, Matilda.'

I could just make out three figures sat together in a circle. Lady Barrington was on the edge of her chair. She wore the brooch on the front of her dress; I doubted that she ever took it off. Next to her had to be the medium, Madame Martineau, dressed in a too-tight bodice and still wearing her hat. In her lap was a little notepad and pencil. The third person was Mrs Jessop. My guts clenched at the sight of her. She didn't look at me. She sat stern and straight with her eyes fixed on the wall.

I went to go. Behind me came a rustling of skirts and the thud of a chair tipping over like someone had stood up too fast. I turned round to see Mrs Jessop on her feet.

'I cannot be a part of this,' she said, wringing her hands. 'Please forgive me, but I cannot stay.'

Lady Barrington hissed, 'Sit down!'

'I cannot.'

'It is an order. Sit down!'

Mrs Jessop breathed in sharply. 'Then it's an order I cannot follow.'

Any second they'd notice me still here. My feet seemed rooted to the spot.

'I need you here, Mrs Jessop,' said Lady Barrington. 'Those silly girls below stairs just wouldn't do. I need someone who will hold her nerve. And you must know what this means to me, you of all people!'

Mrs Jessop stood ramrod straight, though her chin quivered slightly. 'Indeed I do, your Ladyship, and for that reason I cannot stay. Good evening to you.'

She bobbed her head and swept past me for the door.

'Let her go,' said Madame Martineau, patting Lady Barrington's arm. 'If she's not willing, it'll upset the circle. The spirits only come to those who believe.'

'But there's only two of us now. You said we needed at least three.'

Madame Martineau motioned to me. 'Come forward, there's a good girl. You can be our third.'

I didn't think I'd heard right.

'Well come on, then! Quickly!'

She meant me. *Me!*

I felt sick and uneasy. But what could I do? I put down my tray and stumbled forwards. Lady Barrington rolled her eyes. Here I was, a silly girl from the kitchens, but it seemed she had no choice. I picked up the fallen chair and placed it back in the circle. My knees were shaking now; I was glad to sit down.

'You aren't a giddy girl, are you?' said Madame Martineau to me.

'No ma'am.'

'And do you believe in the spirit world?'

I swallowed. 'I do, ma'am. And I sense spirits here in this house.'

'Then you are a welcome addition to our little circle,' said Madame Martineau, smiling. 'Now, take the hand to your left.'

Lady Barrington snatched up my hand and gripped it tight. I squirmed, thinking how rough it must feel to her.

'And now the hand to your right.'

Madame Martineau's palm was sticky and warm. As I took hold, she jerked in her seat. 'You're a live wire, aren't you?' she cried. 'The spirits are drawn to you, I can tell.'

Lady Barrington looked at me then, like she'd seen me for the very first time. I was glad when Madame Martineau instructed us to shut our eyes.

She cleared her throat, took a long breath through her nose. 'Our purpose tonight is to contact Kit, most beloved son of Lady Barrington,' she said, her voice silky like she was soothing a wayward horse. 'This must be our one and only thought. If our minds wander, it will divide the circle and the spirits won't feel wanted. What's more, we must be patient. No grasping or fawning or forcing the spirits to come.'

Lady Barrington's hand twitched in mine. The room fell silent. I sat still, head bowed, listening to the blood pounding in my ears.

Would Kit really come to us?

Last night the spirit had left me all alone in this sad, sad room. I still couldn't shake off the emptiness I'd felt here; I only hoped the ghost was listening now.

No one spoke. The fire crackled in the grate. Nothing was happening. After a while, my mind began to wander. I had an itch on my leg and was dying to scratch it. I could smell the food on the table behind me. Somewhere outside, a fox barked.

Of a sudden a coldness seized me. I started to shake. The hands holding mine gripped tightly. My eyes flew open. Her Ladyship was looking about her nervously.

'Gently now,' said the medium. Her head was tipped back, her eyes still shut. She seemed to be speaking to the spirit. 'You've come far to be with us and we've waited a long while. Take your time.'

The hairs on my arms lifted and my heartbeat

quickened. Yet mixed with my fear was a kind of relief. For tonight, something was different. The spirit wasn't waiting outside the door. This time it was here inside the room.

Madame Martineau's fingers felt ice-cold. She fell back in her seat with a gasp. When she spoke, her voice was strange, all high-pitched, like a girl's. 'Have you come to play?'

The drapes at the window began to sway.

'Then play nicely with us, there's a good . . .'

On the table behind me, the china rattled. I began to feel sick. Lady Barrington's mouth fell open. She stared in horror at something above my head. I turned slowly in my seat, dreading what I'd see. Nothing looked amiss on the table. I glanced upwards.

And froze.

Floating inches above my head was a cup. A *cup*! So close, I saw the maker's stamp on the base of it. Could reach out and touch it. Make it stop. But my arms were heavy. They wouldn't move. I stared and stared, transfixed.

I was dimly aware of Lady Barrington, gasping and sighing in her seat. And the medium's queer girlish voice, saying, 'Listen to the spirit, Tilly. Ask what it wants.'

I blinked. Swallowed hard. 'Spirit,' I said. 'Why are you here tonight?'

The cup seemed to quiver. I held my breath. Then, like some fairground trick, it whizzed over our heads, smashing to pieces in the hearth. The fire hissed and spat. The room fell silent again. It was an eerie, dangerous sort of quiet. Lady Barrington started to weep. My mouth turned dry as the fear in me grew.

'We bring you love, child,' said Madame Martineau. 'Please hear us.'

But the spirit wouldn't reply. An icy draught blew around us, making the lamps flicker and sigh. We'd all dropped hands by now. Her Ladyship's face was deathly pale and streaked with tears. My own heart beat so fast, I feared I'd faint.

Madame Martineau swayed in her chair. 'Do you have a message?'

Silence.

Lady Barrington cried, 'Anything! A sign! A word!'

Madame Martineau's eyes snapped open. She seized her Ladyship's arm. 'Hush now, please. You'll frighten it away.'

Once again, the room fell silent. Lady Barrington sat still, though her earrings trembled against her neck. I gripped the sides of my chair and waited.

Nothing.

The medium leaned towards me. 'Perhaps you should try, dearie.'

Lady Barrington looked bewildered. 'But you said ...'

Madame Martineau gave a solemn shake of the head and indicated me. I sat forward in my seat. It had to be worth a try.

'Please, spirit,' I said, steady as I could. 'Do you have something to tell us?'

For I was beginning to realise. Last night's empty room had been a message for me. Tonight the spirit had another person in its sights.

Madame Martineau had picked up her pencil, her notepad now open on a blank page. She was poised, ready.

All was still.

'Try again, Tilly,' she said. 'I sense it is listening.'

'Do you have a message for one of us?'

I'd barely finished speaking when a strange tapping sound started. It came from over by Kit's bed. The taps were slow and steady, like a ball bouncing, and seemed to inch forwards towards our circle. I fell back in my seat, snatching my feet up from the floor. Her Ladyship twisted round to face the noise. It stopped at her chair. She breathed sharply and turned her huge eyes on Madame Martineau.

'It's me, isn't it? It wants me.'

Madame Martineau nodded. 'The spirit has a message for you.'

And her Ladyship seemed so full of joy, I could hardly bear to look.

'Oh my darling boy, it's you!' she breathed. 'At last!'

But Madame Martineau was frowning and shaking her head. The air felt charged with spite.

How could this be Kit? Dear, sweet Kit?

My head spun with dreadful thoughts.

What if he harmed us? What if he wanted some sort of revenge?

The tapping started again, moving away from Lady Barrington towards the table full of Kit's books. This time the noise was faster, urgent. I hardly dared breathe. Just as it had started, the tapping stopped. The quiet was thick. No one moved. Our eyes fixed on that table. We waited. Nothing seemed to be happening. Then, ever so slowly, one of the books began to move. Only the pages fluttered, first one way, then the other, like they were caught in a breeze. I knew which book it was, all right. Even from my seat, I could see the angel drawings and the page of fancy lettering at the end: 'To my dear ... To my dearest ...'

It was a job not to gasp out loud.

Kit's message! To his own dear mother!

Unsteadily, Lady Barrington got to her feet and made her way to the table. The lamps flickered. She reached out, and as her hand hovered over the fluttering book, its pages stilled. Fingers shaking she began to turn each one, with agonising slowness at first then faster as her face lit up. I was mesmerised. My own heart stirred.

A message to his mother. At last.

But as her Ladyship reached the final page, her hand flew to her mouth. She turned to us. Her look now was one of absolute horror.

'What is it?' I cried. 'What's wrong?'

Lady Barrington touched her forehead. She looked about to swoon. Then she summoned strength enough to take the few steps to Kit's bed. I expected her to collapse onto it. Instead, she crouched down before the little bedside cupboard.

Madame Martineau cried, 'No!'

I felt it too. A jolt ran right through me.

Lady Barrington didn't seem to hear us, or if she did, she didn't respond. She opened the cupboard and pulled a drawer halfway out. For a moment, she swayed. She put out a hand to steady herself. Then she took something from the drawer. At first, I couldn't quite see what it was. But as she stood upright again, she held it before her. The object was flat, the size of a tea tray, and wrapped in brown paper and string. Her Ladyship stared at it like it was poison.

Madame Martineau slumped in her seat, exhausted. One by one, the lights brightened, and the air in the room grew warmer. It was Kit's bedchamber again; a strange, sad place, but nothing more. My racing heart began to slow.

The spirit had left us.

Madame Martineau blinked like a person waking from a long sleep, then wrote something down in her notebook. Once finished, she squinted at the page and drew a long breath.

'Good girl,' she said to me. 'The spirits respond well to you.'

Then she called to Lady Barrington, 'Please join us. Our visitor from the Other Side has revealed its name.'

'Oh?' Her Ladyship didn't seem to be listening. She was turning the package over and over in her hands.

'Yes, it's a short name – three letters, in fact.'

My chest went tight.

Her Ladyship dropped the package and flew across the room. She snatched up the notebook, eyes flitting across the page. Her mouth fell open. Again that look of utter horror. She flung the pad back at Madame Martineau.

'What is the meaning of this? Do you wish to torture me?'

'No,' said Madame Martineau, uneasily. 'It's what the spirit told me to write.'

'Is that so?'

'Why yes. You saw yourself. The spirit isn't happy and it wanted to tell you. And I think it wanted Tilly to know too.'

Lady Barrington stared at me. '*You*? What on earth . . .'

'Please,' I said, 'let me see the writing.'

Her Ladyship gave a wild laugh. But Madame Martineau passed me the notepad and pointed to the word. Though her writing was faint and shaky, the letters were clear. The name wasn't Kit.

It was Ada.

29

AN UNPLEASANT TASK

Madame Martineau watched me like a cat at a mouse-hole. I felt the flush spread across my cheeks.

'Well, dearie, does it mean anything to you?'

Yes, you daft woman, I thought to myself, *it means everything!*

For of course this bad spirit wasn't Kit Barrington! How could I ever have thought it? He'd saved my life. He wanted my help. He'd never do harm to me.

Though the relief didn't last. With a sinking feeling, I remembered last night's dream and how the ice had seemed so close to breaking. Yet Kit still couldn't be free of it. He couldn't rest in peace. This wasn't finished; the truth still had to be revealed.

'I don't know no one called Ada,' I said, which was a sort of lie since I'd encountered her spirit more times than I'd cared to. And on my upper arm, I still bore the bruises to prove it. I reckoned Madame Martineau guessed this; for a moment more her gaze lingered on me.

Then Lady Barrington said sharply, 'Don't pretend you haven't heard the stories. I know what goes on below stairs – all that gossip late into the night.'

'No, your Ladyship, I swear. I in't never heard this name before.'

'… Young girls like you, with your heads full of nonsense.'

'Your Ladyship, please,' said Madame Martineau. 'Tilly has a way with the spirits. Ada didn't want to communicate much with me. It was you two she was drawn to. It might be worth listening to Tilly.'

But I'd nothing to say. I trembled still. All I wanted was a moment to myself to let everything sink in.

I got to my feet. 'May I be excused, please?'

Lady Barrington fixed me with a glittering stare. 'It's you, isn't it? *You* did this.'

'Pardon, m'lady?'

Then she turned to the medium, who was nervously rearranging her hat. 'You're to blame too. You sent Mrs Jessop away, and put this trollop in her place. No wonder it didn't work.'

'But your Ladyship, I can't call spirits that don't want to come,' she said.

'He's my only son! Of course he'd want to come!'

I felt truly awful.

Because Kit hadn't come, had he? Just like he'd not come to her for the last ten years.

'But Ada came, at least,' said Madame Martineau.

'Blast Ada! Blast the lot of you!'

The room fell silent.

Madame Martineau went red in the face. 'Well! I don't expect to be spoken to like this, lady or no lady!' she said, and started to gather her things.

A bit of foul talk didn't bother me. It was the name Ada that I couldn't shake off. And like a lamp being lit inside my head, I realised I *did* know it from somewhere. It was a name I'd seen – here, at the Hall. No surname, just 'Ada'. Even thinking on it made me go cold.

I knew exactly where I'd seen it. That day I'd come to see Kit's grave, it was Ada's I'd found first. I could picture it now, clear as if I was stood before it – that little rusted headstone poking up through the snow, the words 'TAKEN TOO SOON' carved into it.

I felt a lump in my throat. Just last night her spirit had led me here to this room.

This very room. Kit's room . . .

My thoughts took a strange turn.

'Might I say something?' I said, heart thumping.

Her Ladyship didn't look up. She'd picked up the package again, but seemed to have no intention of opening it, holding it from her at arm's length like it was about to explode.

Madame Martineau urged me on. 'Go ahead, dearie.'

I took a deep breath. 'Did Ada ever know Kit?'

Her Ladyship's face went red, then white. She laid a hand on her chest and swayed like she might faint. As I went to help her, she flinched. 'Stay away from me!'

'But she might be trying to tell us something . . .'

'I'm warning you! Stay back!'

I stopped. 'I'm sorry, your Ladyship. I didn't mean to upset you.'

'It's too late for that,' she cried. 'Now get back downstairs and out of my sight!'

'I'll send up Dorcas,' I said, and rushed for the door. Madame Martineau was right behind me.

*

Once I'd shown Madame Martineau out, I took a moment to get myself straight. The passage below stairs was quiet and dark and I was glad of it, since my head was fit to burst with all that had happened, and

I hardly knew what to think. One thought shouted loud above the others.

Kit and Ada.

There was a link between them. I was certain of it. Her Ladyship had got in a lather at just the mention of their names. And what the heck had been inside that package? It seemed to be connected to Kit's sketchbook, and the writing on the last page. One look at all those fancy 'to my dearest's and Lady Barrington had gone straight over to the drawer.

My mind spun off in all directions then, searching out the things I still didn't grasp. But my thoughts came back all jumbled up and silly. I was too flipping tired to even think right. I reckoned it was time for bed.

I headed back to the kitchens, hoping to make myself a quick cup of tea. Dorcas was talking with Mr Phelps in the doorway. They looked up when they saw me. She mouthed the word 'Sorry,' then slipped away. Mr Phelps stepped forward, blocking my path.

'Ah, Matilda,' he said, sternly. 'Since we cannot locate Mrs Jessop, this unpleasant task falls to me. Step into my pantry please.'

'Am I in trouble?'

The tilt of his head seemed to say so. My heart sank like a stone. Tonight had been my last chance to prove myself as a housemaid. In that sense, things hadn't gone well. I followed him into his room. He shut the door behind us. He stayed standing and didn't pull up a chair for me.

'Yes, I'm afraid you are in trouble,' Mr Phelps said, looking at a place somewhere near my chin. 'There has been some sort of . . . commotion . . . upstairs this evening.'

I felt myself go red. 'Please, sir, if I could just . . .'

'It is not our place to comment on such proceedings,' he said, cutting me short. 'However, Matilda, it seems that since your arrival in this house there has been much talk of spirits and the like.'

'I didn't start it! They was all full of it when I got here!'

'Which', he continued, 'is unsettling to the other staff, and deeply unsettling to Lord and Lady Barrington.'

'But that in't my fault!' I said. 'I in't the one keeping a fire lit all day and night!'

'Hold your tongue, young lady!'

I bit my lip. What else I had to say would keep.

'Her Ladyship insists that you leave . . .'

Of course it had been coming. Still, it felt like a punch to the guts. And I didn't want to cry in front of him, so I fixed my eyes on the floor.

'. . . tonight.'

My temper flared. 'Now hang on a minute! That in't fair! I was trying to help her Ladyship, really I was.'

'I hardly see how.'

'But it was her idea. She wanted to contact Kit. And I weren't even meant to be part of it!'

Mr Phelps held up his hand. 'Enough!'

I started to panic. 'But sir, please, I'll do anything! Wash dishes, iron clothes. *Anything!*'

In my mind, I saw our landlord's leering face, and Ma all frail and low. Without me earning a fair wage, we'd be out in the streets within days. And then there was Kit; I couldn't leave now, not when Ada's spirit had been trying to tell us something. Just a bit longer here at Frost Hollow Hall, and I reckoned I'd uncover the truth.

But Mr Phelps was already signalling that I should take off my cap and pinny. 'Go upstairs and collect your things. You can return the rest of your uniform to Dorcas.'

'So you really are chucking me out? At night?'

He nodded gravely. 'Her Ladyship wishes it so. There's nothing more to say on the matter. We'll see you have a light to guide you home.'

30

SNOW-BLIND

Mr Phelps didn't mention the snow. By the time I'd changed back into my own clothes, it was coming down thick and fast outside, though I was too wretched to care. At the back door, Cook took her old greatcoat down off its peg and wrapped me in it.

'It in't right,' she kept saying. 'They should at least let you wait 'til morning.'

What did it matter? What did any of it matter now?

'I knew this séance would be trouble,' said Dorcas, and turned to Gracie. 'Come on, say your goodbyes.'

Gracie hung back, upset.

'You'll be all right, you'll see,' I said to her, mustering what cheer I could. Yet my voice sounded flat and hollow and when I hugged her, she cried all the more.

Eventually, Dorcas pulled us apart. 'Sleep in with me tonight, Gracie. Mrs Jessop's gone off goodness knows where, so no one will mind.'

Out in the yard, there was already an inch or two of fresh snow.

'Go straight home,' said Dorcas. 'And keep to the driveway, else you'll get lost.'

I hardly cared where I was headed. What was there to go back to? I felt lost enough already.

'Well, take care.' Dorcas started to close the door.

I stuck my foot out to stop her. 'Before I go, tell me, what d'you know about Ada?'

'*Ada?* Why you asking that?' she said, startled.

'Just tell me. Quick!'

Dorcas glanced nervously over her shoulder and dropped her voice. 'She was Mrs Jessop's girl.'

'Her *daughter*?'

'No one talks of it now,' she said. 'We haven't done for years. Mr Phelps says we're not to since it caused so much upset at the time. You see, Ada got sick and . . .'

Mr Phelps called from inside, 'Shut that door and bolt it.'

'What on earth went on upstairs tonight, Tilly?' Dorcas hissed.

I went to speak but Mr Phelps's voice cut in. 'Hurry up! And make sure Matilda has a lamp.'

'He can stuff his lamp!' I said, hitching up my skirts. 'Thanks, Dorcas. So long.'

I set off out the courtyard. My head was reeling.

Mrs Jessop had a daughter?

Something Cook had said came back to me, that I looked like someone dear to Mrs Jessop, someone who'd died.

Ada.

The very idea made me shudder. I walked faster 'til my head began to clear. Never mind what Cook said; maybe she needed spectacles, or wasn't thinking straight, or just happened to be sharing a bit of gossip. I couldn't worry about that.

What mattered was Kit and Ada. There were two spirits here at Frost Hollow Hall, and they'd both contacted me.

Two dead children and two grieving mothers.

This was the link between Kit and Ada, or part of it, at least.

As ghosts they were worlds apart. Ada seemed to haunt the back stairs and kitchens mostly, whereas Kit had appeared to me in the lake. And then there were my dreams of holding Kit's cold hands, and his dear face pleading for help. Not Ada. There was nothing dreamy or gentle about her. She was angry and spiteful. As if she was out for revenge.

Whatever connected the pair of them, this Ada person had me gripped. There was so much I didn't know about her: *how did she die? What did she look like? What did she mean to Kit?* Heck, I hardly knew where to start.

And it seemed Ada was fixed on me too. Every night I'd been at the Hall, she'd done something to get my attention. And now she most definitely had it.

Yet it did nothing to improve my mood. If anything, I felt more crushed than ever. Here I was, leaving the Hall so full of questions and with only half the cursed answers.

And it wasn't even my fault!

I set off across the park at a right pace, kicking at the snow and cussing 'til my throat felt raw. What did I care? No one would hear me now.

I went on kicking and cussing for quite a while. But eventually my temper cooled and I saw that I'd covered a fair bit of ground. Snow clung to my skirts, and my legs ached like mad. Behind me, I could just make out the faint lights of the Hall. Up ahead was all dark. There were no paths to follow; I was miles from the driveway. Each way I turned looked exactly the same.

The sweat under my clothes cooled quickly. I started to shiver. It was snowing faster now, in hard little grains that stung my cheeks and caught in my hair. The wind had got up too.

Which way?

I set off with the wind in my back. As I walked, the snow began to play tricks on me. It seemed the ground glowed with light and the darkness was not quite black. I felt dizzy just from looking at it.

Eventually, I stopped to get my bearings. Footprints – my footprints – lay before me, going this way and that like ants. My spirits sank in a trice. *Oh no! Oh heck, no!* I'd been walking in a circle, hadn't I? I'd passed this way before.

Cursing didn't help. Up ahead, I could just make out a dark sort of shape. It might have been a house, or a hedge or a gate onto the road. There was nothing to do but to aim for it. Bunching up my skirts, I set off. In places, the snow had drifted knee deep; it was like wading through mud, and it tired me quickly now, so I had to keep stopping to rest. The dark shape I'd been aiming for seemed to have vanished. I'd got colder too and felt very low. And once the bad thoughts started, they wouldn't stop.

You've let Kit down. You've let Ma down. You can't do nothing right. No wonder Pa took off without you.

Round and round they went in my head. I kept going, one boot in front of the other.

The snow looked as white as sheets on a bed. My eyelids grew heavy. All I wanted was to sleep. I sank to my knees. Really, it wasn't even cold any more; I'd stopped shivering completely. I scooped up the snow into a little pillow and lay back against it.

Tiny snowflakes tickled my face. I stuck my tongue out to catch them and watched as the sleeves of Cook's coat turned white. Blimey, I was warm. Too warm for this greatcoat. I took it off and spread it out, then lay back down and shut my eyes. Just a minute or two's rest would do.

Gently, deliciously, I began to drift off. I imagined I was lying in bed at home with the window wide open. But somewhere out in the lane a dog was barking, and the blasted thing wouldn't stop. And then a person started calling the same name over and over again, getting closer 'til they seemed to be right under my window. I wished they'd just clear off and let me sleep.

The noises were lost in a gust of wind. I opened my eyes and looked about me. There was no dog, no person calling; all I saw was endless, swirling snow. Yet I didn't feel alone.

'Kit?' I said, out loud. 'It's you, in't it?'

The dead don't always answer: I knew that now.

He was here. It was him. The air said so. The snow kept falling and the night got darker. I hoped it might never be morning so it could be like this for ever.

DREAMING: 6

Everything feels light. Kit and me, we're drifting above the trees and fields. We're free of the lake at last. It should feel right but it doesn't quite. Not yet. Being this high up makes me giddy as if I've risen too high too quick. Kit looks startled too. The snow has cleared, and now the stars are out. The cold is blade-sharp.

Spread below us is someone's old coat. On top of it, all curled up, lies a girl with wild dark hair. Her eyes are shut. She seems to be sleeping; I can't quite be sure. Something twists in my chest and I realise I'm looking down on myself. I know this feeling – last time it happened I nearly died. Only now I'm too light-headed to care.

Who'd miss me if I did die?

The answer comes so fast it takes my breath away.

Ma. It would kill her. I'm all she's got left.

I gaze down at the girl, and out the corner of my eye, I see a movement. A dark shape is striding towards her, the lantern he holds casting light across the snow. The person looks familiar.

Will!

He's found me, and I know I should be glad, but in truth I'm torn.

'You can't hold on for ever,' Kit says. 'You have to let go.'

He's so close I can see the colour of his eyes, the shades of blue all mixed up together. The pain in them is fading. He looks tired, ready to sleep at long last. Not yet, though. Not yet.

'The truth is very near now,' says Kit. 'Go back for it.'

The most beautiful smile lights up his face. Just for a moment it dazzles me. He begins to move away from me. I try to hold onto his hand but it's impossible; his fingers are as slippery as ice. And though my heart feels fit to break, I know what this means; I can't stay here. It's not my time. The truth is out there. To find it, I must leave Kit behind.

31

A LIGHT TO GUIDE ME

I grew aware of a hand touching my face. I opened my eyes to see Will crouched in the snow beside me, patting my cheeks.

'Slap me again and I'll kick you,' I hissed.

'Looks like *you* aren't dead, after all,' Will said. But there was no mistaking the relief in his face, and it made me suddenly fearful. Clearly I'd come very close to not waking up at all.

The snow had stopped falling but it was colder than ever, and I felt chilled to the bone. Struggling to sit up, I started to shake. I tried to put the coat back on, but my limbs were so stiff and heavy, I couldn't even get my arms into the sleeves.

Will went to help me.

'I can manage, ta very much,' I said, though it was obvious I couldn't. For I was shaking so hard now I could barely see straight, let alone put a flipping coat on.

'For God's sake, Tilly!' said Will. 'Stop acting like a baby!'

He pulled me to my feet. And before I knew it, he'd wrapped his arms so tight around me I could barely breathe. Cursing loudly, I struggled to get out of his grasp. But it was no good. He held me fast against him, my face pressed into his jacket, so I had no choice but to breathe in his smell of earth and cold air. I was too weak to fight him any more.

The heat from Will began to warm me, making my hands and feet tingle until they hurt. I leaned into him and his arms shifted, so he was holding me gently now, his chin resting on the top of my head. And though it surprised me to feel it, I was very glad indeed that he was there.

'Thank you,' I mumbled into his jacket, like I was testing out the words.

'Did you say something?'

'Thank you,' I said, louder.

He stepped back so we weren't touching any more. I saw he was smiling. And it was, in fact, a rather nice smile, not his usual stupid grin.

'Come on,' he said, gesturing over his shoulder. 'Let's get you inside.'

For that dark shape that I'd seen up ahead had indeed been a house – Will's house at the edge of the village. I'd no idea I'd come so far off course. It looked smaller than I'd remembered it, and scruffier too. As we entered the yard, a great hairy dog set off barking and whining at the end of its chain.

'It was Barney who heard you,' said Will, meaning the dog, who was now wagging his tail in delight. 'He woke me up with his hollering. Good job too, as it happens.'

We went through a door and into a warm kitchen that smelled nicely of baking. The only light came from the embers of a fire. My legs sagged beneath me, and I reached for a chair.

Will took hold of my elbow. 'No sitting down yet. You've to warm up slowly,' he said, and bid me walk about the kitchen 'til my fingers and toes had stopped hurting.

I groaned. 'Just hope your ma and pa don't hear us.'

'Don't fret. They'd sleep through an earthquake.'

In the time it took for me to thaw out, Will had stoked the fire and set two chairs at the hearth. He'd tried to heat some milk up too but managed to scald it in the pan. Even so, I drank it greedily, glad of how it warmed me inside.

'Now,' Will said, letting me sit down at last. 'You'd

better tell me what the heck's happened.'

So I told him about Madame Martineau, the brown paper parcel, and the spirit revealing itself as Ada, though even to my ears it sounded unreal. And when I'd finished, Will said, 'And now you've been kicked out, right?'

'Don't remind me.' I felt hopeless enough already. 'I knew this séance wouldn't work. Kit was never going to show himself. But Lady Barrington just wouldn't listen.'

'That's hardly surprising, is it? It is all so . . . well . . . *unlikely*.'

'You still don't believe me, do you? You think I'm mad.'

He ran a hand through his hair. 'The thing is,' he said, looking almost nervous, 'I *do* think about you, quite a lot as it happens.'

I stared at him. 'Don't be daft.'

He was joking of course. *Wasn't he?* This blasted fire was too hot of a sudden, and I felt myself flush.

'What I mean is,' Will said, hurriedly, 'all this stuff about the Hall and Kit Barrington. My head's full of it. I was wrong to doubt you.'

'Oh.'

A stiff silence followed. We seemed not quite able

to meet each other's eye.

Then Will got to his feet. 'You need some sleep.'

He found me an old blanket that smelled strongly of wood smoke. I wrapped myself in it and quickly felt my eyes grow heavy. Soon I was fast asleep.

*

Some time later, I woke with a start. I knew at once what I had to do. *Go back for it*, Kit had said. It was simple. There was one place where I'd find out about Ada. And sitting here wouldn't get it done. The clock on the mantel said quarter to three. If I went now, I'd just have time; Dorcas didn't rise until five.

Unsteadily, I got to my feet. Will was still asleep in his chair. Tiptoeing past him, I held my breath. Luckily, there wasn't a key in the door. I turned the handle. The door inched open.

'Where you off to?' said a sudden voice behind me. *Drat!*

I shut the door again.

'Nowhere,' I lied, not turning round. 'Go back to sleep, Will.'

But he didn't sound remotely sleepy. 'Not with you

prowling about. Come on, out with it. What you up to?'

I faced him. He might as well hear it.

'I'm going back to the Hall,' I said.

Will's mouth fell open. 'Are you *completely* loopy?'

'Probably,' I shrugged. 'But I've got to do it. If Mrs Jessop's not around still, then this is my chance.'

'For what, exactly?'

'To find out all I can about Ada.'

'But it's the middle of the night!'

I wished he was still asleep. He was beginning to get on my nerves.

'Will,' I said, patient as I could, 'Mrs Jessop's got these books. She makes notes in them, on everything right down to the last broken teacup. There's shelves full of the blinking things in her office but no one's allowed to read them. They go right back to the time when Kit was alive.'

'And Ada,' said Will, latching on.

'Precisely. Surely Mrs Jessop would've have written something down about her own daughter. Especially if it all ended so strangely.'

I glanced at the clock. Time to be gone.

'When I left tonight, Mrs Jessop had taken off somewhere. I'm praying she's still not back, because

this is my chance. I'd never get near them books otherwise.'

'What if you get caught?'

It was a risk, all right. Twice I'd been caught trespassing, *and* I'd just got sacked from my job. There'd
be no welcome for me back at Frost Hollow Hall; this
time they'd be calling the magistrate. I felt sick at the
thought. But I couldn't help myself, not now the idea
had taken hold.

Will made a sudden lunge for the door.

'Don't try to stop me!' I hissed, barring his way.

'You can't go back there!'

'I have to! There's a link between Kit and Ada. And
I bet you there's proof of it in those notebooks.'

'But . . .'

'I *have* to know what happened, once and for all.
Otherwise Kit will never be at peace.'

'They might arrest you, though.'

'Or', I said, 'I might make Kit Barrington happy at
last.'

In my mind, it was well worth the risk.

'Got a key to let yourself back in, then?' said
Will.

My heart sank. 'No.'

'I can hoist you up through a window. And if she's

locked her office, I can pick a lock quick enough. What d'you say?'

'*You?*'

It hadn't occurred to me that he'd want to come too, not after last time when Mrs Jessop had threatened to tell his pa.

'Yes, why not?'

Heck, I hardly knew where to start. But in truth, I'd be dead in the snow if it wasn't for Will Potter. It was one more thing I owed him for. Maybe it was time to start trusting him.

'All right,' I said, slowly. 'But this in't no dare and we're in it together.'

'I know that,' he said. 'This is for real.'

He looked pleased as punch, and though I didn't expect it, I was too. It felt good to have someone by my side.

*

Will knew his way better than I did. We ducked under a fence, then followed a hedge all the way through the parkland until we found ourselves back at Frost Hollow Hall. The house was silent. The windows were shuttered and dark, and thin trails of smoke from the chimneys told us the fires had died down for the night. I headed for the back door. Mr Phelps had ordered Dorcas to bolt it, and true to his word it held fast against my shoulder.

Will pointed to a small window high above the kitchens. 'Reckon you could get through there with a leg-up?'

'I'll give it a go.'

Quick as a flash, Will had hold of my leg. Never mind good manners. He counted to three then swung me upwards. I grabbed at the guttering. Gripped on tight. Then I heaved myself onto the roof. Once up here, it was a job to stand upright. The drop made me dizzy and the tiles were slippery as anything, and the blasted window catch was stuck fast.

'Hurry up!' Will hissed from below.

'I'm doing me best!'

A sharp shove and the window swung open, wafting warm air up into my face. I peered into the kitchens. It was gloomy down there. A couple of gas jets still flickered on the wall, so I could just make out that right beneath me was the kitchen table, piled high with clean pots and pans. It was a good ten-foot drop down. I'd have to shut my eyes and pray.

'All right?' called Will, softly.

'Yes. Come on up.'

He scaled the wall with ease and picked his way neatly over the roof to crouch beside me.

'Wish on a star for luck,' he said, pointing at the sky.

I swallowed. *Oh blimey, do I have to?* I'd sworn I wouldn't, not since that awful night when Pa and Eliza had first gone. But right now I needed all the luck in the world. So I fixed on the brightest, biggest star, and on making my wish, I felt my courage rise.

'Right,' said Will. 'You ready?'

I nodded. Swinging my legs round, I sat right on the edge of the window, feet dangling into the kitchen below. My heart began to race.

'Aim to your left. And try not to land on nothing,' said Will.

I squeezed my eyes tight shut.

'One . . . two . . .'

He didn't get to three. I pushed off with my hands. And I fell for what felt like for ever.

32

ALL ABOUT ADA

The ground rushed up to meet me. My legs buckled and I slammed hard into the table, sending pots and pans clattering to the floor. I landed in a heap amongst them. The din seemed to go on and on.

I've blown it, I thought. *That's it. I'm done for.*

Will landed neat as a cat beside me.

'Great start!' he hissed.

'At least I'm in one piece, thanks for asking,' I muttered, and sat up.

We both froze. Out in the corridor came the sound of footsteps, then voices . . . two voices.

'Oh heck,' said Will. 'Here they come.'

I grabbed his sleeve. 'Don't just stand there!'

We squatted down behind the table. It hardly shielded us at all, but seemed a better option than just handing ourselves over. The door edged open. A candle appeared, then someone gasped sharply. I bit my lip. Any second now we'd be spotted. Instead, to my great relief, the door closed again. And out in the passage, I heard Dorcas's voice. 'It was nothing. Finish your drink now, Gracie and we'll go back to bed.'

She clearly thought this mess was Ada's work, and didn't want to upset Gracie further.

I gave it another few minutes, just enough for the house to fall quiet again and for my heartbeat to slow.

'Ready?' I whispered to Will. He nodded.

I found us a candle stub, and once I'd got the thing alight, steadied myself with a deep breath.

'Right,' I said. 'Follow me.'

Out in the passageway, the darkness closed in on us. No sign of Gracie or Dorcas. The air was colder too, and it was deathly quiet. A shiver ran down my back. We went through the glass doors towards Mrs Jessop's office. The candle gave off little light, but I could see the walls at least, and then up some stone steps to a door. We stopped in front of it. My heart thumped hard against my ribs.

'This is it,' I whispered.

'Step aside then,' said Will. 'And hold that candle close.'

He tested the door to see if it was locked.

'Of course it's locked!' I hissed. 'She's got the

biggest bunch of keys in England. She'd lock *you* up if she could!'

'Thinking like that don't help. Now, if you don't mind . . .'

'Sorry.'

Crouching low at the door, he slid his knife in the lock and jiggled it for what seemed like an age. My arm began to ache from holding up the light.

'You done yet?'

'Nah,' Will said. 'It don't want to budge.'

I tutted irritably. Hadn't he bragged that he could pick a lock? Wasn't that why he was here?

Then he turned his wrist sharply. The lock clicked. Easy as pie the door swung open.

The room was much as I remembered it – clean and orderly and full of notebooks. But this time the lamp was unlit, the grate full of cold ashes. I put down the candle and looked about me. I saw that the desk had drawers. Each one had a lock. But the brass clock on the wall showed it was already nearly quarter past four, so we'd have to get a shift on. The maids would be up at five.

'I'll start with the books,' I said to Will. 'You get those drawers open.'

The notebooks were in date order, one for each

month, their spines all level on the shelf. I counted backwards 'til I got to 1871, the year Kit died. Ten more books and there it was. My throat went tight: 'February 1871'. But this particular book wasn't lined up neat like the others; it was set right back on the shelf. I slid it out, dreading what I might read inside.

Heart in mouth, I opened the book. Page after page was filled with tiny writing. I couldn't make head nor tail of it, so I held it near the candle for a better look. My heart sank. It was all just details of meals and chores and who'd done what. Then I noticed other things written round the edge of each page. They seemed to be little thoughts, *Mrs Jessop's thoughts*.

I shuddered. It didn't seem right to read her private words. It felt uncomfortable, like she was right here in the room with her cold eyes on me. Now wasn't the time to get squeamish. I took a breath and read on.

The first entry was for Thursday February 2nd:

Milk late again.

I skipped forward to Friday February 3rd:

Still no milk. Jug of Monday's milk pass-

ght were meant for his mother
been meant for someone else.

I didn't know how old Ada was. In
a little girl, on account of the words
and the light footsteps I'd heard on

didn't know what to believe.
on down the page, my eyes alighted on
ater that same day:

ives at last! News from the vil-
at the fever's back. Five children
grievously sick, God help their

:

d flew into the kitchens this af-
n. That young housemaid Dorcas
ins turned skittish and said it was a
there'd be a death in the house before
Such superstitions these girls have!

ldn't imagine Dorcas like this, not when she

able for breakfast. Lady B peevish about
K and A making too much noise in the
library. Says they should be somewhere
else.

I guessed 'K' would be Kit, and 'A' would be Ada.
So far, so clear.

K and A chasing up and down on the
back stairs, but now the housemaids cannot sweep up properly or carry things to
and fro. A full chamber pot has been
dropped. Tempers are short. The staff are
complaining. Matters must be dealt with,
though I suspect one of the maids has
done this already. A shows me the pinch
marks on her arm. Tell her not to make
such a fuss.

I shuddered and rubbed my own arm. *The back
stairs . . . pinching fingers . . .*
So.
Ada and Kit had made mischief on the back stairs.
Hardly a hanging offence, but clearly the housemaids

didn't like it, for someone had given Ada a hiding. Her own mother hadn't exactly taken her side. And so by pinching me and terrifying Gracie, perhaps Ada's spirit was getting its own back. Quite by surprise, I almost felt sorry for her. Fancy her own mother not sticking up for her, even when she was all upset! I knew what *that* felt like.

I glanced up at Will. He was crouched by the desk, working his way through its drawers.

'Found anything?' I said.

'Not yet. You?'

'Think so.'

'Keep going then.'

I read on:

Afternoon spent with K and A writing and drawing in quiet part of kitchen. A getting good at her letters now, thanks to what K has taught her, though we all keep this from Lady B. The very idea would irk her further. It is not befitting of an heir to be so free with us, she says. Must take care not to anger her further. For I am blessed to have a position in a

seemed such a steady sort. The next entry was for Saturday February 4th, two days before Kit died. My heart began to thud.

> *The wind has turned nor'easterly. Snow since last night. Hard frost.*

A few lines of what food was cooked and how Mr Phelps had ordered the silver to be cleaned, then . . .

> *A out of sorts today – parched throat, warm head. Put her to bed early with hot water and honey. Said extra prayers, though must try not to fret. Honey is a great healer, I am sure of it. All she wants is 'dear K'. L B forbids it. Insists she must be confined to her room until we know what ails her. She even talks of forbidding me to tend her, my own child! Wretched . . .*

A word had been heavily crossed out. I guessed it wasn't a kind one. Another thought hit me.

Honey.

The smell of it had been a sign that Ada's spirit was

close. I'd smelled it on the back stairs and in the kitchens. And each time, that sickly scent had made me feel ill too. And it quite turned me over to think of Ada so poorly, not from fear like me but from some terrible sickness that in a day or two she'd be dead from.

'I in't found much,' said a voice beside me. Deep in thought as I was, I took a moment to realise it was Will.

'Oh, um, right.'

'I'll try this middle drawer. Looks like it hasn't been opened in years.'

He pulled and cussed 'til the drawer opened at last. Then he stuck his hand right in, and with a sharp gasp drew it straight back out again.

'Quick! Give me that candle!' he cried.

We peered into the shadowy drawer. There, at the back was something dark, all coiled up like a snake. Holding his breath, Will pulled it out.

'Take it,' he said. 'I'll hold the light.'

It looked like rope. But as soon as I touched it, I knew what it was and a thrill ran through me. The hair had been braided into a thick plait about a foot long. Tied with a limp blue ribbon, it felt cool and heavy in my hands. I held it closer to the light. The hair was darker than my own, so dark it was almost black. *Just like Mrs Jessop's.*

Will whistled through his teeth. 'And look at this!'

He'd found a photograph. It was a simple postcard portrait of a serious little girl in her best frock, with her hair all neatly plaited and her hands crossed in her lap. She was sat in a chair that was too big for her, so her feet dangled high above the floor.

'Oh Ada!'

Here she was, a girl of seven, perhaps eight. She looked such a poppet of a thing it made me feel choked and sad. I gave it to Will so he could put it back in its proper place.

'Hang on, what's this?' He seemed to have found something else. 'I reckon this might be her, too.'

He gave me another picture, bigger than the last. An older, handsome girl stared back at me. She was unmistakably Ada.

She might've been my age. Her hair was dark, smoothed neat to her head, and though she wasn't quite smiling, her eyes were bright. At second glance, she wasn't so pretty. But she had a clever, spirited face. It was there in the tilt of her chin, and the strong curve of her mouth. She looked so full of life. Somehow, this made things worse.

'What d'you reckon she died of?' said Will

'She got sick, that's all I know.'

Will turned over the picture in his hand. 'Well it says here, "Ada Jessop – d. sixth of February 1871".'

Everything stopped.

'Give me that!' I seized the picture from him.

As I read the writing on the back of it, a sob broke from my mouth. There it was, clear as day, that date which linked everything together. How could it be? Kit and Ada, dying on the same day? What were the chances of *that*?

For a moment I couldn't speak.

'I'd bet it was scarlet fever,' said Will gently, seeing my shock. 'The village got it bad that year. My brother had it too.'

I looked at him. 'Oh, Will. I'm sorry. I never knew.'

'It's all right. He lived. But they cut all his hair off soon as they knew. They said it was to stop the infection spreading. And no one could see him; the rules were very strict.'

'Well, it seems pretty sad,' I said, my eyes filling up. 'Poor Ada.'

And I meant it too. I couldn't quite see my likeness in the picture. I still reckoned that was all in Cook's mind, since my hair wasn't as dark as Ada's, and it certainly wasn't as neat to my head. But my view on Ada was shifting. Maybe she had good reason to be angry.

'Lady Barrington sounds heartless to me. Fancy keeping such dear friends apart like that,' I said.

'Scarlet fever spreads so quick. She was just protecting her son.'

'But he died anyway, that's what's so strange.'

Will took the picture from me. 'Reckon you've seen enough?'

Before I could answer, I heard footsteps and low voices out in the passageway. A faint light passed under the door. The footsteps stopped. I held my breath. Ever so slowly the door eased open, and two frightened faces gazed into ours.

33

WHAT THE HOUSEMAID SAW

Gracie rushed at me, almost knocking me to the floor.

'Oh Tilly! It's you!' she sobbed. 'We came down for a drink. Then we heard noises in the kitchen and thought . . . oh . . . !'

I wrapped an arm around her and told her to shush. After so much talk of sickness and dying, it was a comfort to feel her next to me, though she trembled like a leaf. Dorcas was right behind Gracie. She was in her nightgown, her hair loose about her shoulders. She didn't look pleased to see us. In fact, she seemed properly vexed. Slowly and pointedly, Dorcas took in the scene – Will with his knife, the drawers flung open, and me with a dead girl's hair in my hand. I shifted uncomfortably. There was no point trying to hide anything. We'd been well and truly rumbled.

'What on earth is going on?' Dorcas fixed us with such a glare, I wanted to curl up in shame.

'It in't what it looks like,' I said.

Dorcas narrowed her eyes at the plait of hair. 'What've you got there?'

Shamefully, I raised my arm. She came closer with her candle, and gasped. 'Why, that looks like Ada's. Good God, Tilly! This is too much!' Her face crumpled and she started to cry.

'Who's Ada?' asked Gracie, bewildered.

I shook my head. *Not now*.

All went quiet but for the sound of sobbing. People like Dorcas didn't cry; not cool, unflappable Dorcas who always kept the rest of us in check. It was deeply unsettling. And for a moment, we were all at a loss; Gracie leaned into me, and Will stared awkwardly at the floor.

Dorcas was right. It was all too much. Ever so gently, I let go of Gracie and laid the hair back in the drawer. But I wasn't finished with the notebook yet. When no one was looking, I slipped it into my pocket.

Once Dorcas had recovered a little, she said, 'This nonsense has got to stop before it turns us all mad.'

'It in't nonsense. Really it in't,' I said.

'Isn't it? Look at us all, you, me, Gracie. Even Will's white as a sheet.'

'I'm fine,' said Will, squaring his shoulders.

'Suit yourself,' said Dorcas. 'But her Ladyship's in a right state, and goodness knows where Mrs Jessop is.' Her grey eyes fixed on me. 'So what *is* going on? You'd better tell me, Tilly. Before Mr Phelps finds out you're here.'

My mouth went dry and I felt sicker than ever. Though what would it matter if I did tell the truth? I'd nothing to lose. Better to be honest than be branded a sneak or a thief. And besides, Dorcas had been working here during Kit's last days, so I reckoned she knew plenty. If only she'd be willing to talk.

'Can we go somewhere else?' I asked, wanting suddenly to be gone from this sorry little room.

After a quick tidy of Mrs Jessop's things, we went back to the kitchens where a scene of chaos greeted us. Pots and pans lay strewn about the floor. A chair had fallen over, and the table was awash with dishes. Gracie stiffened in the doorway. I knew what she was thinking: this looked like one of Ada's tricks. Quickly, I put her straight.

'I came in through that window,' I said, pointing to the roof. And gawd, did it look a long way up! 'But I didn't land too neat, so it was me what made this mess, not no ghost.'

This seemed to ease Gracie a little. Dorcas, though, was less than impressed.

'That still doesn't make it all right,' she said. 'And it'll need tidying up before anything else.'

Once the pots were cleared away, we all sat down at the table.

'Make some tea, Gracie,' said Dorcas. 'And Will, try not to stare. I know we're in our nightgowns and it's not very proper. But it'd help if you didn't have your mouth open.'

Then she turned to me.

'You'd best start talking.'

'All right.' I cleared my throat which had gone awful dry and tight. 'The spirit what's been causing all this trouble, well, we reckon it's Ada's.'

'Which was why you asked about her last night as you were leaving,' she said. 'But what's it got to do with you now? You've been dismissed.'

'The séance proved it was Ada. And now I've lost my job and it in't fair.'

She looked at me in disbelief. 'Is that why you're here? To beg for your job back? Give me strength!'

'No, it in't because of that. Ada's ghost is angry, and I need to know exactly why.'

'Ada was a dear girl. Wilful perhaps but not *angry* . . .'

She stopped. Seemed to hold her breath. Nervously, her eyes travelled the room.

'What's wrong?' I said.

Dorcas didn't answer. The room went very still. I felt the hair on my neck lift as the gas jets dimmed to a queer, flickering half-light. Gracie gasped, and under the table Will's hand snatched at mine. The air seemed to thicken. It turned proper cold. Then with a whoosh, the jets flared up again. The chill vanished. And everything was normal, though my heart still beat hard in my chest.

Dorcas was the first to speak. Her voice sounded shaky. 'Very well, so Ada might've had reason to be angry. God knows she was too young to die.'

'But there's more, in't there?' I said. 'It's right strange that her and Master Kit died on the same day.'

'How d'you know all this?'

'Mrs Jessop's notebooks. It's written down.'

Her mouth fell open. 'And you've read them? Her *notebooks*? Why, you sly creature!'

She had a point; it *did* sound bad.

'But don't you see?' I said. 'Something in't right in this house. And you've been here a while, so ... well ... maybe you know things we don't.'

Dorcas shook her head. I hoped Will might back

me up, but he still had hold of Ada's picture and was staring at it strangely.

'Will?'

He slid it across the table to me.

'The light's better in here. Looks familiar, doesn't she?'

Picking up the picture, I saw immediately what Will meant. My breath stopped. It was there in Ada's eyes, in the set of her jaw. The way she gazed head-on at the camera.

Dorcas leaned forward for a look. 'Gosh! She looks so like you, Tilly! I'd not noticed before.'

I hadn't either. And now my head was reeling.

Gracie rushed to my side. 'Let me see,' she said, then, 'Blimey, you're right! No wonder Mrs Jessop had an eye for you. She's never nice to no one.'

'But she loved Ada,' Dorcas corrected her. 'I hardly saw a more devoted mother. Except her Ladyship, that is.'

I sat back in my seat. So I looked like Ada. It wasn't just a fancy of Cook's, after all. Once the shock had passed, I began to see a sort of sense to it. Not many housekeepers would take on a girl who'd twice been caught trespassing. Then there were those long looks she'd given me, and the ointment for my hands, and what Cook had said about me looking like a person who'd died. All this I could just about swallow.

But what about Kit? For this was the part that stuck in my throat.

Was this why he'd chosen me to help him? All because I looked like a dead girl? When he'd appeared in my dreams, he'd held my hand for dear life. Made me believe I was the only one who could help him. Was it Ada he was really thinking of? Had he not thought *me* brave and capable at all?

I felt foolish. My eyes filled with angry tears. I'd done so much for Kit. I'd stuck my bleeding neck out for him. More than that, I'd believed in him. Believed that I was worthy of this task. *And what for?*

Heck, I'd been second best in my own ma's affections. I'd lived my whole life knowing Eliza was smarter and prettier than me. Even Pa had finally chosen my sister over me. And now once again to be in someone's blinking shadow . . .

I took a deep breath. It didn't help to think like this. I had to stop this nonsense, and trust what I knew to be right. Kit needed me.

Me.

A hot cup of tea was placed in my hands.

'So, what is it you want to know?' said Dorcas. 'I'll

try to help but you better ask quickly – folk'll be stir-ring soon.'

The tea revived me a little and I found my tongue.

'What I really want to know about is Kit,' I said.

Dorcas lowered her teacup. 'I thought as much. You've had notions about him since the day you got here. I saw it in your face.'

Will cleared his throat. I couldn't look his way right now. I kept my gaze on Dorcas. She'd hear the truth from me, no matter if she believed it or not. I cleared my throat.

'I saw his spirit under the water that day I nearly drowned. And I know it sounds mad but he saved my life. His spirit's been out there all this time, and he's desperate to be at peace. But he can't be because something's stopping it. Something's not right.'

I braced myself for a snort or a laugh. But she sat absolutely still.

'He's told me there's a truth I must reveal. And I'm sure it's here in this house. Might you know what that is?'

Her eyes slid away from me. 'I can't honestly say.'

'Is it to do with Ada, do you think? I'm reckoning it is.'

Dorcas's eyes glistened with tears. 'Ada got sick, and

291

when they knew it was scarlet fever, Lady Barrington panicked. She was terrified for Kit, so she sent Ada away to one of the workers' cottages on the edge of the grounds.'

'To stop the infection spreading?' Will chipped in.

'Exactly. Mrs Jessop was banned from seeing her, even though it was very likely that Ada would die.'

I thought for a moment. 'Which might be why her spirit's so angry. Then what happened?'

Dorcas sighed heavily. 'That day's such a blur to me I'm not sure I'll remember it right. You see, we were all worried sick about Ada, then Master Kit drowned. We were in complete shock. It was too much pain for one household to bear.' She sniffed. 'I reckon it still is.'

To think all this happened on the very same day. It shocked me to the core. Dorcas looked pale as a ghost herself and had fallen silent, so I pulled out the notebook. What Dorcas couldn't tell me, I'd surely find in here. As I went to open it in my lap, she tutted.

I looked at her steadily. 'I know you think this is snooping, but I have to find out what happened that day.'

I turned the pages. Only when I got to Monday February 6th, there was nothing there. The dates jumped from Sunday 5th straight to Tuesday 7th. The binding looked puckered. I peered closer then shrank back in my seat, flummoxed.

The page had been torn clean out.

34

HIDDEN

That page might be anywhere, if it still existed at all. And I doubted that it did. Most likely, it was just a heap of ash in a grate somewhere.

'Bet Mrs Jessop's got it stuffed down her bodice,' said Will. 'And I'm not searching her, so don't ask.'

He pulled a face at Gracie, who tried hard not to giggle. I didn't see much to laugh about.

'That in't helpful talk,' I said, irked that we'd got this close only to reach a dead end.

'But *why* would she tear it out?' said Gracie. 'No one went near those notebooks. Why would we? It's only Dorcas and the footmen what can read well enough.'

It was a cracking good point. And a little part of me felt glad that I knew my letters, but the gladness didn't last. Maybe Mrs Jessop wanted to forget that day, to rip it out of her mind, so to speak. Except it didn't work like that. You couldn't make yourself forget people because it hurt too much to think of them. I knew that very well.

No.

Something had been written there, something she'd wanted to hide. The tear looked fresh and white. Which might mean she'd only just done it.

'I'd better tell you,' said Dorcas, suddenly.

We all looked at her.

'What I mean is . . . someone did go near the notebooks the other day.'

'Who was it?' I said.

She let out a long breath. 'Me.'

I was taken aback. Hadn't *she* just given *me* a dressing down for reading Mrs Jessop's notebooks? What the heck was this all about?

I went to speak but she held up a hand to shush me. 'I was trying to hide it, the one for February 1871. Rumour was Madame Martineau was after details about the day Kit died, to help her look authentic at the séance.'

'So you're saying you took the page?' I asked.

'No, not quite. Mrs Jessop caught me red-handed. I hadn't read any of it; it didn't even cross my mind to. But it didn't look good, me in her office like that, snooping through her things. I told her straight out what Madame Martineau was up to, and I think she believed me. Only then she turned quite strange, and I was glad to leave the room.'

'What d'you mean, turned strange?'

'Sort of panicky, I s'pose. Not that I blame Mrs Jessop; no one wants their private journals read, do they?'

'Maybe she's got something to hide,' I said. 'And where's she taken off to, anyway? Don't *that* strike you as queer?'

'Mrs Jessop's not been right since Ada died,' said Dorcas. 'But this séance has certainly stirred things up again.'

'Maybe she just went to Ada's grave,' said Will.

Dorcas raised an eyebrow. 'What, all night? In this weather?'

The mere mention of the place made me shiver. No one in their right mind would go there, surely. Not in the dead of night, not even to lay a single snowdrop.

Somewhere down the passageway, a clock chimed the hour. Dorcas got to her feet. 'I'm sorry but you'll have to go now. Mr Phelps'll be down any minute.'

At the back door, she pulled back the bolts and turned the key.

'Take care. But don't come back here again, not if

you know what's good for you both.'

Gracie hugged me tight. 'God bless, Tilly. And good luck.'

As we stepped out into the courtyard, the stars were already fading, and the trees were black, spidery shapes against the sky. The back door closed softly behind us.

'That page might still exist, you know,' I said.

Will shook his head. 'Not a chance. She'll have destroyed it. Especially if it's as important as we think.'

'But she writes down everything. That's what housekeepers do. And she's kept it all this time, remember.'

'No,' said Will. 'She's nervous. She'll have burned it. She's covering her tracks.'

'Perhaps.'

Except I couldn't quite believe it. What if Mrs Jessop wasn't covering her tracks? What if that page was out there somewhere, waiting for someone to find it?

And then I remembered her antics at the ice house yesterday. It had to be worth a shot.

'Got your lantern still?' I said to Will.

'I left it out here somewhere.' He looked about him. 'Here it is!'

'Save your tinder 'til we get there. Come on. This way.'

*

We headed for the lake. It was a job to find the path, never mind follow it, since the snow came over the tops of our boots and was frozen hard to a crust. It took us an age, and by the time we reached it, the sky was already pale grey. The lake was silent as always, though the ice looked dark, as if the water was pressing up from underneath.

'Rain's on the way,' said Will, looking up at the clouds. 'That ice won't hold much longer.'

'I hope you're right. Come on.'

Under the trees was the ice house. As soon as Will saw it, he understood.

'You saw her here yesterday, didn't you?' he said.

I nodded.

'Makes sense. Ada's grave is over there, see?'

All I saw was the stone wall where I'd found my flint, and beyond it the copse where Mrs Jessop had been.

'Can't see no graves,' I said.

'Further on. Look!'

I saw then where he was pointing. About fifty yards

up ahead was a second, higher wall, the very same one we'd clambered over just a few days ago as a shortcut to Kit's angel. On the other side of it, hidden from view, would be all those sad little graves. I shivered at the thought.

Of a sudden, Will tensed up. 'Listen. Can you hear it?'

'Hear what?'

'A rustling noise. Someone's coming.'

'Oh heck!'

His eyes were fixed on something in the copse. We both stood still for what seemed like an age. Then Will relaxed.

'It was probably just a deer. Anyway, it's gone now.' He turned to me. 'So, where exactly did you see Mrs Jessop yesterday?'

'Right here. On these steps, with some paper screwed up in her hand.'

Will drew a long breath.

'Exactly,' I said. 'If it was the missing page, then she might've hidden it inside.'

'Wouldn't hurt to look.'

The door to the ice house stuck fast. We grabbed hold together and gave a specially sharp tug. The door snagged against the ground, then swung open. The air inside smelled rank. My heart was racing now.

'Stay here and keep watch,' I said to Will.

'Take this, then.' He lit the lantern and handed it to me.

I edged my way in slowly. The lantern didn't help much; in fact, it made the dark seem darker. Up close the walls were grimy brick, the floor a foul-smelling mess of wet straw. The roof pressed in on me so that I was almost bent double. The only sound was the slow drip of icy water draining away at my feet. Up ahead was the pit of ice. I felt the chill of it even from here. My spirits sank. Nothing else looked different. Nothing had changed. Before I knew it, the same hot panic rose up in my chest. I had to get out. Now.

I groped my way back to the entrance. Just as I reached it my fingers touched something rough in the wall. I stopped. Holding the lantern up, I peered closer. One brick jutted out an inch from the rest. My hands shook as I gripped it. It came away easily enough. And there, stuffed in the damp space where the brick had been, was a scrunched-up piece of paper.

Outside, I showed it to Will.

'Blimey! You were right!' he said, his eyes all wide. 'Have a quick look and then we need to get out of here.'

He cleared the snow from the top step. I was glad to sit down, for my legs were shaking. And now I had the thing right here in my flipping hand, I felt ill at the thought of reading it. I breathed deep, made my eyes focus on the page.

35

FEBRUARY 6TH 1871

It didn't make sense on first sight. For this diary entry wasn't like the others. There was no mention of cleaning tasks or who'd eaten what. This was all thoughts, laid out like a broken list on the page. It didn't appear to have been written all in one go but in snatches during the day; the dashes at the edge of the page seemed to show this.

It started angrily:

> *– Sick at sight of Lady B this morning, breakfasting happily with her dear son, when my darling child lies ill in a stranger's house, and I cannot go to her. Such agony! I anxiously await news of how she does. Cannot eat for fear it will be bad.*

Then some time later:

– An ugly big crow flew into the kitchens and sat on top of the dresser, eyeballing us all. Dorcas kept quiet about deaths today, but I saw the look she gave Cook. Everyone fears the worst, I know it.

– Word comes from the cottage – the news is bad. A's fever rages. She cries out for me and for Kit. O how am I to bear this?

– Still Lady B refuses my plea to go to A. She speaks as if I've forgotten my duty to Frost Hollow Hall. We only have one heir, she says. We must keep infection from the house, no matter what. Hateful, hateful woman with no heart of her own! Is she not a mother too?

– And what a change there is in K! Now he mopes in his room. His mood is foul, with not a kind word for anyone. Does he not care for his friend any more, when just a few days ago she was his 'dearest'? How fickle he is! It seems he has truly forgotten A. Am I the only one wishing to see her? Is he really, truly *heartless? I am sunk too low. I fear I will put the pen right through the page if I write any more.*

— The strangest thing has just happened. I came into the kitchen and swear, swear, I saw my A wiping dry the china. My heart leapt for joy. I was sure she was recovered and come back to me. Only she put down her cloth and went out of the back door. I rushed after her into the courtyard, but there was no sign of her. It was as if she had disappeared into thin air.

— Calmer now. Luncheon over. Place is quiet. No one will notice. I have to go to A. I have no choice.

I turned the page over, confused. I'd not expected to feel pity for Mrs Jessop. Yet now I did. The stuff about Kit threw me even more. Was he really such an uncaring toad?

The next entry, in a different pen and with much crossing out, seemed to have been written later that day. Reading it, I went completely cold.

– I have done a terrible thing. My hand trembles so much I can hardly write, but there may be some comfort yet in getting these words onto the page.

I stole away from the Hall with a heart full of dread. The way to the cottage took me right past the lake. There, some distance from the bank I saw a person skating on the ice. It was a cruel sight to see someone so joyous, so carefree, today of all days. It was then I noticed that the ice looked thin; in places, the water was already coming through. I stopped to call out a warning. I think I even cleared my throat. Then I saw who the person was.

Master Kit.

A sudden rage seized me. What foolish mother would let her son come skating when the lake was not properly frozen? And why was he here? What right did he have to enjoy himself when my baby lay dying in her bed? He was heartless, like his mother. If he fell through the ice, if he perished, what would she feel then?

An agony just like mine.

I didn't shout a warning. I walked on by, and reached the cottage too late. My darling girl never knew I'd come. By the time I reached her, her eyes were shut, her breathing changed. And I knew that what I'd seen earlier in the kitchen was her departing spirit come to see me, come to say goodbye. She died fever-warm, in my arms. It was over. And I was now dead without her.

It was agony to leave again. But some time later, I set off back to the Hall. Yet Death still stalked me. At the lake, o horror, I found Master Kit face down in the water. God knows I tried to pull him free, but he was too heavy, too cold. Too long dead.

I was to blame. I could have saved him. This terrible deed was all mine.

How I got home I don't recall. Somehow, I raised the alarm and the men went to bring Master Kit home. That my pain as a mother would now be shared –

doubled – was no comfort at all. I believe I lost my wits for a time.

Now as I lie here in my room, my hand no longer shakes. The doctor's draught has helped me, or maybe the act of writing down these words is a balm to my soul. I think not. My heart has been torn from my chest and the wound left deep and open. I wonder that I am still alive, since this is the worst agony of all. I wish . . . no . . . pray that I might be dead of it come morning.

– Mr Phelps has just been. He tells me Kit's body is laid out in his bedchamber. Great fires have been ordered. Her Ladyship thinks the warmth will revive him. She fools herself. Her son is too long dead. He was cold when I found him, much colder than my Ada. And now I hear a terrible wailing noise from somewhere deep in the house, and the opening and closing of many doors. I feel nothing. It is even an effort to breathe.

I became aware of Will rubbing my shoulder.

'Say something, won't you?'

I opened my mouth but the words seemed to stick in my throat. I took a few shaky breaths and blew my nose in the hankie Will held out to me.

'Tell me what it says,' he said, gently.

'Mrs Jessop . . .'

But I didn't know where to start so I thrust the page at him. 'You'd better read it yourself.'

I got to my feet. My head felt full. One word of warning, that's all it would've taken. Just one flipping word and Kit might be here now.

My temper flared. I couldn't keep still, pacing up and down 'til the snow wore thin and the grass underneath showed through. I sure as hell didn't feel sorry for Mrs Jessop any more. I fancied ripping her measly eyes out.

Will gave a low whistle once he'd finished reading.

'A right old mess, isn't it?' he said, rubbing his jaw. 'No wonder she wanted to keep it secret.'

'She could've saved Kit, and she didn't!'

'She was upset. Her daughter was dying.'

'That don't mean what she did was right!'

''Course it don't. But it don't make Mrs Jessop a villain, neither.'

'You've changed your tune,' I said. 'Back in the kitchens, you was on Lady Barrington's side.'

'It isn't that simple. 'Specially not now I've read this.'

Will handed the piece of paper back to me. I stuffed it in my pocket, suddenly unsure of any of it, when what I really needed was answers.

'So, who *is* the villain, then?' I said.

'Heck, I don't know. They both did a pretty shoddy thing.'

I didn't want to hear this; *someone* was to blame for Kit's death all right, and Mrs Jessop seemed a good place to start. As I turned it all over in my mind, I grew aware of how the wind had got up. Birds circled unsteadily above the tree tops and the air felt soft against my face.

'It's getting warmer,' I said.

Somewhere behind us a gate clicked shut.

'Sssh!' Will went still.

Men's voices carried on the wind. A dog yammered like it was on the scent of something. Someone shouted.

Will met my eye in alarm. 'We'd better get out of here.'

We picked our way down the path, keeping low and hidden under the trees. We didn't speak a word, though already a plan was forming in my head. When we'd almost reached the courtyard again, Will made to go off down another track.

'This way,' he said. 'Cut through here and we'll be at the gates in no time.'

I stopped. 'I can't go yet . . .'

Behind us, something crashed through the bushes. We turned to see a huge black dog hurling down the path towards us.

'Run!' cried Will.

I couldn't move. A blur of teeth and tongue barged past me. I staggered but somehow didn't fall. Will was already running. The dog raced after him. It gained on him in no time.

Will's head whipped round at the dog's first bite. He kicked with all his might, sending it sprawling into the snow. Snapping and snarling, it lunged at him again. A scream rose up in my throat. I waved my arms like a mad thing. I yelled. I roared, running straight at the dog. One look at me and it stopped in its tracks, then sloped back off into the bushes towards the men's voices. They sounded closer now.

I rushed to Will's side. 'Can you walk?'

Gingerly, he raised his trouser leg. The bite was deep and ragged. Blood poured down his calf into the snow.

'It don't look good,' he said, gritting his teeth.

Three men were now coming down the path with the dog at their heels.

'Here they are!' said one, slapping a thick stick against his palm. I recognised him at once. It was Jake, the thug who'd caught us last time.

Will turned pale beside me. A figure came running out from the courtyard, dark skirts bunched up in her hand.

'Leave those children alone, do you hear me?' she cried.

The men stopped. Jake slipped his fingers through the dog's collar. I felt Will sway against me and caught him just in time as Mrs Jessop came striding through the snow towards us.

36

THINGS TURN NASTY

The fear took hold of me. We'd been caught fair and square. Things were about to turn nasty. I braced myself for it, but one look at Will's leg and Mrs Jessop ordered Jake to carry him straight inside. I followed right behind. The household was up now, the kitchens busy. Gracie's mouth fell open as we trailed blood in through the back door.

'What is it? What's happened?' she cried.

I shook my head at her. No one else stopped to explain.

We went to Mrs Jessop's office where, with a grunt, Jake dropped Will into the nearest chair and disappeared sharpish. Mrs Jessop closed the door behind him. She stood very still, her arms folded across her chest. I hovered uneasily at Will's side. Any second she'd spot a notebook out of place and guess what we'd been up to. Yet the fear in me was fast turning to anger. I knew her guilty secret now, the part she'd played in Kit's death.

Mrs Jessop didn't seem interested in her book-shelves, or even poor old Will. She was looking straight at me.

'Well,' she said.

Briefly, I met her eye. Then my gaze fell to her snow-crusted boots. Dead leaves were caught up in her skirts. *Odd*. There weren't any trees on the lawn where she'd found us.

'I believe you have something of mine,' she said.

Will coughed nervously. I felt my cheeks burn.

'Like what?' I said, though my blasted hand went straight to the greatcoat pocket.

'You know very well.'

I felt myself go redder, as if that gaze of hers could see right into my soul.

That's right, Mrs Jessop, I do know very well. I know exactly what you did.

She held out her hand, palm upwards, twitching her fingers at me.

'Come on, give it to me.'

I stood my ground.

'I'm warning you, Tilly.'

'I can't believe what you did!' I blurted out. 'Kit might've lived if you'd warned him!'

Her eyes flicked over me. 'You don't know what you're saying.'

'Oh, but I do. It's all written down.'

'Give it to me!'

She lunged at me. I jumped back smartly. She stopped, breathing hard. A lock of hair had come loose across her face.

'You'd better hand it over, young lady, or else I swear I'll . . .' And she went for me again, her arm raised like she was about to clout me one.

'Blimey Tilly, just give it back to her!' cried Will from his seat.

I wasn't scared of a walloping. But Will was right. I'd got what I needed. I knew what had happened. What did I care about a lousy scrap of paper? My hands shook as I took it from my pocket. It was damp and crumpled, and the ink was beginning to run.

'Here. Take it.' I held it out to her.

Mrs Jessop hesitated. Her lip quivered. Then she took it between thumb and forefinger like it was the finest silk in the land. Ever so gently, she folded it into neat squares and put it in her pocket. There was something desperate in her look. With a shudder, she composed herself again.

'He needs a doctor,' she said, meaning Will. 'And you, Tilly Higgins, had better stay right here until I decide what's to be done with you.'

With a rustle of skirts, she left the room, pulling the door shut behind her.

'I'm for it now,' I said, beginning to panic. 'Why did I have to go and mention Kit? I should've kept my gob shut just a bit longer . . .'

Will shrugged. 'It's not your strong point, is it? But she'd have done us for trespassing anyway, with or without the notebook.'

'How did she know what we were up to?'

Will looked at me like I was stupid. 'Where do you think she went last night?'

With those leaves on her skirt, it didn't take much working out. 'Ada's grave, which is right near to the ice house.'

'Exactly. I did tell you.'

'And it wasn't deer you heard in the woods,' I said. 'It was her.'

I flopped down heavily into a chair.

'So now what do we do?' said Will.

He'd gone a funny shade and there was sweat forming on his brow. Blood had pooled on the floor by his foot, and his trousers were plastered against his leg. It didn't look good at all. Quickly, I made him a sort of bed with cushions and chairs, so his leg was up high and the blood began to slow. And since he was shivering, I covered him over with the greatcoat. Then I took his hand.

'I'm all right really,' said Will. 'You mustn't fuss.'

'Let's just see what the doctor says,' I said, trying to sound cheerful though the amount of blood bothered me. 'Now lie still and be quiet.'

'You don't have to stay with me.'

'I in't leaving you here, not with *her*!'

'Mrs Jessop isn't going to kill me.'

'I don't trust her,' I said.

Will's face darkened. 'So you've made up your mind from one poxy notebook, have you?'

'Well, if she'd only . . .'

'*She* didn't kill Kit. *He* was an idiot for going out on the ice in the first place.'

'Don't say that!' I cried. What was it with Will Potter? Even with his leg in shreds, he still got right up my nose.

Will looked at me gravely. 'Think about it. I bet this isn't the whole story. So don't waste your time sitting here with me.'

True enough, it wasn't what I'd hoped for either.

Just then, Gracie peered round the door. 'Oh Tilly, how is he?'

'He'll live,' I scowled, then saw that she was carrying a bucket of coal. 'Where you going with that?'

She looked flustered. 'Upstairs, to Master Kit's bedroom. Her Ladyship wants the fire building up. And Dorcas says I *have* to do it, no excuses this time.'

I tided my hair and smoothed down my skirts. Mrs Jessop might be back any minute. And Will was right about one thing, I certainly didn't need to sit here holding his flipping hand.

'Right. Give it to me then.'

'What?'

Before Gracie could stop me, I'd snatched the bucket from her grasp.

'I won't be long.' Then, feeling suddenly guilty, I added, 'Look after Will. Keep his leg up. But if he asks you to, you don't have to hold his hand.'

I rushed past her. She called out for me to stop. But I wasn't slowing down for anyone.

37

A FIERCE ATTACHMENT

Lady Barrington was stood by the window with her back to me. The air felt thick and close. And for the very first time I noticed a strong smell of stale bed sheets and unbeaten carpets. The chairs were still set for the séance, though the dishes and black cloths had been cleared. Kit's boots were here, his open books, his folded clothes. A lump formed in my throat as it hit me all over again.

This room was so full of sadness.

'What a commotion outside, Gracie,' Lady Barrington said, her back still turned. 'And is that blood I can see down there in the snow? Whatever's happened?'

'A boy got bit, your Ladyship.'

Her shoulders tensed at my voice. She turned round slowly, knowing I wasn't Gracie at all.

'What in heaven's name . . . ?'

I put the coal bucket down and as I went towards her, she threw up her hands in panic.

'Come any closer and I'll scream!'

'I mean no harm, but please, you must listen.'

She looked feverishly ill. And very capable of screaming the whole house down.

'You've done enough harm already. Now get out!'

'But I have to talk to you,' I said. 'About Kit.'

'Why should I listen to you? You're a charlatan, just like Madame Martineau.'

'I'm nothing to do with her!'

Lady Barrington tossed her head. 'Of course you are. She sent you here, didn't she? You should be ashamed of yourself, playing with people's grief!'

I bit back my words. *She'd* employed the blooming medium, not me, though it wouldn't help to say so.

I tried again. 'That day I went through the ice, I should've drowned. It's a miracle I didn't. And that's because Kit saved my life.'

She blinked. Her hand went to her cheek.

'What *exactly* do you mean?'

I knew I'd got her then.

'Kit's spirit haunts the lake,' I said. 'He's cold and restless because there's a truth that in't being told.'

Her Ladyship froze. Her face drained of colour and she sank into a nearby chair. I wondered if I'd said too much, too quick, but I wasn't about to stop now.

'And he comes to me in my dreams, almost every night.'

'You dream of him? *Every night?*'

'Yes, your Ladyship.'

She looked stunned.

'And what does he speak of? How does he seem?'

Like an angel, I so wanted to say. And it might've brought comfort, but it wasn't the whole truth. 'Well, he in't happy. He wants me to help him so he can be at peace.'

'*You?*'

'Yes,' I said, uneasily.

'But why you, when I, his own mother, dream of nothing?'

It was a question I'd asked myself too.

She shut her eyes in a long, painful blink. When she looked at me again, her gaze was clear.

'I knew from the moment I saw you, didn't I? You bear a striking resemblance to her.'

My stomach lurched. She meant Ada, of course.

'Kit was very fond of poor Ada,' she said, shakily. 'Too fond probably, but then he got that from his mother. It's our weakness, you see, to form these fierce attachments.'

I felt my cheek flush. Kit had held *my* hands tightly.

He'd even saved my life. Surely that meant I was a fierce attachment too.

Lady Barrington continued. 'When Mrs Jessop's husband died, we agreed to take both her and Ada on. She came to us with glowing references, and for all her ways, she's proved herself a remarkable housekeeper.'

Anger stirred in me. Mrs Jessop was remarkable, all right. If her Ladyship had an inkling of what she'd *really* done, she'd get rid of her like a shot. *Just like she'd done with me.*

It was on the tip of my tongue to tell her, but I held back: it could wait. Now that I'd got Lady Barrington talking, I didn't want to throw her off course.

'Only Ada and Kit became firm friends. She was like family to him, almost the sister he never had. I didn't really approve of it but it seemed harmless enough at first.'

Her Ladyship paused, clearly troubled.

'Over time, they became inseparable,' she said, eventually. 'It started to cause problems. People didn't know their rightful place. You have to understand, Kit was heir to a fortune, and Ada was destined to be a maid. Such an attachment couldn't continue for ever. Nothing would ever come of it, don't you see?'

She fell silent. My gaze drifted away from her, to the

unmade bed, the too-hot fire; this shrine to her be-loved Kit. This was her fierce attachment, wasn't it? Even to me, who knew how special Kit was, it all felt too much.

'You find it strange?' she said, watching me. 'Most people do, even those who've lost someone dear. They might wear a locket or keep a curl of hair. But the thing I wanted most of his had vanished. This is how I keep him close.'

It still seemed mawkish, somehow.

'What was it, this thing you wanted?' I asked.

She sighed. 'A gold ring we'd given him for his birthday.'

My heart stopped.

'It was a beautiful thing,' she said. 'Made from fam-ily gold with his name engraved inside it.'

I know, I thought. *I know.*

'He wore it on his little finger. He swore he'd never take it off. But when they found his body, he wasn't wearing it. It had gone. I had hoped one day he'd pass it on to someone special, someone very dear to him.' She frowned. 'We even checked that he'd not some-how given it to Ada.'

I wanted to cry out: *but he did give it to someone dear to him! He gave it to me!* Because I saw more than ever now what that ring really meant. And when I thought of what had happened to it, I could've died of shame. If only I'd returned it to Lady Barrington right at the start. Instead, it was most probably in a pawn shop somewhere, or stashed away in Eliza's trunk.

'And now, with your story,' said her Ladyship, 'maybe it fits that there is part of him still out there in the lake.'

She fell quiet then, though her hands fidgeted madly in her lap.

'Kit says there's a truth that needs revealing,' I said.

Lady Barrington shuddered. 'Ah yes, the truth . . .'

A sharp knock at the door stopped her. She passed a hand across her brow, calling out, 'Not now, please.'

The knocking carried on. Her Ladyship rolled her eyes.

'What on earth is it?'

As the door opened, my heart sank. It was Mrs Jessop. And she looked ready to wring my neck.

'Forgive me, your Ladyship,' she said, then sharply to me, 'You were told to wait downstairs!'

A look of alarm crossed Lady Barrington's face, as if I might well be a trickster after all. Then she said, 'Mrs Jessop, you'd better come in and sit down. We're discussing something that involves you, and we should have done it long ago.'

Mrs Jessop blanched. But she collected herself and took a seat next to her Ladyship.

'You too,' Lady Barrington ordered me.

I sat down. My palms were sweating.

'Matilda has news of my son,' said Lady Barrington.

Mrs Jessop turned pale. She knew nothing of my dreams, of course. She reckoned I was about to spill her secret, to tell her Ladyship what I'd read on that torn-out page. And I was dying to. Only not yet.

'Please continue, Matilda,' said her Ladyship.

Their eyes were on me. My mouth went dry. Here I was, a tatty little housemaid, only I couldn't even call myself that any more. Why the heck should they listen to me?

Yet they were waiting for me to speak. I had to hold my nerve.

38

A MOTHER'S LOVE

The room was airless. It made my head hurt, and I felt my frock turning damp under the arms.

'Can you think of why Kit's not at peace, your Ladyship?' I said, bold as I could.

Mrs Jessop coughed. Lady Barrington shot her a dark look. Seeing the pair of them sat inches apart like this, I could almost *taste* the ill will between them.

'Kit was loved. More than any boy could ask for,' she said.

'But it's strange his ghost never comes to you. You said so yourself.'

Her Ladyship stiffened. I glanced over at Mrs Jessop, who hadn't moved an inch. But now a red flush was creeping up her neck.

'We had … an argument,' said Lady Barrington. 'His last words to me were …' Her lip trembled. 'Well, let's just say they were cross words.'

I sat forward at this. Strange how Mrs Jessop's

notebook spoke of mother and son all cosy together at breakfast. Yet Lady Barrington's account was different.

'What did you fight about?'

Lady Barrington stared at me.

'Ada.'

Mrs Jessop gasped. The room was too hot. If only I could open a window.

'Let me finish, Mrs Jessop,' she said, though the housekeeper hadn't yet spoken a word. 'There is an angry spirit in this house. And though it upsets me to say so, I might know why.'

Mrs Jessop had her hands over her face. 'I don't want to hear this,' she said. 'Please stop.'

'But you must,' Lady Barrington insisted. 'Because maybe . . . maybe Ada's angry with me.'

And she'd have reason to be, I reckoned, struck again by what Lady Barrington had done on the day Kit died. *You kept her from Kit, and her own flipping mother! You let her die all by herself!*

Whose side was I on now? I didn't have the faintest idea.

For a long moment, we sat in stunned silence. A steady dripping noise came from the gutters outside. Eventually, Lady Barrington turned in her seat. She glanced at the window, then back at me and Mrs Jessop. Touching the brooch at her throat, she took a deep breath

'Mrs Jessop, please believe me when I say this,' her Ladyship said. 'Kit loved your Ada. Really, he did. Yet he loved her too much for a boy with his responsibilities. It wasn't right for them to be so close. It couldn't go on.'

It was uncomfortable to hear. Though by now I reckoned it was near to the truth. Mrs Jessop's hands dropped away from her face. Her Ladyship took it as a sign to keep talking.

'When Ada got sick, Kit was desperate to see her. He'd made a gift for her and he so wanted her to have it. They'd worked on it together, you see.'

She glanced quickly at me. 'At the séance I took something out of a cupboard, do you remember?'

I nodded. Of course I remembered it.

'Well, that package was Kit's gift to Ada. I kept it all this time. You see, Kit didn't care about the infection, not in the slightest.'

I went cold all over.

Oh no.

'All he wanted was to see Ada and give her his gift,' her Ladyship said. 'But I forbade him to go. He begged me to say where she'd been sent, but I wouldn't tell him. He'd have just gone there anyway, I knew he would.'

I could hardly bear to look at Mrs Jessop.

'I was terrified for him.' Lady Barrington sounded choked. 'Children in the village were dying, and I saw how fearful you were, Mrs Jessop. But when Kit knew how ill Ada really was, he grew incensed. "There's danger everywhere!" he said to me. "I have to see her. You can't protect me for ever!"'

Mrs Jessop slumped in her seat.

'He was in a rage. And then he went out on that ice just to spite me, just to prove his point,' her Ladyship said. 'I don't know what he was thinking of.'

Mrs Jessop's face was wet with tears. 'What did I do?' she whispered. 'What on earth did I do?'

Her Ladyship looked confused. 'I don't quite understand.'

It was agony. I'd rather have watched them tear each other's eyes out. Because I knew what was coming next, and I almost begged Mrs Jessop to keep her secret where it was, since I wondered what good it might do now.

Mrs Jessop squared her shoulders. The tears still fell but her voice was steady. She raised her chin as she met

Lady Barrington's gaze. It made her look defiant. And so like Ada.

'I did a most awful thing that day. I've lived with the guilt ever since.'

Lady Barrington leaned forward as if to comfort her, but she pulled away.

'Please. Let me explain. Tilly knows what I did, how awful it was.'

Lady Barrington looked at me, then back at Mrs Jessop. I felt sick to the pit of my stomach.

'I saw Kit out there skating that day, and I knew it wasn't safe. But I was so angry with you. And I thought . . .' She paused. '. . . That Kit didn't *want* to see Ada, that he'd forgotten her. I was angry with him too. I wasn't thinking properly . . . I never meant to . . .'

She broke off, sobbing. Lady Barrington sat back in her seat. There was no attempt to comfort Mrs Jessop now.

'What are you trying to tell me?' her Ladyship said, coldly.

Mrs Jessop took a big shuddery breath. 'The ice was too thin for skating on. I could see that, even from where I was on the path. I should have shouted to him. Not a day's gone by when I haven't wished I did. Because, don't you see, if I'd warned him, he'd

329

most probably have survived. But instead I pretended I hadn't seen him. I walked straight past. And when I came by the lake again later, he was already dead.' She let out a cry. 'And I did try to revive him, I did try to pull him free, but I couldn't . . .'

She crumpled in her seat. Her mouth gaped open. Huge sobs shook her whole body. The sound of her despair was awful, like an animal caught in a trap. I couldn't move.

Lady Barrington went white. She didn't say anything. After what felt like eternity, she spoke in a low, flat voice.

'You could have saved him. One word from you and Kit might still be alive.'

I'd thought this too at first. I'd been ready to blame Mrs Jessop fair and square. Now I wasn't so certain.

Lady Barrington, though, looked set. She got to her feet. Coolly, calmly, she stood over Mrs Jessop. My eyes followed.

'You could have saved my son,' her Ladyship said again.

One moment she stood still. The next she lunged forward. Arms flailing, hair flying, she went for Mrs Jessop like a wildcat. The housekeeper shrank back, horrified.

'Lady Barrington! Please!' My own voice came out strong.

I rushed to her and tried to grab her arms. She twisted from me. Went for Mrs Jessop again, swiping at her face. The force of it made her stagger. As she almost fell, I grabbed her round the waist. Locked both my arms right round her. Flip knows what I was doing, touching a lady like that. But it was the stillest part of her. Even so she was strong, lunging and kicking with all her might. Mrs Jessop cowered like a cornered dog. It was pitiful.

'You must stop!' I cried.

'But she could have saved him!'

I held her tighter. Her skin burned hot through her frock.

'It's too late,' I said. 'It won't bring him back.'

Her Ladyship shuddered. Suddenly, she went limp. Her legs sagged and I seemed now to be holding her up. Then, quite feebly, she shrugged me off and crossed to the window.

'One word. Just one word,' she whispered, her breath misting up the glass.

Mrs Jessop sobbed quietly, but I watched her Ladyship close, not sure what she'd do next. What she did was simple.

She stood gazing out over the gardens to the lake beyond, as if all the answers lay there. At last, she looked away. Her hand went to the small gold brooch at her throat and she returned to her chair again. Tears poured down her cheeks and dripped unchecked off her chin.

Watching her Ladyship, my own eyes filled up too and that ache was in my chest again. It grew and grew 'til it spread up my throat and I could barely breathe.

No one spoke. No one moved. The pain passed between us like a queer energy, holding us tight together.

I wondered at my own grief, so strange and strong. Only now I realised what was hurting. And it wasn't all about Kit. I was hurting for my own ma, who'd lost a daughter, and for Pa who'd chosen his dream over me. It was too much to think of at once. I thought I'd die if I tried.

I don't know how long we sat there. Drops of rain streaked against the window, and the room had grown chill. In the grate the fire was no more than a heap of ashes. Eventually, Lady Barrington saw it too. She gave a small sigh, nothing more.

Thinking her still dazed, I got up to add more coals.

'Leave it,' she said.

I stopped, bewildered.

More gently, she said, 'Please be seated. I have something to say.'

I put the pan down and took my seat again.

Lady Barrington turned to Mrs Jessop. In a faltering voice, she said, 'It was monstrous of me to keep you from Ada. I should have let you go to her.'

Mrs Jessop looked stunned. 'But I did go to her,' she said, her own voice thick with tears. 'I went against your word. I had to. That's where I was going when I passed by the lake.'

'Oh.'

Her Ladyship seemed to weigh this up for a moment. Then with a firm shake of her head, she said, 'No, we must realise. Kit chose to go skating. We cannot change that. Really Mrs Jessop, no one is to blame.'

'But don't you see . . . ?'

Lady Barrington stopped her. 'Enough. This doesn't help us now.' She hesitated. 'Tell me, did you reach Ada in time?'

'She died moments after I got there. She didn't know me, but I was able to kiss her goodbye.'

Her Ladyship reached for Mrs Jessop's hand. 'Then I'm glad you had that much at least.'

Nobody said a word.

Yet to me it looked like forgiveness.

And the queerest sensation ran through me, like a great stone had been rolled off my chest, and I could breathe again at last. We were still surrounded by Kit's own things, unchanged for ten whole years. Everything seemed just as it was. Yet it wasn't. Something had shifted. We'd heard the truth at last.

What Will had said had been right, too; Lady Barrington and Mrs Jessop had done shoddy things, kept secrets, told lies. And they'd both lost someone dear. Yet what they did, they did for love, though it mightn't have always looked that way. This was what Kit and Ada never realised.

I'd imagined what this moment might be like, when I knew Kit might finally rest in peace. But any gladness I'd expected didn't come. Instead, I felt strangely flat. And ever so, ever so weary.

'You're exhausted, poor girl,' Lady Barrington said to me.

I was. Tired to my very bones. It was morning and I hadn't even yet been to bed. I rose from my seat. Mrs Jessop stood up too and caught hold of my arm as I swayed on my feet. She gazed at me almost tenderly. It was a look I'd seen on my own ma's face when we'd parted company just a few days ago.

Of a sudden, my heart was full.

I'd not reckoned on my mother's love. As long as I could remember, she'd favoured Eliza over me, and it was Pa who'd always loved me best. Or so I'd thought until now. Because I'd seen the pain of what it is to lose a child, and yet my pa had walked out on me without even a backward glance.

Not Ma. She'd always been there, and always would be. No dream would take her away.

'I want to go home,' I said.

'Get some sleep first,' said Lady Barrington. 'Let's not do anything rash.'

She came towards me and cupped my face in her hands. 'You've done us a great service today. You've opened our eyes to each other's pain.'

Then she crossed to the window and raised the sash. Sweet, fresh air flooded in.

39

IN THE COMPANY
OF ANGELS

I woke to feel sunlight on my face. Gracie was sat at the foot of my bed with a tray of food on her lap.

'Morning, sleepyhead,' she grinned. 'You've been asleep ages. Almost a whole day and night, I reckon.'

'Blimey, have I?'

I sat up and rubbed my face. Here I was, back in our attic room, where just a few nights before we'd talked of ghosts. It felt like an age ago, though Gracie didn't seem in the mood for reminiscences. She put the tray down with a thump and started tugging at the covers.

'I've orders to get you out of bed,' she said, all excited.

'I'll be leaving soon as I'm dressed. Don't worry yourself.'

'You in't leaving yet.'

'What d'you mean?'

She didn't answer, muttering instead about fetching hot water. 'We'll need you to look your best,' she said,

336

and shut the door behind her.

I didn't have a clue what she was on about; I was still half daft with sleep. Bit by bit it came back to me, all that had happened.

Then it hit me hard.

I'd slept all this time and not dreamed of Kit. Not once. I sank down into the bed again, feeling wretched. Maybe I'd just slept too long and deep. Perhaps it'd come back to me later, the way dreams sometimes do. But the emptiness inside me felt real. I was fooling myself, wasn't I? I knew what this meant. I'd known it yesterday. It was over.

Kit was gone.

The sun kept on shining through the little window in the roof. A downpour would've suited me better. Or perhaps Kit was smiling, and maybe, just maybe, the sunshine was his way of showing it. And if he was at peace, then I should surely be glad. I'd done the thing he'd wanted me to do. The truth around his death had been revealed. And what a sad sort of truth it was. Two mothers blinded by love.

Gracie bustled in again with a pitcher of steaming water and my own frock, which looked all pressed and clean.

'Come on then,' she said. 'Look lively!'

'I'm going straight home. You don't need to fuss,' I said.

'Not yet you're not. Someone wants to see you first.'

'Who?'

'You'll see.'

She was hellbent on getting me ready, bidding me wash and dress in the blink of an eye. She even tried pinning my hair as I bent over to lace my boots.

'Ouch!' I cried as she stabbed my scalp for the hundredth time. 'What's the flipping hurry?'

And then I remembered Will.

I seized her hands. 'It's Will, in't it? Is he all right? He in't taken a turn for the worse?'

Gracie laughed. 'He's taken *quite* a turn, now you ask. He's driving Cook mad, playing the fool!'

The relief quite hit me. I even had to blink away a few tears.

*

Gracie rushed me down the back stairs. She didn't seem to bat an eyelid, not even at the darkest bits of the staircase where there weren't any windows.

When we reached the bottom, I said, 'Any bother here last night?'

She shook her head. 'Not a thing.'

I couldn't feel sad. In fact, a little shiver of excitement ran through me. It was happening, wasn't it? It *really was* happening. Kit and Ada were now at peace. And wherever that peaceful place might be, I hoped they'd be there together.

As we stepped into the passageway, two maids I'd not seen before went by. Each was carrying an end of a heavy-looking trunk. Oddly, as they passed us they seemed to want to catch *my* eye, to bid *me* good morning, in a way that had me blushing since I didn't even know their names.

'What's going on?' I asked.

'You'll see,' Gracie said. 'And folk is all saying it's down to you.'

What the flip was she on about?

Mr Phelps stepped out of his pantry. My guts turned. *Oh heck*. He wouldn't want to see me again.

'Good day to you, Matilda,' he said. 'I trust you are suitably refreshed.'

Gobsmacked, I looked at Gracie. This was getting stranger by the minute.

'Just say summat nice,' she hissed in my ear.

'I . . . ummm . . . yes. Thank you.'

And we went on our way.

At the baize door, Dorcas was waiting. She looked different, in a smart grey dress with no cap and no pinny. Then I saw the bunch of keys at her hip.

'Mrs Jessop's leaving us for a while, and I'm stepping in as housekeeper.'

'Mrs Jessop? Where's she going?'

'You and your questions!' Dorcas smiled.

So she'd got her dream. I was glad for her and wanted to say so, only she was set on rushing me on.

'I'm to take you up to her Ladyship.'

I stopped, more confused than ever. 'Hang on. I thought we was going to see Will.'

'Will Potter'll keep.' She tucked her arm through mine. 'Besides, she's been asking for you all morning. It seems you've made quite an impression.'

A thrill ran through me again. It wasn't just the back stairs that were different this morning: the whole place seemed changed. Dorcas led me out into the hallway and up the stairs. At the top we turned right towards the front of the house. I stopped dead.

'Oh no, not Kit's room, I can't go in there. I can't bear it.'

'Go on. She's waiting for you.'

Dorcas tapped at the door, then nudged me forwards as Lady Barrington called from inside. Feeling sick, I went in.

And gasped.

All the windows were wide open, making the room feel cool and fresh. There was no fire lit; the grate had been swept clean. Packing cases stood open, their straw spilling onto the floor. The bed had been stripped, the books and pens almost cleared. Bobbing her head in my direction was another new maid. She put down her work and left the room.

It was only then I noticed her Ladyship. She was stood as usual by the window, and she looked so small and slight I'd have hardly known it was her. Her frock was as fine as any I'd seen her wear. But this time it wasn't black: it was the colour of doves. She still wore the brooch over her heart and indeed it looked well on her.

On seeing me, she rushed to my side like some long-lost friend. I was mightily taken aback.

'Tilly! You're awake at last!'

She'd even called me Tilly. I didn't know quite what to say.

'I can see this is a shock to you,' she said. 'I'm trying to be brave, myself. But it's no good holding on to these things of Kit's, is it? It'll never bring him back.'

'No, your Ladyship.'

And she was right, of course, but it did make me low, seeing Kit's things in boxes like he really was gone. The last dream I'd had came back to me then, of Kit and me high above the snow, and his fingers slipping out of my grasp. Here we were, doing what he'd wanted us to do. We were letting go at last.

'Are you still set on leaving us?' said Lady Barrington. 'Can I not tempt you to stay?'

Just a few days ago, I'd have given my eye teeth for this job. But our weasel of a landlord didn't scare me now. What Ma and me would face, we'd face together.

'We're desperate for money, it's true. But my ma needs me and I need her. We'll think of something, somehow.'

And though I didn't say so, the real reason I'd come here was for Kit. Now he was gone, Frost Hollow Hall was nothing more to me than a big old house with far too many floors to clean.

Lady Barrington smiled. 'A mother would be blessed to have such a daughter.'

I felt my cheeks flush with pride.

'And don't fret about money. Arrangements will be made. I cannot ever repay you for what you've done.'

Then she held out her hand like she meant me to shake it. I gave mine a quick wipe on my skirts and held it out to her. She took it and pulled me close.

'I have to tell you. Something extraordinary has happened.' Her voice had dropped to a thrilling whisper.

'Really?'

'Can you believe it? Last night I had a dream.'

My heart leapt. 'Oh! Tell me!'

'I dreamed I was in this very room. It was filled with sunlight and birdsong, and Kit was here, standing right where you are now. An angel appeared – it was calling to him, beckoning for him to join it. He wanted to go, but before he went he took my hand.'

I bit back the tears.

Lady Barrington let go of me then, moving to her place at the window and tilting her face to the breeze. 'He said something to me. Just one simple word – that was all. But heavens, how I needed to hear it!'

'What was it?'

She turned to me, her whole face smiling.

'Live.'

40

SOMETHING QUITE REMARKABLE

I found Will in the kitchens eating cake. Just the sight of him made my eyes fill up. Before I could stop myself, I threw my arms right round him and blubbed into his shoulder.

'Thank God you're all right!'

'Watch out for old waterworks!' he laughed.

Yet his arms went round me too, and we stayed like that for a long moment, with my face nestled into his shirt front. Then he tipped his head slightly, smoothing back my hair so I felt his mouth warm against my ear.

'Clever you,' he said in a voice so low that only I could hear it.

I shivered with happiness.

'I couldn't have done it without your help,' I said.

He squeezed me tight. It made my insides go fluttery and strange. I pulled back, sharpish. *What the heck was the matter with me?*

Fumbling about for a chair, I saw the smirk on Cook's face. I sat down with a bump.

'So,' I said, trying to act normal, 'is your leg better, Will?'

It was hard to look at him. Each time I did, the fluttery feeling came back. I'd never noticed that his eyes were so dark, nor how his face went all soft when he smiled. He was fine-looking, all right. No wonder he was always so pleased with himself.

'Didn't know you cared,' he said.

Cook laughed. ''Course she does, you daft thing! Anyone with half a brain can see that.'

I did my best to ignore her and said to Will briskly, 'You up to walking home, then? Only I want to go today.'

'I could give it a go,' he said.

He pulled up his trouser leg, wincing. The bite was bandaged up so there wasn't much to see, but his leg looked stiff and swollen.

My spirits sank. 'You can't walk on that.'

'Try getting a ride with Mrs Jessop, then,' said Cook. 'Go to the front of the house and you'll catch her. They're loading her things onto the coach.'

I felt a sudden pang in my chest. 'Is she leaving right now?'

'She is. Going to the coast to take the air. Long time coming, if you ask me.'

I raced out the back door and round to the front steps. Mrs Jessop was stood amongst a pile of cases, wearing a brown coat and smart straw hat. She shielded her eyes from the sun as she saw me coming.

'Hullo,' she said, as I skidded to a halt in front of her. 'Seems we're both leaving today.'

Before long, the coach set off up the driveway. Will and me had squeezed ourselves into one seat with Mrs Jessop facing us on the other. Except she didn't look our way, not once. She gazed out the window the whole time. I bet she was thinking of Ada.

The main Frostcombe road was all potholes and slush, throwing Will against me with every lurch. We laughed a bit and he excused himself. But as the road evened out, I noticed how his arm stayed touching mine.

Just before the village, we stopped at Will's house to let him out. Then it was my turn, though our lane was too narrow for a carriage.

'This'll do me,' I said, jumping down.

'Just a moment.'

Mrs Jessop climbed out after me, telling the driver to wait. My eyes prickled; I prayed she didn't have notions of walking me right to my front door.

'Let me show you something, Tilly.'

She opened a bag and pulled out a parcel wrapped in brown paper. My heart lurched. It was the same flat package Lady Barrington had taken from the drawer at the séance. Kit's final present to Ada.

I dithered uneasily, not sure I wanted to look at such a personal gift. But the packaging itself had already come loose, so I guessed I wasn't the first to have a peek inside.

'Go on, open it,' Mrs Jessop said, nudging it into my hands. 'Her Ladyship kept it all this time, and today she gave it to me.'

With shaking fingers, I pulled back the wrapping. What I saw was beautiful, so beautiful it made my chest hurt. For here was a pencil drawing of the most lovely angel I had ever seen, lovelier than the statue at Kit's graveside, lovelier even than the drawings in his sketchbook. There was no fancy writing, no gushing 'to my dearest . . .'s. What he'd chosen instead was simple. At the bottom of the picture in a copperplate hand were the sweetest words: 'To Ada.'

His gift was perfect.

Yet Ada never lived to see it.

'It's so lovely,' I said finally, and handed it back to

Mrs Jessop. 'Maybe Kit was Ada's special angel. He certainly was mine.'

She put the package back in her bag, then took my hand. 'I often wondered why you didn't drown that day. There's something about you, Tilly. Something quite remarkable.'

I knew if I looked at her, I'd cry.

'Go home now.' Letting me go, she climbed back into the carriage.

I cried out, 'Mrs Jessop, wait!'

She pulled down the window.

'I must ask, do *you* think I look like Ada?'

She smiled sadly. 'At first I thought so, yes. It quite unsettled me. But I don't think you look like her any more.'

'What's changed?'

'You. Me. Everything,' she said. 'And I hope we'll be better people for it.'

I didn't stay to watch the carriage go. I ran straight to our house and lifted the latch. Ma leapt up so fast, her mending work fell in a heap on the floor.

'What's happened? What you gone and done?' she cried.

'Nothing, Ma,' I said, though it wasn't exactly true. 'But you'd better sit down again.'

As simply as I could, I told her. She half-laughed, half-gasped, and by the time I'd finished her eyes were bright with tears. We fell quiet, like two people unsure what to do next.

Then she held out her arms to me. 'Come here, child.'

So I did.

DREAMING: 7

I'm stood near water, barefoot. This must be the lake at Frost Hollow Hall but it looks so different, I hardly recognise it. The trees are in bud, the banks full of snowdrops and the lake all silky smooth and sparkling like the finest, bluest eyes.

Everything is beautiful.

Above my head, I hear wing-beats. Two white birds – they look like doves – are lifting off into the air. The sight of them makes my heart soar. Beneath my feet, the grass is warm. I reckon I could stay here for ever.

Yet someone is calling to me. It's time to go. I turn round to see a figure coming towards me across the grass. The sun's behind them. I shield my eyes for a better look. Now I see their smiling face, a face so dear to me I could burst.

41

THE RIGHTFUL PLACE

Early next morning I found a basket of food on our doorstep. It was sent from the Hall, with a note from her Ladyship saying our rent had been 'arranged' so we'd nothing to fear, and that she'd write me the best character a maid could ask for. Ma made me read it over and over, and even then it took a while to sink in.

After a fine breakfast of bacon and bread, Ma settled to her work and I did the pots and scrubbed the floor. It felt good to be busy at something. For not far beneath the surface, I reckoned we were both still sad. But then, it *would* take time, wouldn't it? Up at the Hall, it had taken years. Ma and me, we'd made a start, at least.

The day itself was bright and warm, so I kept our front door open as I worked. Anyone might've walked right in, I wouldn't have cared, though I'd have made them take their boots off so as not to ruin my floor.

But no one did come.

And as the day wore on, I hoped a particular *someone* would call by. I listened for footsteps up the path, and decided to clean the windows for an excuse to keep an eye out. And just as I knelt to scrub the front step *again*, our gate swung open at last.

'I'll get it!' I said, leaping to my feet.

'If it's that nice lad Will Potter, be sure to invite him in,' called Ma.

Blushing, I turned to see not Will at all, but a man in a dark uniform and hat. My heart sank.

'Matilda Higgins?' he said.

'That's me,' I said.

'I've got post for you.'

He handed me a thick envelope. I peered at it. I'd never had a letter in my whole blooming life. And now I'd got one, I wasn't sure what to do with it. One look at the envelope and I went hot then cold all at once. I knew that handwriting anywhere.

It was from Eliza.

I didn't dare take it back inside. I went a little way down the lane to a low wall, where I sat and waited for my heartbeat to steady down. I couldn't bring myself to read the damned thing. Instead, I left it unopened in my lap and shutting my eyes I listened to the black-birds singing. The sun was warm, the air smelled of earth and wet grass. If I stayed here just like this, Eliza couldn't hurt me any more.

It was no good. I had to read it.

I picked up the envelope. The postmark looked like 'Liverpool', though the 'ool' was hard to see against the little black stamp. I took a deep breath.

The letter was only short. Even so, it was a job to focus on the words.

Dear Tilly,

By the time this reaches you, you might of forgotten us already. Or cut us from your lives — I wouldn't blame you for that. But you must know that I couldn't bring myself to pawn your ring. It just weren't right, not when I saw the name inside it and what with all you'd said about your queer dream — though where you got such a thing God only knows. But, see, I do have a heart, after all.

Pa wanted you to know something. Last Sunday, when he nearly came home he saw you. You was with Will Potter on the road heading towards Frost Hollow Hall. He said you looked excited and happy, like a person heading off on an adventure. And he was glad that you weren't sat at home waiting for him. Seeing you so purposeful made him strong. It gave him the guts to follow his dream. He thinks you'll be better off without him. Lord knows you'll be better off without me!

In two days' time, we set sail for America on board a vast ship called the Britannic. Pa still has this little dream that you might come after us. So if you change your mind we're staying at . . .

I didn't read the rest.

I shook the envelope like a mad thing. A small gold ring fell into my hand. I grasped it tight, and started to laugh, since the joy was too much. And then of a sudden I was crying. The tears fell fast and hot. My whole body trembled, but I didn't hold back. I let myself weep. And as I sat and sobbed 'til my throat ached, the ring turned warm in my hand, just as it had a week ago when I'd found it in the hem of my frock.

Eventually, my tears stopped. I folded up the letter and pushed it to the deepest part of my pocket. Eliza was right; it was too late. Things were different now.

It hurt, though. Deeply.

So Pa had seen me with Will on our way to go skating. Had I been excited that day? *Really?* I didn't think so. I'd been miserable because Pa hadn't yet come home. Will and his skates were just a distraction. Or they had been then.

Yet it was also the very start of things. I'd been heading towards the lake, towards Kit Barrington. An adventure *was* about to start. He was right about that. Perhaps Pa knew it before even I did.

There was one thing I did know. I'd not be chasing after him and Eliza. Though I'd miss them both every day for the rest of my life, I'd not leave my ma. Not for anything. That didn't stop it hurting. Yet I knew what it was, this feeling. I was losing something dear to me, my own flesh and blood.

I was letting go.

I looked up to see Will limping towards me along the lane. Quickly, I wiped my face and hoped I wasn't a complete state, though I knew he'd seen me looking worse.

'I was just coming to call on you,' he said.

I patted a place on the wall next to me. He eased himself down. Straight away he saw Kit's ring in my hand.

'What on earth you got there?'

I held it so he could see it properly. My hand was shaking hard. 'This belonged to Kit Barrington,' I said, and told him about Eliza and the letter in my pocket.

His eyes went wide in wonder. 'So there really was a ring.'

'You didn't believe me, did you?'

'Not quite. Not at first.'

I shrugged. 'Well, I can hardly blame you for that.'

He sat quiet for a moment. I noticed how close we were sitting, how our hands were nearly touching. My stomach did a little somersault.

'Reckon you're done with this business now?' said Will.

'I think so.'

He took a deep breath.

'Any chance I might get a look in, then?'

I stared at him. 'What? *You?*'

'Why not?' he said, all easy. 'Up to you of course, but let's just say I've never come second best to a ghost before.'

Damn Will Potter!

I bit back the urge to be sharp. Because in a way, he was right, wasn't he? The Kit I'd known hadn't been real. He'd been a thought in my head, an idea of a person. And because of him, I'd got off my backside and done things I was proud of. Kit would always be dear to me.

Will seemed to sense my shift in mood. He said

gently, 'You did right by Kit Barrington. He's a lucky chap.'

I gazed at the ring, then at Will. 'That's all done now.'

For here was Will Potter, sat so close I could almost feel the warmth coming off him. Goodness, he was lovely to look at. And he was real.

'So what you going to do with it?' said Will, meaning the ring.

'I'll give it back to her Ladyship. Its rightful place is with her now, not me. But that can wait 'til tomorrow. I can't face Frost Hollow Hall today.'

'If you like, I'll come with you.'

'Ta,' I said. 'I'd like that very much.'

Will got down off the wall and stood right in front of me. His eyes were the deepest brown.

'I've got a dare for you, Tilly.'

My mouth must've fallen open in horror, since he said, 'Now then. Be fair. It *is* my turn, after all.'

'Go on then. What is it?'

He folded his arms across his chest. 'You've to invite me in. Properly this time, for tea and everything.'

I tried to keep a straight face, um-ing and ahh-ing until he started to look quite vexed.

'Oh all right then,' I said finally. 'On one condition.'

'Now what?'

I jumped down off the wall and I held out my hand, hoping more than anything he'd take it.

He raised an eyebrow, then smiled the handsomest smile.

'Very well,' he said. 'It's a deal.'

And he took my hand in his.

It wasn't just any old handhold, neither, for it made me flush. Our palms seemed to fit together perfectly. His fingers felt so warm, so sure, I felt certain I'd never let them go.

We walked back up the lane, dawdling a little just for the joy of it. As we reached our gate, I stopped to take in the clean front step and the curl of smoke coming from the chimney. Inside, I pictured Ma still hard at work. Or perhaps she'd seen us coming and had already put the tea on. Either way, my heart was full. This was my house, my home. I wondered if it was right to feel so happy.

'Pinch me, would you? Just to check I'm not dreaming,' I said.

Will pinched my arm.

'Ouch! Not that hard!' I laughed, pinching him back.

Really I was glad because I'd had enough of dreams.

What I wanted was the here and now. To live my life with what I had, not what I hoped might be.

When we reached our front step, I held the door open wide.

'Come on in,' I said to Will.

He let go my hand just long enough to take off his cap. Then with his fingers in mine, he stepped inside. And as the sun streamed in through the windows, we took our tea together, Will Potter, Ma and me. It was very fine indeed. Better, in fact, than any dream.

ACKNOWLEDGEMENTS

This story started life as a scene on a frozen lake. With the help of some special people, that scene became Frost Hollow Hall.

Firstly, I'd like to thank The Arvon Foundation's Totleigh Barton Centre for creating the spark, and to the Axe Valley Community College for being supportive ever since.

Thanks to all on the Bath Spa Writing For Young People MA. Course Director Julia Green is an inspiration. To my class – Sue, Carol, Bernie, Maria, Ros, Kirsten, Naomi – it was an honour. Special thanks to my wonderful tutor Steve Voake, who was there from the very start. Thanks also to my mentor Marcus Sedgwick.

Huge thanks to my brilliant agent Jodie Marsh for sending Tilly Higgins out into the world one snowy February afternoon, and to Jane Willis for journeys further afield.

To the team at Faber, thank you for making my dreams come true. To Susila Baybars for saying 'yes', and to Leah Thaxton for agreeing. Warmest, deepest thanks to my amazing editor Rebecca Lee, whose skill made this a better book. Thanks also to superstar copy-editor Eleanor Rees.

Heartfelt thanks to my early readers, Naomi Rich, Kirsten Harvey, Karl Watson, Becky Howat, Eliza Hall, Pam and Maurice Hall. It meant the world to share this book with you.

To my mum and dad for a lifetime of love. And to my husband Owen, who did everything else so I could write; my biggest thanks of all is to you.